perfected
by girls

Alfred C. Martino

Coles Street Publishing
Union City, New Jersey

ya
Mar
pb

Requests for permission to make copies of any part of the work should be mailed to the following address: Permissions Department, Coles Street Publishing, 1700 Manhattan Avenue, Union City, New Jersey 07087.

www.AlfredMartino.com

Library of Congress Cataloging-in-Publication Data
Martino, Alfred C.
Perfected By Girls / by Alfred C. Martino.
p. cm.
Summary: Melinda Radford, the lone girl on her high school wrestling team, grapples family and school pressures for the opportunity to compete in a varsity match, something no girl in school history has ever done.[1. Wrestling-Fiction. 2. Family problems-Fiction. 3. Friendship-Fiction. 4. Competition (Psychology)-Fiction. 5. Michigan-Fiction.] I. Title.
[Fic]- dc22 2011934850
ISBN 978-1-59316-600-7

Text set in Sabon
Text and Cover Designed by Jenn Martino Design
Edited by Karen Grove

First edition
ACEGHFDB

Printed in the United States of America

For Mom

Acknowledgments

In hindsight, perhaps it's not surprising that I'd write a novel centered on girls' amateur wrestling. In the mid 1980s, two of my cousins, Kari and Veda, competed admirably—and successfully—on the boys' wrestling teams of their respective New Jersey hometowns of Roselle Park and Tewksbury. At the time, a female amateur wrestler was an anomaly. Today it is most certainly not, as girls (and women) compete at every level of wrestling, including the Olympics. It is a welcomed development in our sport.

During my research for *Perfected By Girls*, I had the opportunity to speak with dozens of former and current female wrestlers about the obstacles that they had to overcome in order to compete, their thoughts on being teammates with and opponents of boys, and, ultimately, what the sport meant to them. Some were kind enough to offer comments on the book cover as it was in development, as well. Their insight helped me a great deal. Though I'm sure I'll forget a few, and appologize if I do, I'd like to thank Leigh James, Joey Miller, Rowan Pilger, Stephanie Marino, Uilani Kaneao, Jennah Brennan, Amanda Ayotte, Arial Fitzner, Alaura Seidl, Kailee Ball, Aubrae Putnam, Michele Levy, Amy Granton, Amy Fazackerley, Kiki Lane, and a special thanks to Danielle Hobeika.

Most importantly, I am indebted to Kayla Percy, the other member of our two-person writing group and a fine novelist herself; Karen Grove, masterful editor for all three of my novels; Alexes R., who generously took time from her ice hockey schedule to critique the novel; Elizabeth, for her support; my sister, Jenn, for her fine design work; and Alisa Weberman, publisher at Coles Street Publishing, for having the wisdom to publish *Perfected By Girls*.

Alfred C. Martino
July 2011

perfected
by girls

Chapter 1

Sometimes I wish I were a guy.

I know that sounds stupid, probably ridiculously stupid—my best friend, Jade, would certainly say it does. So, before word gets out at Ashton High that I might be considering "augmentation" to my south-of-the-border region, let me clarify: I wish I could be *like* a guy.

I'm envious of them. Everything about guys—the things they do and the way they do them, from irrationally impulsive to single-mindedly determined, and all shades in between—seems to originate from their bodies. It's like watching one of those animal shows where a lion is sprawled out lazily on the savanna, then the moment strikes and he takes off, his muscular body charging through the grassy plains, mane swaying, to knock the snot out of some hyena.

I envy guys' muscles and the arrogance those muscles give them. I envy that it seems like they don't need to do anything special to be sturdy and broad. They don't have to flex. Or pose. Or strut. It just *happens*. When they move; when they don't move. They can just be, and yet it's impossible to ignore how their bodies are so...

I'm not sure what the right word is.

Intimidating, I suppose.

Or powerful.

Alive, maybe.

Yeah... Sometimes I really wish I could be like a guy.

Chapter 2

"Oh...my...God..."

Jade is definitely the excitable type. Right now she's squeezing my arm and squealing in my ear in one of those ways where I'm concerned she may not be able to keep her thoughts discreetly contained in her head. It probably won't matter anyway, given that we're sitting among my JV wrestling teammates at the top row of our standing-room-only high school gymnasium bleachers, looking down on hundreds of classmates and teachers, parents and neighbors, shouting and clapping for the pride of Ashton, Michigan: our state-ranked varsity team.

Jade leans in. "Did you hear me?"

We've been sister-tight since we terrorized Brownies Troop 77 together, like, eight years ago. She comes to every wrestling match and even watches the action on the mat as intently as I do, though usually for much less sports-related reasons.

"Do you *see?*" She's downright giddy.

I roll my eyes.

It's the third period of the 170-pound match. Trey Fignorelli, our team co-captain (my brother, Cole, is the other) and three-year letter winner, just hit a standing switch that took him and his South Lyon opponent out-of-bounds.

"No points," the referee shouts. "Same way."

Trey, reddish floppy hair sprouting from under his headgear, picks himself up and shakes out his hands. The South Lyon wrestler stands up, as well.

That's when Jade blurts into my ear, "Are you even *looking*?"

I am. At Trey.

He's tired. He always shakes out his hands between drills near the end of practice. It's his little quirk. Why I notice these things, I'm not sure. But I do.

I take a gulp from my water bottle. I'm still in my singlet and warm-ups. My sweat isn't totally dry. Bet I'm a bit smelly, too. Our JV team won, but I didn't. I wrestled in one of the "exhibition" matches after the regular lineup was done. Got my clock cleaned. I don't think my opponent was too thrilled to be wrestling a girl, so he dispensed with any semblance of chivalry and took me down with a double-leg, then cross-faced me, without any respect for my button nose, into a far-side cradle. I was behind 5–0 before my brain unscrambled. I did have an escape in the second period—for what it was worth (very little)—but then gave up another takedown in the third for a 7–1 shellacking.

I glance at the clock. Fifty-four seconds left; Trey's up 4–2. But that's not what Jade sees.

"He's *huge*," she says, giggling.

I purse my lips but don't look at her—that'll just egg her on.

"I know you notice," she says.

"I don't."

"You do."

"I'm watching my *teammate*."

Jade laughs. "Teammate?"

"Yeah," I say, without any conviction whatsoever.

"Mel," she says, "if it wasn't for Cole, Trey wouldn't even know your name."

"Yeah, well—" I start to say, but I know she's right.

Trey kneels down at the center circle, taking a last deep breath before he sets himself in the down position. His opponent is facing the South Lyon coach, who sits on a folding chair at the corner of the mat.

"Gotta turn him," the coach shouts. "Off the whistle, grab an ankle and Turk. Then put in the half."

Reasonable, but rather obvious, suggestions.

When the South Lyon wrestler turns around, Jade's distraction is more than apparent. His white singlet with a gold-colored band running diagonal across his chest, at just the right angle, seems as sheer as satin and, for a moment, it's as if he's standing on the mat wearing only red wrestling shoes, a yellow sash, and an abundantly filled jockstrap.

Jade squeezes my arm harder and practically howls. I glance around us. Thankfully, the crowd's cheering has begun to swell in anticipation of the referee's whistle and nobody seems to notice.

Ashton's a wrestling town, has been for decades— that's what our legendary Coach Hillman reminds us of in practice every day. And if he didn't, the long list of state champions and place-winners displayed prominently in our wrestling room would certainly hammer the idea home. Ashton fans know what they're seeing. They're seeing their co-captain, less than a minute away from securing an early December season-opening team victory, in the bottom position in the center circle, while his opponent waits for the referee to motion him on top.

"Mel—" Jade says.

I shush her.

"Don't shush me."

"Watch the wrestling," I say, gesturing down toward the mat.

Jade purses her lips and goes into pissy mode, pulling a cell phone from her handbag.

"I'll just check my messages," she says in an annoying way. "Why don't you check yours? Oh, that's right, you can't."

I offer my best bitter smile. Mom put the kibosh on my texting and calling when I went a little overboard one month (actually, two) last summer. So now I'm practically the only person at Ashton High who doesn't have a cell phone.

"Just watch," I say to Jade.

The referee blows the whistle and the third period continues. Trey holds his base for the first few seconds, arms braced against the mat, triceps totally bulging. The South Lyon wrestler grabs a near ankle and drives Trey down to the mat. Then he forces in a half nelson.

Ashton fans yell, "Look away! Look away!"

Trey manages to get to an elbow, but he's obviously tired. I *knew* it. Now, both sides of the gymnasium are really rocking.

It's as if the South Lyon wrestler wants to wrench Trey's arm out of his shoulder more than try to turn him to his back. He's driving as hard as he can, while Trey fights to get back to his base. The willpower from both guys is amazing—one using every bit of his energy and strength to pull the upset, the other enduring pain and fatigue to hold off the challenge.

As the clock ticks down, I imagine myself in Trey's place and wonder: In front of a packed home crowd, could I be as tough and gritty as I'd need to be to get the win? My stomach tightens. I doubt it. I don't know if it's a girl–guy thing. Maybe it is. Maybe if I had ripped arms and broad shoulders and thick quads that stretched out my singlet... Maybe.

"Come on, Trey!" Jade shouts.

She's doing her best impression of an interested fan, though I know she's more concerned about whether we're going to hang out later tonight than Ashton winning this dual meet.

"Get to a base," I say.

I'm surprised to hear my own voice. I'm not one of those wrestlers who cheers on every teammate. I'm usually silent. I like to analyze what's happening on the mat, wondering why a takedown setup worked, or which wrestler had better balance in a certain position. My dad told me once that I'd make a good coach someday. I'd like to make a good *wrestler* first.

I watch Trey get to his hands and knees.

"Crank down on the arm!"

It's my voice again, but this time it's loud and comes at a lull in the crowd's cheering, so my words are as clear as a boat horn on Whitmore Lake.

Trey suddenly raises his body a little, then cranks down on his opponent's arm. The South Lyon wrestler falls to his hip, allowing Trey to step over smoothly for the reversal.

I can feel the know-it-all grin on my lips. A few Ashton fans glance over their shoulders and nod their approval, though none of my JV teammates do. That's fine. They probably figure I only know this stuff from being around my brother. Or, maybe, they just don't want to admit a girl can have more wrestling smarts than them.

Back on the mat, Trey rides his opponent for the last half minute of the period, jumps to his feet at the buzzer, then has his arm raised in victory.

I still feel flush, sitting straight up with my chest puffed out. I'm sure people are listening to hear what I'll shout during the 182-pound match.

"Uh...hate to disappoint you," Jade says, putting a hand on my shoulder, "but no one's waiting for your next moment of brilliance."

I roll my eyes to deflect her snarkiness, and then finish the rest of the cheese sandwich that I hadn't eaten after weigh-ins.

Soon enough, the dual meet is over. The Ashton varsity has started the season with an important, but expected, victory. Jade and I stand, then wait for fans to move down the bleacher steps. It takes a few minutes.

"Hey," Jade says to me. "Good job earlier."

"With what?"

"Your match."

"I got my butt handed to me."

"Maybe," Jade says. "But you had a nice escape in the second period." She steps down a row, then another.

"You saw that?" I say, following her. I think she's smiling. "I figured you'd be too busy watching other *things*."

"Mel, my darlin', I promised you over the summer I'd make it to every one of your JV matches *and* pay attention. I'm keeping that promise."

Well, that's kind of sweet.

"Besides, I'm waiting," she says.

"Waiting?"

"Yes."

"For what?"

She gestures down to the mat.

"And?"

"You, the first chick to wrestle varsity for Ashton," she says. "And I'll be able to say, 'I knew her when she was regular ol' Melinda Radford.'"

I can't tell if Jade's teasing me or she's serious. Either way, our conversation makes me majorly uneasy. I look around to see if anyone's heard what we're talking about. They'd probably think Jade is out of her mind.

"Things are fine the way they are," I say.

"Fine the way they are?"

"Yes."

"That's it?"

"Yes, that's it."

"You don't ever think about it?"

"No," I insist.

"Liar."

"I'm serious," I say. "I don't." But maybe I don't sound very convincing.

"What about someday?" Jade says.

I roll my eyes. "Okay, someday."

"Or sooner."

"Jade..."

"Suit yourself," she says, with a shrug.

Then she grabs my hand and we hurry down to the bottom row. "Now, let's go find Trey and Cole," she says, her almond eyes sweeping across the gymnasium floor. "While they're still in their wrestling outfits."

"Outfits?" I say, incredulous. "They're called singlets, Jade. *Singlets.*"

But she's not listening.

Chapter 3

Jade dives onto my bed with this week's *People* magazine, sweeping the pages to check out the latest Hollywood breakup, or starlet arrest, or celebrity rehab. She's enthralled.

"Keep it if you want," I say.

"You're finished?"

"You know I don't read that trash."

Jade gives me a look. "Excuse me, Einstein."

"My mom got it," I say, pulling off my warm-ups. I'm standing in my singlet. "There's a dress in there she thought would look good on me."

"Which one?"

"I forget."

The magazine hits my butt. "Don't BS me," Jade says. "You know *exactly* which dress." She jumps up and walks to my closet, pulling open the mirrored sliding door. "I'm the one who got you interested in fashion and now look—a black strapless dress from, hmm..." She turns out the label. "BCBG. And this? A Calvin Klein sleeveless." She pushes aside more clothes. "Galliano... Another Galliano... Anne Klein, St. John Collection, DKNY..."

"Okay, okay," I say.

"So?"

I sigh. "It was a BCBG black satin halter dress that hits here." I show Jade—a few inches below the bottom of my singlet, just above my knee.

She says, "I'd totally look fabulous in it."

I hear my brother coming down the second-floor hallway. Jade apparently does, too.

"Hey, Cole," she calls, as he passes by. "Really great win tonight." She gives him one of those gee-aren't-you-wonderful looks, and I think her already-full lips suddenly become poutier.

Cole stops. He smiles at Jade and his eyes lock onto her as if she's the only person in his world. It's enough to make me sick.

"Oh, please," I mutter. "Just go away."

"I'll be downstairs in five minutes, chubby," he grunts at me. God, I really hate when he calls me fat. "Be ready," he says.

"Do I have a choice?"

"What was the score of your match?" he says.

"Never mind."

"Did ya even score a point?"

"Yes, actually," I say.

"Whoa, break out the champagne," Cole says, with a forced laugh. "Mel scored a whole point."

I shake my head. "You're such a supportive, loving brother."

Cole grins, in that obnoxious way that only he can do, then looks toward Jade and, with a cowboy-on-a-whitesteed wink, says, "Coming to my next match?"

Jade feigns being coy. "Maybe…"

"Leave us alone," I interrupt and slam my bedroom door closed. It's not like I haven't seen Cole flirt with Jade before, he does it all the time. I know it doesn't mean anything (and it better not). I'm just not in the mood to see it right now.

Jade turns to me. "Anyway, what were we talking about? Oh, yeah, all these gorgeous clothes."

I pull the straps of my singlet off my shoulders, then roll it past my underwear and down my legs.

"Whoa, Mel…"

"You better not say I'm chubby."

"No, you're *way* muscular," Jade says. I can't tell if she's impressed or busting on me. "Starting to look like *that* chick." She gestures toward the poster on my wall.

"I wish," I say. "That *chick* is Tricia Saunders. She's, like, the best female amateur wrestler from the US, ever."

"Yeah, yeah… You've told me this a million times. And a million times, I've told you, 'whatever'."

"Not 'whatever'," I say. "Four-time world champ, eleven-time national champ. Never lost to another American female wrestler. Not once. She, my dear Jade, was a bitch in a singlet."

She looks at me, unimpressed.

"Anyway," she says, "soon you're not going to fit in these dresses anymore. It'd be a shame to have to get rid of them. Guess I'll have to be the benevolent friend and take them off your hands."

"Benevolent," I say. "That's an SAT word. I'm

surprised you knew how to use it properly in a sentence."

Jade flares her nostrils. "Thanks. Let me try it again. That South Lyon wrestler wasn't very *benevolent* when he wiped the mat with you today."

Then she gives me the fakest of smiles, and we both laugh.

While Jade sifts through my closet for more of what she hopes will be hand-me-downs, I pull out a T-shirt, long-sleeved shirt, two pairs of sweatpants, and a hooded sweatshirt from my drawer. Soon, I have them all on.

"Hey, are we still getting a mani-pedi tomorrow?" Jade asks.

"Yep," I say.

"Good, my nail polish is chipping."

I look at my own. My nails are a mess. "I'll be back in twenty-five minutes," I say, before leaving my bedroom.

"Take your time," Jade says. "There's no way I'm going home."

Then she gives me a look that I know all too well. Her father must be in one of his moods. It doesn't help that her mother hasn't been around for years. We never talk about that. Jade doesn't like when I feel sorry for her. But I do anyway.

Cole and I run almost every night. After practice. After matches. On Sundays. He never lets me off the hook, no matter how I feel or whether I want to or not. He waits in the laundry room off the kitchen, where we keep our running shoes. When mine are on, he tells me where we're going. He's got four routes. One is hilly. Another is long and mostly straight. The other two are a combination.

Together, without talking, we walk from the back of the house down the driveway, stretching along the way. Once we get to the street, Cole takes off sprinting. After he's a quarter mile or so down the road, he stops and bounces on his toes until I catch up. It's the same every time we run.

"Keep going," I want to tell him. "I'll make it home."

He doesn't need to make sure I'm all right every step of the way. I'm fine. I mean, not completely—my legs feel totally heavy and I'm pretty sure my period's going to start tomorrow or the next day. But it's not like something's going to happen to me running—or more accurately, slogging—a couple of miles.

But I know he'll never leave me behind. And not because of some sense of brotherly love. I'm pretty sure it was a parental edict. "Look out for Mel," Dad probably said. "She's your sister, and a *teammate*." I'll bet Cole laughed at that. There's no way in the world he considers me a teammate. It's clear I'm not one of the guys.

As I approach my brother, I do my best to pick up the pace. The moment I'm close, he sprints away again.

A small part of me wishes he'd wait. I could use the company. We wouldn't have to talk or anything (like he'd ever want to), we could just run side by side in silence. But, the truth is, I really don't mind facing this drudgery by myself. It allows plenty of time for thoughts to rattle around in my head, if sometimes obsessively.

Like, properly capturing the far knee when finishing off a hi-crotch…

(Working on it.)

Or making it through the season without a teammate or opponent "accidentally" copping a feel...

(Unlikely.)

Or drilling with Brook Evans in practice, who smells as good with a little sweat on him as he looks wearing athletic shorts and a tight T-shirt...

(Very, very distracting.)

I push through the back door into our laundry room, leaving my brother to run a few more miles. I bend down to untie my running shoes, then I pull off both pairs of sweatpants, sweatshirt, long-sleeved shirt, and T-shirt. My mom comes in from the kitchen.

"Put whatever you need washed in the wicker basket," she says.

I'm standing in my underwear and sports bra, sweating. Not a lot, but enough. I notice Mom eye me up and down.

"What?" I say, though I know what she's thinking. Probably doesn't like that she can count each of my ribs, or that my skin looks as thin as a silk top, or that I'd asked her to buy me a few bras—a size smaller than usual. "Mom, my ribs seem like they're showing because I just got done running," I say, though I know that makes no sense at all.

"I didn't say anything."

"And I probably look a little thin because I'm sweaty." Which makes even less sense.

"Not a word," she says.

I put my hands on my waist and frown. "I *needed* new bras, mine were totally old. I wanted a smaller size because"—I hold my boobs—"these get in the way. You try wrestling with them."

"Yes, I'm sure it's a problem," Mom says. She pulls a bath towel from a shelf and puts it over my shoulders. "Jade's staying over?"

"Yeah."

"If you two want something to eat, let me know. Now, get upstairs, my little warrior princess, before you catch a chill."

Chapter 4

I'm in deep on the double-leg. Head on the outside of the hip. Arms around my teammate's legs, hands on his calves.

But I'm on my knees, and I have that fraction of a second to realize I'm going to pay for it big time. Mark Wexler doesn't care that he's one weight class heavier than me. He doesn't care that he's a junior and I'm a sophomore. And, most of all, I don't think he's particularly pleased that a girl's on the team.

So he kicks his legs back and crashes all of his weight on me—it's a nasty sprawl. I hear him grunting. He's definitely trying to make this as painful for me as possible. If this was the beginning of practice I might make a real effort to hold on, improve my position, and look to finish off the takedown. But it's late, and I'm wiped out, and my arms are practically useless. I hate the feeling of giving in. But I know that's what I'm doing, just holding on until the minute-long shot is over so I can take a seat to the side and catch my breath. It's okay, I tell myself. There'll be other shots, other drills, other practices.

Mark doesn't let up. He jams my head—my face, really—against the mat with his hand. When this indignity sparks a mild anger inside me, I raise my head. And that's when Mark cross-faces me, forcing the bony part of his forearm against my nose, then my eye socket, as a rather nasty way to move my head from his hip. I can taste blood. Literally. Finally, Mark spins behind easily for the takedown.

"Time!" Jim Geiger calls out from the middle of the room. It's his first season as Ashton's assistant coach. Cole says he's a Pennsylvania AAA state champ from a few years back, which isn't surprising since he definitely knows how to run a tough practice. "Next group on the mats," he says. Then, after a moment, he blows the whistle to start the next shot.

I find the nearest wall and slide down. I just got schooled in a major way. My neck aches and my nose is sore. Mark stands not far from me. He still has this intense look on his face. He's ready for more.

I'm not.

Instead, I look for my brother on the "champions" mat—reserved for varsity starters and contenders—at the front of the practice room. Cole doesn't notice me. I doubt he even cares what happens on the adjacent "runners-up" mat, where the rest of us toil. Coach Hillman's the same. He spends all of practice watching the varsity. Which, on a day like today, isn't the worst thing in the world. At least on the runners-up mat, I can wrestle like garbage in anonymity.

"Time!" Coach Geiger calls. "Next group. Gotta push yourselves, Ashton."

I pick myself up, secure my headgear, brush strands of hair from my eyes, and step back onto the mat. Mark crouches in his stance; I do the same. Right foot forward, hands in front, head up.

Off the whistle, I circle. Mark, however, comes right at me, forcing a tie-up. It's not a position I want to be in. But it's too late. He's already captured my arm with an underhook, and has my other wrist. I know what's going to happen even before it does. He sweeps my legs out and crashes me to the mat, then covers on top.

"Heard the cheer squad has an open spot," he says in my ear.

Oh, *that* pisses me off.

I start to work off my stomach. I need to get my hips under me. But Mark presses every ounce of his 120 or so pounds down on me. By the time I realize he's reached under my armpit, he's already cupped the back of my head with his hand. And by the time I realize that, he's already out to the side, grinding my face into the mat. And by the time I think to look away—which I shouldn't even have to think about—he's already circling with the half, prying my arm over my head and wrenching my shoulder from its socket.

I want to scream. Or cry. Or both.

But I don't. I fight it. And I fight Mark. As best I can. But he doesn't let up, putting me to my back. I try to bridge, but can't. I try to turn and slip my arm through, but can't. Then he goes chest to chest and squeezes.

"Time," Coach Geiger calls out.

Mark pushes off of me.

As the second pairs of wrestlers find space on the mats, I struggle to my feet. My shoulder's killing me. The end of practice can't come soon enough. Again, I slump against a wall. I have no idea why I let Mark tie up my arms. What'd I expect to happen?

I'm frustrated. Bruised. And exhausted.

Then I hear Coach Hillman's gravelly voice. "Hold on, Ashton," he says, stepping onto the champions mat. "This has been a doggone awful practice."

I look toward the front of the room. Coach Hillman never raises his voice, but he always makes it clear when he's annoyed. I guess when you've been one of Michigan's best coaches over the past twenty-four years and your teams have made it to the Division 2 finals eight times, capturing seven championships, you don't need to yell.

"Take a look around you. Go on," he says. "Maybe you've forgotten, this is the wrestling program's legacy, *your* wrestling program..."

Every wrestler—varsity and JV—focuses on the practice room walls. On one are the names of the school's district and region tournament champions; on another, the state place-winners. On the front wall, each of the school's twenty-nine state champions is honored with a plaque, going back almost seventy years when the Ashton program first began.

"Now, we've got a week until the Christmas tournaments," Coach Hillman says. "That's not a lotta time. Let's raise the intensity level for the last twenty minutes to where it should be for every practice. Next group of wrestlers get set."

Pep talk over. Now I can go back to hanging my head.

"Wexler," Coach Hillman says.

I look up. Why's he calling Mark's name?

"Find another partner," Coach Hillman says. "One who's going to push you."

Oh, great...just great.

I'm alone in the girls' locker room. As usual, winter track and basketball finished much earlier. It's just one of the differences between wrestling and other sports. Coach Hillman works us long and hard. Every practice.

I lie down on one of the wood benches and close my eyes. Sometimes my mind wanders and I wonder if one of the school's janitors is going to creep around the corner, pretending to be mopping the floor, so he can catch me in my underwear. But tonight, all I can think about is how lousy I was at practice. Dad says these things happen. That's little comfort. An ass-kicking is an ass-kicking. I can't just dismiss it. Worse, Coach Hillman was watching. The last thing I need is to give him any reason not to want a girl on the team.

I think about checking my weight. However, the scale is kept in the boys' wrestling locker room and I just don't have the energy. The school won't put one in here. Parents, teachers, feminists, fat girls would all be up in arms, insisting that a scale promotes an unhealthy focus on body image, leading to bulimia, anorexia, binging, purging, etc. All I want to do is weigh myself.

The locker room door opens. I bolt upright and cover my bra with my hands.

"You in there?" It's Cole.

"Yeah."

"Let's go," he says.

"Hold on a second," I mutter, pulling my gym bag out from a locker.

"Now."

I quickly slip on a sweatshirt and sweatpants, then carefully put my wrestling shoes and headgear on one side of my gym bag so that they don't mess up the folded outfit and flats I wore to school on the other side.

"We gotta get home and run," Cole says.

"I'm coming."

I shake my head. I just want to get home and crawl into bed.

Chapter 5

Holiday music fills our house.

Last night it was Elvis Presley; tonight, it's Dean Martin, an even older dead guy. Every year, Dad promises he'll play something from a cool band that I like. But he never does.

I look at myself in my closet-door mirror. My black DKNY cocktail dress is flawless and smooth, as are the set of pearls and gold bracelets Mom allows me to wear on only the most important of occasions. But that's not what catches my eye. It's my shoulders. And arms. And upper chest. And calves. I turn sideways to look at my butt. I'm buff there, too. Not big, mind you, definitely not like Trey or Cole or any of the guys on the team. But the muscles I have are cut.

I close my bedroom door, then strike a double-biceps, bring-down-the-house pose. Not a whole lot of cleavage, but definitely hot.

"Mel, are you ready yet?" I hear Mom call out. "Reservations are at six thirty."

"Gimme two seconds," I say.

I pick up the shoes I had set aside for the evening and

slip them on. They're black Steve Madden leather four-inch heels. Jade would just die if she saw them on me.

Cole pushes my door open. "Well, well, well," he says. "Guess you're not running."

"Running? I'll be lucky if I can walk in these," I say. "Wrestling shoes, they ain't."

"You're going to make up the miles tomorrow night," he informs me.

"Whatever." And when I see he hasn't left, I say, "Don't you have something better to do? Aww, you sad that it's a holiday dinner for just me, Mom, and Grandma?"

He leans against my door. "Like I'd want to go."

"I'll tell Grandma you said hello," I say, sarcastically.

He shrugs. "Yeah, whatever."

"You're one fine grandson."

"Just watch what you eat, chubby."

"Buh-bye," I say, turning away and fastening the buckle on my other shoe. I don't want him ruining the night before it's even started.

Cole leaves, finally. I straighten up and take one more look in the mirror to make sure the reflection is perfection...

What's that?

I step closer to the mirror. Then even closer. How did I not notice this? I touch my fingers to my cheek. Is that a bruise? If it's not, it's sure close. And my nose... was that scratch there earlier? And the mat burn over my eyebrow... Whoa, I look like I've been in a fight.

"We've got to go, Mel," Mom calls from the bottom of the stairs.

"Coming," I say, wondering what in the world to do. The only answer is an obvious one: Call Jade.

Thankfully, she picks up the phone immediately. Her suggestions, however, are ideal for someone who has solitary access to a bathroom for the next hour. "Warm compresses and cucumber oils," she insists.

"Jade," I say, doing my best to control my nerves, "I'm going to dinner *now*."

"Oh," she says. "Then blush. Lots of blush. Tons of blush."

I hang up the phone, put on my coat, and grab some blush—I'll brush it on in the car. I race out of my bedroom and slide, like a dork, the moment my heels touch the wood floor of the hallway. I hit the banister hard.

"Everything all right?" Mom asks.

"Fine," I manage. "Just peachy."

I rub my leg. What's another bruise or two? Lesson learned: All those agility drills we do in practice aren't too helpful when you're wearing high-heeled shoes.

Of course, it could've been worse. "Uh...sorry, Coach Hillman," I imagine having to say. "I'm afraid I can't finish the rest of the season because I wrenched my ankle trying to make it to dinner in pumps."

Yeah, that'd go over well.

Chapter 6

Light snow is falling as Mom pulls our Lexus to the front entrance of Crystal Fog Country Club. The headlights shine on two valets dressed neatly in red wool overcoats and black leather gloves. One walks in front of the car to the driver's side, while the other opens my door.

"Good evening, ma'am," he says in a surprisingly deep voice. His cheeks are rosy and his smile is confident. He's way cute, and just a couple of years older than me, I figure.

"Thank you very much," I say.

"Be careful of your footing," he says, offering me his hand. "It's slippery out here."

I step out of the car and stand up, then feign a wobble.

"I've got you," he says, grabbing my arm with one hand and closing the door behind me with the other.

As I hold his arm, he walks me under the canopy leading to the club's main doors. He's got muscles, I can tell. And, even in the cold air, I can smell his cologne. I wonder if he's a member's son trying to make extra money during his college winter break. Finding that out is first on my must-do list before dinner is finished.

"Have a pleasant dinner, ladies," he says, opening the door of the club for Mom and me.

"Oh, you, too."

I wince. I can't believe I just said that. How goofy. How yes-I'm-really-just-fifteen sounding. Couldn't I have come up with something sophisticated? Or at least a little witty?

Mom gives me one of those looks. "Surprising how you're suddenly very steady on your feet," she says.

"Yes, quite surprising," I reply.

That was kind of witty.

At the top of a short flight of stairs is the main foyer and, beyond that, the grand ballroom. Though I've been to the club many times before, I still marvel at the framed paintings, the ornate wood paneling along the ceiling, and the antique crystal chandelier lighting the foyer's immense Oriental rug. Piano music plays in the lounge, while a fire crackles in the brick hearth to our right.

Even when I was younger, I looked forward to dressing up and having weeknight dinners or Sunday brunch with my grandmother at the club. It thrilled me to have my coat taken and hung in the cloakroom, and I loved the way the waiters would ask me directly what I'd be having, instead of looking to my mom and dad for my order.

A gentleman in a flawless charcoal suit steps up. "Ladies, may I relieve you of your coats?"

Mom and I oblige. Being treated special never gets old.

"Mrs. Drake is waiting in the lounge," he says, with a nod.

I can see my grandmother through the open doors, sitting neatly and properly, setting down a goblet of red wine. When she notices us walking in, she smiles grandly. My steps quicken.

"Grandma," I say, giving her a big hug.

"My little Melinda," she says. She *always* calls me little.

"Sorry, we're late," Mom says, kissing her cheek.

"A few more minutes," my grandmother says, "and I might have had to ask one of my fine gentlemen friends to take your place."

I play along with her. "Really, Grandma? Which one?" I scan the crowded lounge and immediately notice a rather handsome older man who is dressed in a black suit with a bold red tie and sitting alone at the back of the room. "How about him?"

"My dear," she says, matter-of-factly, "none of these men can keep up with your grandmother."

I believe it. She's been running Drake-Dreshner Industries for, like, forever. A market leader in Michigan and Ohio, she always tells me. Her husband died in a boating accident long before Cole and I were born. Because of that, I never thought of him as my grandfather; my grandmother was always enough for me. I love that she's a big deal in business, even if I don't know that much more of what her company does than its logo: *DDI—Chemicals for Everyday Living*. Sounds kind of cool, though.

I point to a brooch in the shape of a horse pinned to the shoulder of her suit jacket. "That's pretty, Grandma."

"Twenty-four-carat gold with six inlaid diamonds, half carat each," she says. "It'll be yours when I'm gone."

"Really?"

She gives me a look.

"Don't worry, it doesn't have to be soon," I say, with a wink.

A little while later, the maitre d' leads us into the ballroom. My grandmother knows everyone. She shakes hands, or gives a cheek-kiss, to men and women at nearly every table we pass. I'm introduced as the brilliant, beautiful, and talented granddaughter who took time out of her busy high school schedule to have dinner with her grandmother. Of course, she doesn't mention that I wrestle. (She hates that I do—she's never even been to one of my matches.) But I do shake a lot of hands, and have ready answers to all of their questions.

I'm a sophomore at Ashton with a decent grade point average (sort of)…

My favorite classes are business and microeconomics (they're not)…

Oh, yes, I've been waiting excitedly all week to have dinner with my grandmother (true)…

Sometimes I have to embellish a bit, but I certainly don't mind the attention. And, who knows, maybe one of them will turn out to be the grandparent of the cute valet.

Mom and Grandma are deep in conversation, talking about things like revenue and product development, tax abatements and cash flow. Which is fine, frankly, because I'm engrossed in my appetizer. Of course, I don't want to eat too much, but when a plate of escargots bathing in butter and garlic sauce is sitting in front of me, my defenses are weak. So, with each delicious forkful that I put in my mouth, I calculate how much extra running I'm going to have to do with Cole tomorrow night after practice. A quarter mile... Another quarter mile... Oh, that one's definitely a half miler—

"Melinda?"

I look up from my plate. "What, Grandma?"

"I suggested to your mother that it might be beneficial for you to gain some experience this summer."

"Experience? What kind of experience?"

"The work kind," she says.

"I *do* work," I say. "You know that. You've come by the mall to see me."

"Ah, yes, Happy something-or-other."

"Happy Holidaze," I say.

"A positively, enlightening establishment," she says, with a dismissive wave of her hand. "No, I'm talking about more substantial work experience. An opportunity that few people your age get, my dear."

A second waiter comes to clear our plates, then scoop crumbs from the tablecloth. When he steps away, I eye my grandmother suspiciously. "And..."

"I'd like you to start spending some time at DDI. Perhaps a few hours during your Christmas vacation, and whenever you get a day off from school," she says. "You'd be a kind of intern."

"An intern?"

"An intern whose grandmother owns the company," she says. "But, yes, an intern nevertheless."

I love my grandmother, but I *really* like it at Happy Holidaze, especially after the school year ends. Jade works as a receptionist at Nails Galore, across from the store, and we mostly spend our lunch hours flirting with the guys from Sport Mart. A few times last summer we even snuck beers that the guys kept in their cars. Raven, my manager, never noticed. Most of the time, she was buzzed anyway.

"I appreciate your generous offer, Grandma, but I've made a promise to Happy Holidaze."

"So they'll go out of business if you're not there?"

I feign indignation. "Grandma, I'm an integral part of their product procurement team, a liaison to the merchandising division, and the primary customer service contact."

"You're a store clerk," she says.

I grin. "And a darn good one."

My grandmother purses her lips. She's not mad, I can tell. Maybe just a little disappointed. Fortunately, the maitre d' presents himself at just the perfect time. He asks if we're ready for our entrees. Grandma tells him we are. And with a gesture toward the kitchen, a waiter brings out our dinners. Lobster tails for me. And even more running for tomorrow night.

"Besides, Grandma, what if I don't like my boss?"

She smirks. "What if my intern is a slacker?" Touché. But then my grandmother puts a firm hand on my arm. "I want you to give this some thought," she says, with unexpected seriousness. "It's never too early to gain the work experience and business knowledge you would get at DDI. Can you make that commitment?"

Her expression surprises me. "Now?" I ask.

"Yes," she says. "For me."

I hesitate, then say, "Sure, Grandma, I'll do anything for you."

Just as quickly, her demeanor eases. Thank God. For a little while, I wonder what exactly I made a commitment to, but Grandma doesn't bring it up again and the rest of the dinner goes swimmingly, so I don't concern myself too much.

Instead, I listen as Mom tells us about a divorce case she's handling at her law firm. It's a well-known political couple in Ashton. She's not supposed to disclose any of the sordid details about who did what to whom because it's all hush-hush. But she does anyway, and the three of us have a huge laugh. Then, before dessert, I excuse myself from the table.

"I need to use the ladies room," I say.

Standing in front of the bathroom mirror, I feel fluttering in my stomach and my legs are the slightest bit unsteady. It would definitely be nice to have Jade here to give me a pep talk. Guess I'll have to do it myself.

"He's just a guy," I say to my reflection. "He should be thankful I've got any interest in talking to him."

That works to get my confidence up, for the moment. He's not from Ashton, which is a good thing. I'm sick of the guys at school, since most of them think it's weird that I wrestle. And, of course, there's no way in a million years I'd date anyone on the team—not even Brook, cute as he is.

I take a few deep breaths.

"Remember, he's only a guy."

A pretty cute one, though.

And just when a hint of doubt creeps back into my mind, I shake my head and smile one of those smiles that tells me I've got it together and I'm not going to let anything—or anyone—get the best of me. I pull lip gloss from my handbag and spread it on my lips, check my mascara and eyeliner, then smooth my dress of any wrinkles. One last look.

"Totally hot."

I leave the bathroom and walk into the main foyer where the well-dressed gentleman who took our coats has just greeted a couple of club members.

"Madame, how was your dinner?" he asks.

"Lovely," I answer. I figure "lovely" is something one of the club's ladies would say.

"May I assist you with anything?" he says.

"Why, yes," I say. "I need to get a pair of winter gloves that my mother left in our car. But I seem to have forgotten the name of the valet."

"Could that have been Stewart?" the gentleman says.

"The one without a mustache."

"Yes, Stewart," he says. "A fine, young man. Happens to be the golf pro's son. Works here at night and on the weekends. An excellent member of our staff. Shall I have him bring your car around?"

"No, no," I say. "Thank you, but I'll just ask him myself."

With a smile, I make my way down the stairs to the main entrance, feeling very full of myself for being so sly. I don't have a lot of time to waste, especially since I forgot to pee (and, at this point, I *really* have to), so I push open the door and hope that Stewart's alone.

Must be my lucky night. He's standing by himself under the canopy. When I walk toward him, he gives me a curious look.

"Need something?" he asks.

"Work here often?" I say. Oh, geez, I can't believe *that's* what came out of my mouth.

"Why, you want my job?" he says, smartly.

I hug my arms and scrunch my shoulders to hold off the cold. "Does it look like I want your job?"

"Probably not."

"Actually, do you know where I can get golf lessons?"

"Golf lessons?" he says. "I can help you with that."

"Really?"

"I'm team captain at Grand Hills High."

"What a coincidence," I say.

"Wait a sec..." he says, suspiciously. "Did you know I played?"

"Now how would I know that?" I say. Then with a rush of boldness that surprises even me, I ask, "Got a pen on you?"

He reaches for one in his jacket. I pull the glove off his hand and write my phone number on his palm. "I gotta get back to dinner," I say. "Don't want to miss dessert."

"Hey, are you going to tell me your name?"

"Melinda," I say. "And you?"

"Stewart," he says.

"Okay, Stewart." I turn to go back inside.

"You play any sports?" he asks. "Kind of looks like you do."

"I'll take that as a compliment," I say, slightly suspiciously. "And, yeah, I wrestle."

He looks at me funny. "Wrestle?"

I roll my eyes, knowing what he's thinking. "No, not the mud or Jell-O kind." I take a few steps toward the club entrance.

"Girls wrestle?"

"This one does."

"Who?"

"Guys," I say. "I'm on the team at Ashton High."

"No joke?"

"No joke."

"Is it weird wrestling guys?"

"Not really," I say.

He nods. I smile and open the club door. But before I step in, he says, "You're *really* on a guys' wrestling team?"

I stop, take a deep breath (God, I'm tired of answering this question), then turn and say, "When you call, I'll tell you all about it."

Chapter 7

Owings is our family's short-haired tabby. He spends most of the day in my bedroom, and most of that time under my bed—unless I'm getting ready for sleep. While I put away my heels, Owings strides over and rubs his head against my leg. I can hear him purring. I hang the cocktail dress neatly in my closet, then pick him up and cradle him in my arms.

"Did you miss me, boy?"

Owings nuzzles my face with his. He was originally Cole's cat. Or at least Cole got to name him. Which is a shame because I would've come up with something cute, like Iggiddabooggi, or Iggy, for short. But Cole had just read a book about Olympic gold medalist Dan Gable, whose only loss in high school and college was in the NCAA finals of his senior year to this guy, Larry Owings. Cole figured anyone tough enough to beat Gable must've been special. Too bad for Cole, Owings found his place in my bedroom the moment we brought him home.

Owings takes his usual sleeping spot on a pillow beside me. I give Jade a call to see if she's finished the homework for tomorrow. She hasn't. So we (sort of) do it on the phone, while I tell her about dinner. Jade, however, is disgusted by snails and less than impressed with Stewart, even when I tell her he's captain of the Grand Hills High golf team.

"You can do better," Jade says. "You need to go out with a guy who plays something as tough as wrestling."

"Wrestlers don't play," I remind her. "We wrestle."

Besides, I tell her, if that's going to be the criteria for whether or not I date, then I'm probably going to be sitting at home most of my life. She reminds me that's already true. But her reaction to Stewart is nothing compared to the outburst when I make the mistake of telling her I might start working at DDI.

"Are you *kidding* me?" she yells. "You already have a job."

"Relax, Jade," I say. "It'll just be a couple of hours when I'm free. Maybe one day after Christmas."

"What about the summer?" Jade says. "*Our* summer."

"The summer? Where's that coming from?" I say. "I just told you—a few hours—like, when we have a day off from school."

"Yeah, sure. You know your grandmother," Jade says. "First, it'll be just during Christmas break; by June, she'll make it the whole freakin' summer."

"Trust me," I say. "I'll spend a half day at DDI. My grandma will be thrilled. Then she'll drop the whole thing."

But Jade's not convinced. "Mel, I knew you shouldn't have gone. I just knew it."

"You mean, to dinner?"

"Yeah."

"Jade, I *like* having dinner with my grandma."

"Why'd you two even talk about working for her?"

"She brought it up."

"Why?"

"I don't know," I say, with a slight hesitation. "I guess she doesn't think I'm serious enough about stuff."

"What stuff?"

"I don't know...stuff."

"School?" Jade asks. "You get good grades."

"B's and C's."

"No way. You've gotten, like, one C," she says. "Plus you wrestle, which is super serious."

"I'm second-string on the JV team."

"And you worked hard last summer," she says. "We both did."

"Come on, Jade, be honest. We got to work late most days and sometimes took an hour for our half-hour break. And I don't have to remind you what we did a few times during those breaks."

For a while, there's silence. A very frustrated and annoyed silence, I can tell.

"Mel, whose side are you on?" Jade says, eventually.

"Yours. I mean mine. Ours. I'm on *our* side."

"Working at DDI? Think about all those chemicals you're going to be around," Jade says. "The fumes, Mel, the *fumes*. Breathing them in. Filling your lungs. They're going to make you mental. Or sterile. Maybe kill you."

Jade, always the drama queen.

"I'll just be in the office part," I say.

"Then you'll die of boredom."

Jade is so endearing sometimes. And persistent. I tell her she'll be a great lawyer someday. Again, there's silence on the other end. I forget how much she hates lawyers. Her father lost a big court case a few years ago. I never really understood what it was about. But, ever since, he's complained about "getting bent over and run up the A-tunnel" by the legal system. I think he's just an aloof, angry man. He rarely pays any attention to Jade and me, and the few times he does he has this creepy way of asking about my favorite wrestling moves, when I know he doesn't care at all. I'm sure he just wants to hear me say, "hi-crotch" or "chest to chest."

There's a knock at my bedroom door. Before I can answer, Cole pushes his way in. I whisper to Jade to hold on, and slip the phone under my pillow.

"What'd you eat?" he asks.

"A salad."

"What'd you *really* eat?"

"An endive salad with white wine vinaigrette," I say. "Then some gazpacho."

"What the hell's that?"

"Tomato soup—cold—with a little garlic, basil, salt, and pepper."

"Sounds like crap," Cole says.

"To the uncouth, it might," I say. "For the refined, it is the perfect entrée. Minimum calories, maximum enjoyment."

Cole folds his arms across his chest. "Mom already told Dad what you two had for dinner—snails, lobster, tons of butter." He shakes his head. "I'm going to be down in the basement lifting weights. You coming? Your fat ass certainly needs to."

"Please don't bother me, Cole," I say, loud enough for my parents to hear. "I'm doing homework."

"Homework?" Cole scoffs, as he leaves my bedroom. "Tell Jade I said hello."

I ignore him and wait for him to close my bedroom door. "What'd he say?" Jade asks when I get back on. "Nothing," I answer, then we pick up where we left off.

"Mel, I have a new mission," she says.

"A mission?"

"Yep. I'm going to help you nip this whole DDI thing in the bud."

I don't bother arguing with Jade. If she wants to make this her mission, fine. She tells me she'll have a plan figured out in a few days. Then we say goodbye and hang up.

I step down the basement stairs and take a seat.

"Need a spot?" I ask.

Cole looks up from the bench. "No," he snaps, as if I should've known the answer. He sets his hands, then his feet on the floor, arches his back, and with a grunt lifts the barbell from the rack. His body stiffens—like a controlled spasm—as he begins his reps, his chest and arms and shoulders easing the weight down, then pressing it up. One...

Two...

Three...

The fourth is a real struggle. My instinct is to help him just enough so he can lock out his arms. But I don't. Cole wants to experience that moment when his muscles give up but his brain doesn't. That's when the battle begins, he always tells me. That's when you find out if your mind controls your body, or your body controls your mind. Whatever that means. Guys have a lot of ridiculous sayings and stupid philosophies they apply to workouts and competition, and winning and losing, that seem insightful until you think about what they actually mean, and then you're like, "Huh?"

But this time I feel myself edging off the stairs. The barbell isn't moving up. And Cole's muscular forearms are quivering. I'm ready to help. Ready to jump up and give my brother a spot. Is the barbell sinking?

I lean further, ever so slightly...

And, then, it's like that moment when the Grinch (it was on TV the other night, okay?) has that epiphany about Whoville and becomes insanely strong. The barbell does not dip lower. Instead, Cole presses it up, locks out his arms, then racks it with a loud clank. God, I can't believe he got that one. Face flushed, he stands, thrusts out his chest, and gives me one of his patented maniacal looks.

"Mind over body," he growls. "Mind over f'ing body."

I roll my eyes. Okay, Socrates.

As much as I like to mock my brother's quotable quotes, I can't play down his wrestling talent. And I'm pretty proud of him, though I'd certainly never tell him that. He was 29–5 last year and a Division 2 region runner-up. He could've done well at the states, if a nasty stomach flu hadn't hit him the night before (he puked his guts for two days). But he made up for that disappointment in the spring and summer, placing in five freestyle and three Greco-Roman tournaments, winning two. In July, he went to the J. Robinson camp at the University of Minnesota and another that Coach Hillman held at our high school.

"Well..." Cole says to me.

"What? You want me to leave?"

"I want you to do a few sets."

"I'm tired."

"You're goddamn lazy."

That's not exactly a fair assessment. Besides feeling bloated from dinner, I just don't have the single-mindedness about wrestling that he does, living the sport year-round, training and practicing and drilling moves all the time.

"You need to get stronger," my brother says. "I see you getting your ass kicked in practice sometimes. It's embarrassing."

"Leave me alone," I say, standing up.

He shrugs. "Suit yourself, quitter."

"I'm not a quitter."

He gives me a funny look.

"Wait a sec," I snap. "Who says I'm a quitter?"

He doesn't answer. And now I can't tell if he's messing with my head or not.

"Tell me," I insist.

Again, nothing.

"You're a jerk, Cole."

But a totally weak insult like that means nothing to my brother. As I walk up the stairs, I hear the collars being taken off, and when I reach the kitchen, more metal plates sliding onto the barbell.

Chapter 8

Jade's really good at consoling people. She always has been. She's compassionate, kind-hearted, and she makes you feel as if your problem is the most important thing to her at that moment. I guess it's one of the reasons why she and I are best friends. Especially since I'm not particularly sensitive, and I'm definitely not nurturing.

I remember this one time when we were in sixth grade. We were in Jade's father's den. I didn't like being in Jade's house much (still don't), and I liked being in her father's den even less. It was weirdly neat, with floor-to-ceiling bookshelves on all four walls of the room and a pair of reddish leather chairs facing a huge wood desk. The books lined up perfectly, and there wasn't a pen or paper clip out of place.

Jade came up with the idea for a friendship pact. For some reason, this was very important to her. I thought it was kind of strange that she gave this any thought, since her mother was once again in the hospital and her father was away on a weeklong business trip. I would've figured those things were more than enough for her to be concerned with.

But instead, she sat tall in the desk chair, which she liked a lot because it had a high back that she said made her feel like a queen during the Renaissance (which we were learning about in history class). Then she reached into the top drawer of the desk and pulled out a pad of paper. As if playing a role she was perfect for, she slipped into that intensely earnest, so-close-she's-like-my-sister way that made Jade, well...Jade. She leaned over the desk and looked at me intently.

"Mel, we're like best friends, right?"

"Sure," I said.

"Think we'll still be in high school?"

I shrugged. "I guess."

"What if we don't have classes together?"

"We only have one class together now."

Jade frowned. "But what if we get in a fight?"

"A fight?" I said. "About what?"

"I don't know," Jade said. "Anything. Who's more popular? Who wears cooler clothes? Who do boys like more?"

"We both know you win," I say. "So there's nothing for us to fight about."

"One of us could say something, like, super mean," Jade said. "By accident, even."

"So neither of us will," I said.

She sat back. And though the chair looked huge around her, she didn't seem particularly small. She brushed the hair away from her face, her eyes passing over the room, but I could tell she wasn't looking for anything in particular. Then she said, as if she'd come to a reasonable, if not brilliant, solution, "This pact will have five truths in order for us to stay best friends."

"Truths?" I said.

"Five of them," she said, while scribbling on the paper. "One, we keep our secrets secret from anyone else. Two, we always help each other in geometry and English."

"Really?" I said, rolling my eyes.

Jade gave me a crooked smile. "Okay, okay, so that one's mostly for my benefit."

"Can we get out of here?" I asked. "Let's go over my house."

"Here's one for you, Mel, in case you ever do a sport. Three, we must be supportive of each other's athletic endeavors."

"Need me to spell endeavors?" I said, smartly.

"Like I care," Jade said.

"Are we done?"

"Nope," she said, then sort of whispered to herself. "We need a fourth... What's *really* important?" Her eyes suddenly widened. "Four, our friendship always comes before boys." And before I could comment, she added, "Number five, we never hurt each other."

"Now are we done?"

"Nope," she said, putting her hand up. "And yours."

"This is dumb."

"Just do it."

Reluctantly, I did. We pressed our hands together.

"The pact is sealed," Jade said, seeming very pleased.

I'm not sure why that came to mind, except that now I'm standing with Jade in the girls' bathroom as she comforts our friend Annie who's bawling her eyes out. Jade is definitely in her element. She wraps her arms around Annie, and with a soothing voice assures her that everything is going to be okay. She shoots me *that* look, the one that says, "Hello? Can you be, like, a human being?" So I give it a try. I nod my head in agreement and do my best to seem solemn but hopeful; sympathetic but not patronizing.

I have to work on it. But that's nothing new.

Annie's boyfriend, Georgie—and I use the word "boyfriend" in the loosest of ways—who's also on the wrestling team, just dumped her. Everyone at Ashton High, except Annie, knows he's the biggest sleaze in the sophomore class. I feel like screaming at her, "You didn't see this coming?" I mean, I know for a fact he's told Jade how hot she is, like, a hundred times. And he's winked at me twice—during practice, no less—even though I've told him to his face that I think he's majorly sketchy. There are even stories going around that he sucked face with a freshman at a party last month, after Annie left only a few minutes earlier.

"He...he...said..." Annie says, between sobs, "that... he can't...um...devote...enough time...to me and him..."

"What a jerk," Jade says. She's appalled. "Right at Christmas, no less." She pulls a tissue from her handbag and dabs Annie's eyes. "Did he give a reason?"

"Rrr...rrrr...wrrrestling," Annie manages to get out.

"Wrestling?" Now, *I'm* appalled. He's not good enough to use wrestling as an excuse.

"I really...I really liked...him," Annie says.

Jade shakes her head. "Forget him, Annie."

"I...can't..."

"You can," Jade says. "And you will."

"But he...but he was my...my boyfriend," Annie wails.

Jade gives me that look again. I shrug. I have no idea what to say. This is the best thing for Annie, though she probably won't realize that for a while. Georgie's been playing her for months. It was so obvious. Not to her, I guess.

"I got an idea," Jade says. "Let's start a nasty rumor about him."

"Like what?" I say.

"I don't know. Something bad." Then Jade's eyes widen. "Georgie can't get it up."

I laugh.

"Or that it's smaller than this." Jade sticks out her pinkie.

Annie sort of smiles. "I wouldn't...know..." she says, trying to catch her breath. "Maybe that's why...he broke up...with me."

"If *that's* the reason, then screw him," Jade says. "Guys are such dogs."

I nod. "Yeah, like my brother."

Jade looks at me. Then she turns on the faucet of one of the sinks. Annie leans over and splashes her face with water. It seems to calm her a bit. Jade pulls out a pack of Menthol Ultra Lights, lights up, draws in a breath, then gives the cigarette to Annie. Jade cracks open the bathroom window and blows out the smoke. Annie does the same. They don't bother offering it to me; they know I

49

don't smoke. For a few minutes, Jade and Annie pass the cigarette back and forth.

Jade gestures to me. "Can't you beat his ass in practice?"

I shrug.

"Well?" she says.

I turn to Annie. "Is that what you want?"

"Yes," Jade answers. "Use one of those moves on him. Like a leg-breaker. Or that crotch-crunch."

"Hi-crotch," I say.

"Yeah, that," she says. "Mel, this is for Annie. And for every one of us that's been screwed over by a guy."

Geez, now I'm the defender of all womanhood? As if I don't have enough to worry about. I nod toward the clock on the bathroom wall. "Time for class."

Annie checks herself in the mirror. So does Jade. So do I. When we're all satisfied, Jade tosses the cigarette out the window, sprays herself and Annie with perfume, and the three of us walk out into the hallway together.

Later, Jade and I meet at one of our secret places—the school auditorium balcony, midway down row four. It's always unoccupied during lunch period.

"What took so long?" she says, annoyed. Something must be up.

"I was hungry," I say. "Is that all right?"

She doesn't answer.

I park myself next to her. Last year, we figured out if we sit low enough in the two seats in front of the lighting and mixing board, we could stay hidden from any teacher who might look in from the balcony entrance, or up from either of the main floor aisles. We're safe for as long as we want to be there, or until the next drama class takes the stage.

"Stewart never called," I say.

"Who's Stewart?" Jade asks.

I frown. "The guy from the country club."

"The *valet?*" Jade says, with palpable condescension. "Forget about him."

But I can't. I gave him my number. And I looked totally hot that night. Totally. There's gotta be a reason why he didn't call. Maybe he washed his hand by accident. Maybe he doesn't want to date a girl who wrestles. Or, who knows, he could be gay. That explanation makes me feel a little better.

"Besides," Jade says, "we have more important things to discuss. I've devised a plan to keep you from working at your grandmother's company no more than one day. Two, tops."

"You devised a plan?" I mock.

"This is serious, Mel," she says. "You're only thinking you'll have to work there on days we have off from school. But your grandmother has you headed for the most boring, worst summer of your life, locked in the dungeon that is DDI. It'll be misery. And if your summer is ruined, then *my* summer is ruined."

"Okay, okay. So what's the plan?"

Jade looks me dead in the eye. "Sabotage."

"Sabotage?"

"Yes."

I'm about to answer with an emphatic "no," when we hear the door open on the main floor below us. Jade slaps her hand over my mouth, and we both slump lower in our seats. The click of heeled shoes moves down the center aisle toward the stage. Jade peeks over the front of the balcony, then whispers that it's Mrs. Fournier, the school's drama teacher. Soon, we hear her turn and walk back toward the auditorium exit.

When the door closes, I nearly shout, "Sabotage? Are you insane?"

"No, I'm not insane. And, yes, sabotage," Jade says. "Your grandma is forcing you to work for her, right? But that doesn't mean she can force you to work *hard*."

"You want me to sit there and do nothing?" I ask, incredulous.

"No, no, of course not," Jade says. "If you work super hard, she's going to like it and force you to come back over and over. If you don't work at all, she's going to be really pissed and force you to come back over and over to make up for it." Then Jade smiles and nods her head in such a way that tells me she thinks she's put together a brilliantly foolproof solution. "Here's the kicker. I call it Being Goldilocks. If you do just a very average amount, not too much or too little, then sprinkle in a few mistakes—which is, of course, because you're tired—then your grandmother'll think it's not worth having you work there anymore."

"I don't want my grandma thinking that about me," I say.

"Don't worry, you can make up for it in college," Jade

says. "We're young, so we're allowed to mess up."

"I don't know..."

"Our summers are at stake, Mel," Jade snaps. "And don't kid yourself. Working at DDI is going to totally mess up wrestling for you. You'll be too tired for weekend summer tournaments and too busy for camps."

Jade's given this way too much thought. "How do you know?"

She takes a deep and obviously frustrated breath. "Because that's what serious work does. It ruins fun. Look at my dad. He's miserable and he works *all* the time."

"My parents work hard," I say. "They don't seem *too* unhappy."

"Mel, Mel, Mel," Jade says, shaking her head. "Think your dad prefers spending a July day in a hammock sipping iced tea under the shade of a tree, or dragging his ass to work. And your mom? She didn't get to be the envy of all the tennis ladies in the neighborhood because she practices her backhand at the office."

Jade can be pretty convincing. "I told ya you'd make a good a lawyer," I say. "So, you want me to consider this Goldilocks plan?"

"No, I want you to follow it," Jade says, then adds, with her typical melodrama, "You may only get one chance."

I'm kneeling off to the side of the runners-up mat, waiting for the whistle to blow, re-adjusting my shirt clinging to my shoulders and upper back. I'm sweating like crazy.

Brook is next to me. We're partners for these final half-minute shots. It's something I never mind. He's a sophomore and a 113-pounder, too, though he has to cut to make weight. My walking-around weight is a few pounds under 113, but Coach Hillman told me at the beginning of the season that he wouldn't allow me to try to make 106—even if it was my certified weight class. No discussion. No explanation. His edict. Case closed.

The whistle blows. "Next group," Coach Geiger says.

Brook and I find a spot on the mat. He adjusts his headgear and crouches in his stance. I do the same. Our foreheads nearly touch. After an hour and a half of practice, he still smells nice. I'm not sure if it's cologne or the soap he uses. No, I bet it's his shampoo. I wonder if I should consider breaking my rule of not dating a teammate.

Oh, geez, did I actually just *think* that?

"Wrestle," Coach Geiger calls out.

I'm too slow to react when Brook shoots in for a double-leg. But I kick my legs back and sprawl, dropping my body on top of his. I try to control his head, but this is Brook's favorite takedown and he knows to keep his head tight to my hip. He's got his arms around my waist and curled down to the backs of my calves. Then, in one quick motion, Brook sucks in my legs, lifts one high and sweeps the other. I'm in midair for a split second before crashing down, with him on top.

We're at the edge of the mat, but Brook doesn't ease up. He wraps one arm over my head and snakes the other around my near leg, looking for a nearside cradle. I try to free my leg, but can't. I try to pull his hand off my neck, but can't. Brook then circles hard to break me down. I look away. I feel the cradle get locked up, just as we go off the mat and my feet bang against the wall.

Brook lets go of me. "Sorry."

Sorry? I'm not a Barbie doll. I pick myself up from the mat. I know Brook's just being nice, but way worse than getting my ass kicked is being handled delicately because I'm a girl. I can get tossed into a wall like anyone else in the room.

Back on the mat, we reset. This time I shoot first, drop-stepping in for the single-leg, my head on the inside. Brook puts in a wizzer and tries to hip into me, but I trap his leg with my own.

The whistle blows.

"Grab a different partner," Coach Geiger says.

Time to take care of unfinished business.

Georgie's on the other side of the runners-up mat. He has that smug look on his face. Not for long. I walk up and say, "Let's go."

We find open space, then face each other. At the whistle, I step forward and we tie up. Georgie grabs me tight. He wants to overpower me. Fine. I drive into him; he pushes back. Again, I push forward, making him back up. It's frustrating him, I can tell. Georgie hates the idea of being manhandled by a girl. So he drives into me again. That's when I use his momentum to hit a headlock hip throw.

Georgie lands on his back with a thud. My right arm is wrapped around his head, the left securing his arm. In a match, I'd be up 2–0 and getting back points. But I want more. So I squeeze my arms as much as I can and lean into him. "This is for Annie," I whisper. Georgie's shoulder blades inch toward the mat.

Closer...

Almost there...

"Hey!" I shout.

It takes a second to comprehend what I just felt was Georgie pinching the side of my boob. Thankfully, I never let go of his head. Now I crank it, way beyond anything legal.

Coach Geiger blows the whistle.

But I don't stop wrestling. Neither does Georgie.

"Time!" Coach Geiger shouts.

We stop.

I push Georgie away and mutter, "Loser," then stand up and walk off the mat. When I look over my shoulder, Georgie's still sitting there, rubbing his neck, with an expression on his face that's a mix of being pissed and embarrassed.

I'll remember that for a long time.

The next morning, Jade, Annie, and I have a big laugh in the girls' bathroom when I tell them what I did to Georgie.

"Wish we could've seen it," Jade says, putting on lipstick in front of one of the mirrors.

"When I was done with him," I say, "he sat there like a little boy who'd had his head handed to him by a girl."

Jade presses her lips together, then pulls out a tissue to fix a smudge. "He deserved it."

"He did," Annie says, nodding. Then she gives me a hug. "Thanks, Mel."

"And get this," I say. "He pinched my boob."

Jade spins around. "What?"

"Yeah, right here," I say, pointing at my shirt.

"He's so gross," Jade says with disgust. Then she looks at Annie. "Why in the world did you ever like him?"

Annie shrugs, timidly.

Jade returns to the mirror. "What'd the coaches do when you told them?"

"I didn't."

"You didn't? What's up with that?"

"Georgie would've just denied it. He would've said I was imagining things," I say. Jade's unconvinced. "Look, I don't need to cause any distractions for the team."

"That's ridiculous," she says.

"It is what it is," I say.

Chapter 9

There's an envelope from my friend Odessa waiting for me on the kitchen table. It's something nice to come home to after another killer practice. So I run upstairs, hop on my bed, give Owings a tickle under his chin, then wedge an eyeliner under the flap and tear it open.

I can't help but laugh.

It's a holiday photo of the model black family...sort of. Odessa's mom and dad are standing to one side of their fireplace, prim and proper in their green and red sweaters, while, on the other side, Odessa's in her stance, bent at the knees, elbows in and hands forward, wearing the biggest smile in the world—and her maroon team singlet. Along the top, it reads, *All The World's A Mat, And We Are Truly Wrestlers*... And, on the back: "Mel, have a great season! Love, O."

Odessa's from Royal Oak. Her father was a football player at Michigan, a long time ago. Now he's a professor at Wayne State. Odessa says she got her toughness from him but, thankfully, not his big belly. I think she got her perfect teeth from her mom. Two years ago, we met at a summer wrestling tournament. I was there to watch Cole;

she was there to compete. When I found that out, I was blown away.

At that time it never occurred to me that a girl could wrestle for real. I mean, I'd always kind of wondered about it, but I was never taken seriously by my mom and dad. I think they figured I was just trying to be rebellious, which was strange since I'd grown up around wrestling mats, watching all of Cole's matches. And, plenty of times, when he was on the rec team, I was his bedroom practice partner when he wanted to work on an arm-drag or shrug.

"Watch it up there," Dad would shout from the living room. "And, Cole, don't hurt your sister."

He never did. Never came close. He just needed somebody in front of him as a pretend opponent. I'd watch his eyes. They'd turn hard and his body would move so sharply, yet fluidly, even though it was just for practice in his bedroom.

At the tournament, Odessa sat by herself in her singlet on the bottom row of the stands. No one talked to her. And, as far as I could tell, she didn't have any teammates or coaches with her.

"I'm going to get candy," I said to my dad. "I'll be back for Cole's next match."

Instead, I went into the hallway off the gymnasium to check the brackets. In the lightest weight class, I noticed a girl's name: Odessa Dunn. She'd lost her first match, 7–4, against a guy who was seeded. I returned to where Odessa was sitting.

"You wrestled, right?" I said.

"Yeah," she said. "I lost."

"Close, though."

"I guess."

"That's not bad."

"It's a loss..." she said. "But thanks."

I sat down beside her. She didn't seem to mind. I told her my name; she told me hers. I noticed that people walking by would look at her, some even stared. No one said anything, at least not anything either of us could hear.

Later, we talked on the phone and soon became good friends. Last summer, she came out to our family's beach house on Lake Michigan. And in November she stayed over one night. Odessa's a junior, so she's into the college search. She said she has her heart set on Menlo College in California, so she can try out for their women's team. The rest of the night we talked about school and guys and the upcoming season. Odessa said she expected to be Royal Oak's varsity starter at 120.

"That's amazing, O," I said.

"What about you?" she said. "Gonna cut to 106?"

"I don't think so."

"Mel, you'd be good there."

"Yeah, well..."

I didn't want to tell her that Coach Hillman won't let me. I'm not sure why. I knew she'd understand.

I've got to call her soon, I tell myself. Then I sit down at my vanity and pull out a bunch of holiday cards Mom and I bought at a Hallmark store. I write Odessa's name and address on an envelope and pick out the card I'd set aside for her.

It says: "Success is like holding a dove… If you let it go and it returns, it was always meant to be… If it doesn't, then hunt it down with everything in your arsenal…"

Chapter 10

"You ready?" Cole yells from our front hallway.

"Hold on," I yell back.

I grab a pair of wool mittens and walk through the kitchen from the laundry room. I've got on a T-shirt, turtleneck, Ashton Wrestling sweatshirt, and Lycra pants. As I pass the living room and gaze at the presents sitting under the tree, Mom comes down the stairs. I give her a hug and a kiss.

I remember how wonderful Christmas used to be—before I started wrestling—when I'd open my eyes in the morning and realize I didn't have to think about school or homework, then I'd run down the stairs in my pajamas and grab every colorfully wrapped box that had my name on it.

Not anymore.

"Dad went out to get some bagels and lox," Mom says. "We'll have breakfast when you two get back. And don't forget your grandmother's coming over later."

Cole shakes his head. "We're not eating today."

"Uh, hello, I can speak for myself," I say.

"We're *not* eating," Cole repeats. "I've got the Ann Arbor Invitational in two days; you've got the Southfield JV tournament this Saturday. I'm not letting you pork out and embarrass me by not making weight."

Enough said, apparently.

We step outside, then down the front path. It's an overcast, cold morning, but that does little to wake me up. My body is standing in the driveway, but my mind is still back in bed with Owings nuzzling my hair. Cole begins his usual routine, rolling his ankles, stretching his hamstrings, then bouncing on his toes. I don't do much—except cough twice and shiver—I'm always sort of limber. It's one of the benefits of being a girl, I guess.

"We'll run together," Cole says.

"Together?"

"It's my gift to you," he says, motioning for us to start down the driveway.

"No, no, no," I say. "You better've gotten me a *real* present. One morning of running together isn't going to cut it. I run alone all the time. It's no big deal."

"So I'll run ahead," he says, as we turn onto the street.

But he doesn't. Maybe he's doing this to cull some favor from me, or maybe he just needs an excuse to take it easy. Either way, I don't totally mind. Though I'd never admit it to Cole, there are advantages to having your older brother be a high school sports star. Even last year, as a freshman, teachers treated me differently once they knew we were related. I also get the benefit of the doubt with grades—at least according to Jade. She thinks I should thank Heaven for my last name. She says it's like having street cred without having done anything important.

"How's your weight?" I say.

Cole glares at me. That's always his answer. He's never had a problem making weight, mostly because he'll do anything humanly possible to cut that last quarter or half pound. Once, I watched him stick his finger down his throat to barf. That's "old school" cutting weight, he said, before spitting out the last few chunks. It was gross. And plenty of times I've been the one to pile blankets on him while he wears a garbage bag with holes cut for his arms and legs. After an hour, it's remarkable—and disgusting—how much he can sweat.

"Ready for this weekend?" Cole asks.

"Yeah," I say.

"Better be."

This'll be my first in-season tournament, and it's single elimination. Last July, I competed in a summer tournament in Beaufort. Got pinned twice. Total time on the mats— less than two and a half minutes. It was pretty awful.

Even worse, I was the only girl competing. All the locker rooms were being used by the guys, so the best the tournament director could do was have me change in a bathroom at the other end of the school. Then, after my second loss, I was looking for a place where I could have a few moments to myself before my dad came down from the stands to console me. Out of nowhere, some big fat woman got entirely too close.

"Honey, honey," she said to me. "You all right?"

"Huh?"

"Does your mom know you're here?"

"What?"

"Now, tell me," the woman said. "Why in the world would you wanna be on these dirty ol' mats with boys?"

I didn't have a clue what to say.

"You're an adorable young thing," she said, just as my dad came up. "You should be, uh...on the twirl team, or cheerleading. Wouldn't that be more ladylike?"

How do you answer something like that? Well, I didn't. My dad didn't say anything either. He did when we got in the car, though. He told me how proud he was to see me wrestle. What I was doing was an accomplishment, he said. Anyone who thought differently was just an overweight ignoramus. Then he took me to Dairy Queen.

Cole and I continue down Algonquin Avenue. There aren't many cars on the road. It's kind of peaceful and pleasant. Cole motions for us to turn right at the Unitarian Church, and we head down Ford Park Drive. I can tell he's taking it easy. He doesn't have that usual intense look on his face. Still, we're going long enough that I start to feel my neck and shoulders getting sweaty. Even early on Christmas morning, it's not that bad of a feeling.

I'm staring at a Tiffany's sterling silver jewelry box with "Melinda Drake Radford" engraved on the top. I'm so in awe, I haven't even untied the bow around it.

"Merry Christmas," my grandmother says, sitting at the end of my bed.

"Grandma, this is incredible," I gush.

"I'm glad you like it," she says.

"Oh, I do," I say, placing the jewelry box on my vanity and stepping back to admire it.

"I wanted to give you something you'll have a long time," she says. "So, my dear, did you get everything you wanted?"

"Are you kidding?" I say. "With this jewelry box, and all the stuff Mom and Dad got me? It's been the best Christmas. Check this out."

I reach for the stack of presents on my desk. Mom came through in a major way, getting me a flower-patterned Von Fürstenberg sundress that I lay on the bed to show my grandmother.

"Very nice," she says.

"And look at this—a Louis Vuitton handbag." I hold it up, along with a pair of Palladium leather boots. "She also got me a camera and a subscription to *Teen Vogue*." I jump on the bed beside my grandmother and hold out the camera in front of us. "Say cheese!" Then I snap the photo. It's a good one. "And Dad, he got me a DVD player and the sweatshirt I'm wearing." I point to my back. "See what it says? *Wrestling. Invented by Boys. Perfected by Girls*. Pretty cool, huh?"

"Quite cool, I suppose," she says. "And what about Cole? What did he get you?"

"A pedometer with a calorie counter," I say, rolling my eyes. "How lame is that?"

"Entirely lame."

"It sure is."

"My brother never gave me good presents either," Grandma says. "Perhaps that's just what happens with brothers. But, of course, I never complained. I'm sure you don't complain to Cole, either."

"Doubt he'd care anyway," I say.

Then Grandma takes on a thoughtful look. "But that lets them off scot-free, doesn't it?"

"Yes, it does," I say.

"This is why it's important to only depend on yourself," she says. "Then you'll never be disappointed." Uh-oh, Grandma's doing that thing where she slips a life lesson in the middle of some cheery conversation. "I never thought I'd be running a multi-million-dollar company," she goes on. "But here it is, many years later. Life gives you surprises, good and bad. You must be prepared. I've always found it better that way. You have the world ahead of you. You can do anything you want, even if no one expects you to."

I put on my most solemn face. "Grandma…"

"Yes, dear?"

"You're not dying, are you?"

"Okay, I understand," she says, with a knowing frown. "Enough with the overbearing grandmother routine."

"No, I really enjoy our talks," I say. I notice Owings poke his head from under the bed. I reach down and pull him out, then hold him in my arms. "Owings never lets me down," I coo. "He'll always love me."

My grandmother touches my shoulder. "Oh, you know what I forgot? There's a little something for Owings, too. Inside the jewelry box."

"Owings? Really?"

I step over to my vanity, untie the bow, then lift open the top of the jewelry box. "Oh...no...way..." I look back at my grandmother. "For me?"

She smiles. "The collar is for Owings. The other is for you."

My hand is practically shaking. I reach in and pull out a gold necklace with five diamonds set in a crescent.

"My husband—your grandfather—gave it to me for Christmas forty-three years ago," she says. "He told me it was only to be worn by the prettiest girl in the world. So now I pass it on to you."

Looking in my mirror, I put the necklace around my neck. And touch it again. God, it's beautiful... I turn to Grandma and practically knock her over with a hug. "Thank you, thank you, thank you!"

"So you'll be working at DDI this summer?"

Huh?

I'm pretty sure my jaw just fell open. Jade was *right*. She kept going on and on about this, and I thought she was crazy. I guess she wasn't.

I pull back and look at my grandmother, but her face gives away nothing.

Is she serious? I've got no idea what to say. I don't want to work at DDI. I want to work at Happy Holidaze again, and flirt with guys at the mall, and hang out with Jade on our lunch breaks.

Then, after a long, truly awkward silence, my grandmother says, "Got you, didn't I?"

"Oh, geez, you were only kidding?" I say, letting out a long and anxious breath. "Then, yes, you totally got me."

"I'm pleased," my grandmother says.

Then I give her a smirk. "Though if you'd waited a few seconds," I say, "I might've said yes."

She flashes a smile, then suddenly turns serious in a business-y kind of way. "So, I think next Friday would be ideal for you to come to DDI. I'll show you our warehouse and manufacturing facility and introduce you around the office."

"Office?"

"You can get started with some data input work."

"Data input?"

"It'll be an important learning experience for you."

I'm pretty sure I don't look very enthusiastic.

"My... That necklace looks just perfect on you," my grandmother says. "I wanted to keep it in our family. More importantly, I wanted to give it to you because you understand its significance. And its beauty. I'm pleased. Perhaps you'll wear it to the office."

I stare at the necklace in the mirror. "Uh...sure, Grandma."

"Good," she says. "Very good."

Chapter 11

I lie on my bed, weary and hurting.

Another backbreaking practice. Literally. During one drill, I tried to lift Brook and sweep out his legs. But I wasn't strong enough to get him completely off the mat. So, instead, he grabbed me in a bear hug and dropped me straight to my back.

I think I'm still a little woozy.

The phone rings.

I'm too beat-up to bother. I'm sure it's Jade, anyway. Probably wants to talk about making New Year's resolutions. That's her new kick. After figuring out a plan for me to sabotage my work at DDI, now she's on to something else: making a fresh start. A clean slate. For both of us. *From what?* I ask myself. Who in the world knows?

On, like, the tenth ring, I pick up the phone and say, annoyed, "Yeah?"

"Hello, is Melinda there?"

It's a guy's voice. A sweet voice. One that sounds vaguely familiar. I sit up. Who could it be? Someone from school? Maybe—fingers crossed—some junior or senior who's been checking me out. That'd be totally insane. Jade would just about die. Then again, it could be some loser freshman or sophomore who managed to get hold of my phone number. I'll play along.

"M'linda?" I say, in a voice I've practiced for just such an occasion, the one of a ten-year-old British girl. "M'linda who?"

"Did I dial the right number?" he says. "I'm looking for Melinda."

His confusion nearly makes me laugh.

"From where is you callin', Guv'nor?"

"Uh...my kitchen table," he says.

"Gettin' a bit snarky, ain't we?"

"No, I mean—"

"You is da bloke what phoned 'ere."

"Look, if there's a Melinda there," he says, "can you put her on the phone?"

"No trouble, Guv'nor. Oo's callin'?"

"Tell her it's Stewart. The guy who's going to give her golf lessons."

Oh, shi—

I cover the phone with my palm. *It's him! The valet!*

And, then, I suddenly get annoyed. *Now* he calls? Geez, waited long enough, didn't he? I mean, it's *way* past the three-day rule. I run over to my bedroom door and close it, then jump back on my bed. I get comfortably situated, then take a deep breath.

"Who's this?" I say, in my normal voice.

"Melinda, I'm Stewart, the guy you met at Crystal Fog," he says.

"The guy parking cars, right?"

"That's the one. You busy?"

"Not really," I say, pushing away the issue of *Cosmo* that my mom left on my bed. "Just reading."

"So, who answered the phone?" he asks.

"My kid sister."

"Why's she have an English accent?"

"She watches the BBC a lot."

But being a bit of a wiseass isn't exactly working.

"Hey, sounds like you're in the middle of something," Stewart says. "Nice talking—"

"Don't hang up," I say. "I'm glad you called. I was worried you might be..."

"What?"

"Not into girls," I say. "I figured that's why I hadn't heard from you."

"I've been working a lot lately at the club," he says. "Trying to save up for college. Classes are kind of expensive, you know."

But I don't. I don't think about college. Or how much it costs. My parents or my grandmother are going to take care of it, I guess.

"Yeah, sure," I say.

"And I *am* into girls," Stewart quickly adds.

"Good," I say. "That's good."

It's an odd thing for me to say, but this *is* a pretty odd conversation. I think he feels the same way. And for a few very uncomfortable moments, there's silence.

"So..." I say, finally.

"Yeah?"

"Guess we should start from the beginning."

"Sure," he says. "The beginning."

"So...what's your last name?"

"Marshall," he says. "Stewart Johnson Marshall III."

"That come with a trust fund?"

"I wish," he says. "My family's nothing like that."

"Seems a good fit for Crystal Fog."

"My dad's just the assistant golf pro," he says. "Doesn't make us rich, but it did get me the valet job. And during spring and summer the club lets me on the practice greens. At the end of the day I also get to play the front nine, after the last group goes out."

I don't even know what that means. "Must be fun parking cars," I say, which sounds really dumb since, after all, it *is* just parking cars. "Except, I guess, when it's snowing. Or cold. Or raining. Or humid. Or really hot."

"Well, when you put it like that," Stewart says, "it does sound like a crappy job."

"Oh, you know what I mean," I say.

"Being a valet isn't too bad," he says. "Sometimes I get to drive cool cars, even if it's just in the parking lot. Like, last week, I parked this cherry-red, six-speed Lotus Elise." But his enthusiasm is totally lost on me, which he catches onto quickly. "Not much into cars?"

"Nope," I say.

"And I'm going to guess you don't really want golf lessons, either," he says.

"And you'd be right," I say.

"So you just wanted me to call you."

"Pretty much," I say.

"Okay," he says, "that's fine with me. But you should try golf sometime. There's nothing like it."

Personally, I don't find golf even remotely interesting. Seems like one long walk with very little excitement. Kind of pointless, if you ask me. But it obviously isn't to Stewart.

"The thinking and strategizing," he continues, with enviable excitement. "Each shot is different, and yet each one counts as much as any other. Then you have all these factors to consider: the height of the grass, sand traps, the direction and speed of the wind, whether it's been raining or dry..."

Golf seems the opposite of wrestling. In wrestling, the conditions are always the same. The mats are nearly all the same dimensions. Matches are indoors. Singlets and wrestling shoes are pretty much the same. It's just you and your opponent. For three two-minute periods.

"...I'm not that great yet at reading greens," Stewart adds, with a hint of frustration.

"Of course," I say.

He pauses. "You know what that means?"

"Yeah," I say, for some reason.

"Really?" he says. "So what's it mean?"

"What?"

"Reading greens."

"Uh..."

"You have no idea," he says.

"I don't."

"It's understanding the contour of the green and whether the ball is going to break—turn—one way or the other, or not at all, when you putt. My dad's incredible at reading greens. Actually, he's pretty great at every part of golf. But to be like him takes time—time out on the course. Practicing shots. Over and over. And over."

"That's cool, I guess."

"What kind of stuff are you into?" Stewart says.

I feel myself shrug. "You know...stuff."

"Shopping?"

When he says it, I just happen to be admiring my closet full of clothes. "No, not shopping," I say.

"Fashion?"

I push the *Cosmo* off my bed. "No," I say, just as strongly.

"What then?"

I hesitate for a second. I'm into wrestling. Not like Cole, but pretty into it. My doubt surprises and annoys me. I mean, I like wrestling a lot. I like competing for myself and the team. I like depending only on myself when I'm out there against a teammate in practice, or an opponent in a match. How much does that mean I'm into it? I'm not sure how to measure that.

"Uh...hello?" Stewart says.

"I'm thinking," I say.

"If you have to think about it, maybe you're not really into anything."

"I am."

"I'm not saying that's a bad thing."

"Yeah, you are." I'm getting kind of annoyed.

"I'm not."

"You are," I say, then sort of blurt out. "Wrestling. I'm into wrestling."

"Really?" Stewart says. "I thought you were joking that night."

"Why would I joke?"

And we sort of hit that moment when it seems the conversation could go one of two ways: end abruptly and irreparably, or be saved by one of us reaching out to smooth over the awkwardness of learning about each other.

Stewart opts for the latter, and it totally works on me because as much as I'm mad that I question my own commitment to wrestling, I do like talking to him. And I really like his voice.

"Ever get to travel for wrestling?" he asks.

"Not really," I say.

Cole's been to summer tournaments in Ohio and Fargo, North Dakota, and camps in Minnesota and Wisconsin. But not me. Not yet. Just this part of Michigan. Just within a half hour or so of Ashton.

"Last August, my dad and I went out to play at Pebble Beach. Ever hear of it?"

"No," I say.

"It's in California. It was so amazing. Some of the holes are right near cliffs. And the views of the Pacific Ocean—as you're playing—just blew me away. I think it's my favorite course. But, then again, there are so many around the country that I want to—"

There's a loud knock on my door. I put my hand over the receiver, just as Cole walks in.

"What do you want?" I say.

"If you're going to my tournament tomorrow, we're leaving early," he says, then closes the door.

I take my hand off the phone.

"Sorry about that," I say to Stewart.

"Gotta go?" he says.

"Kind of. My brother's co-captain of the varsity wrestling team. They've got a tournament in Ann Arbor tomorrow, but everyone's gotta be at our high school early to take the team bus over."

This wasn't a bad first conversation. I'm disappointed having to hang up. I think Stewart is, too. He tells me his phone number and I write it down.

"I'll call you tomorrow night," he says.

"Bye," I say, letting that thought settle into my mind as I hang up the phone and lay my head on my pillow.

Chapter 12

It's a cloudless morning. Those are always the coldest. The car heater's on high, but it's not helping. I cross my arms for warmth. Cole's in the backseat and Dad's driving; none of us is saying a word. It's always that way the day of competition.

When I was younger, I always wanted to go to my brother's rec and middle school matches. I watched how he prepared, meticulously checking and re-checking his equipment bag for his singlet and warm-ups, knee pad, socks, and wrestling shoes. And he always had an intense gaze, breathing shallowly and deliberately. I'd wonder what was going on in his head, but I never asked. I preferred not knowing. It always felt like something exciting was going to happen. I liked being part of that, if only as a tagalong.

"I brought a bottle of Gatorade for you," I say to my brother.

My voice sounds almost odd in the quiet car. I glance back over my shoulder. Cole doesn't look at me, but simply nods.

He's seeded first at 160 pounds. He's undefeated so

far this season and should remain that way by the end of the day. The pressure's overwhelming, I can tell, and it'll only get worse as the season goes on. Everyone expects him to win. Every match. It doesn't leave much room for error. None, in fact. He can't afford to have a bad match, or even a bad period.

I close my eyes and sink into the front seat. I have no idea how he handles it.

"Nooo," I hear myself say. It sounds more like a gasp.

Cole's at the edge of the circle, on his knees, holding his left wrist and grimacing so badly that I'm sure if he wasn't so crazy tough he'd already be bawling. I want to run over to him, but there are ropes to keep fans and teammates from crowding the mats.

"What happened?"

I look to my left. It's Trey.

"Cole was fighting a single," I say. "The guy from Pioneer drove him off the mat. Cole put his hand down to stop the fall."

"Hear anything pop?"

"Pop? I don't think so," I say. "That's good, right?"

"A pop would probably mean a torn ligament," Trey says. "He'd be done. And the team would be screwed. Hopefully, it's a sprain."

Coach Hillman walks out on the mat, as I watch my brother clench and unclench his fist. At least he can do that. I know it would be devastating for him to default. It's been, like, a year since he didn't make the finals of a tournament.

As injury time ends, Cole stands up. He and Coach Hillman have a brief but heated discussion. Cole shakes his head, then does it again, but even more animated. Coach Hillman is not happy. He walks back to the corner of the mat. I lean over the rope to listen.

"What's your decision, Ashton?" I hear the referee say to Cole.

Cole gives him a thumbs-up.

"You sure?"

He nods.

"Let's go then," the referee says, gesturing to the Pioneer wrestler.

When people in the stands realize Cole's going to continue, they begin to clap, and Ashton fans shout encouragement. This fires up our varsity wrestlers, who cheer for their co-captain. It gives me a chill. I look at my dad, who doesn't seem the least bit relieved, then at the scoreboard.

There's 1:09 left in the third period. Semifinals. Cole's behind, 6–5.

Right from the whistle, it's obvious the Pioneer wrestler wants to force Cole to use his left hand. He pulls in Cole's right arm and drives him to the mat. Time ticks away as my brother seems unable to brace or push off with his injured hand. I look over. Coach Hillman is standing at the corner of the mat. He seems ready to put a stop to the match. It never even occurred to me that he could do that.

Then, somehow, Cole frees his right hand and steps to his feet. The Pioneer wrestler is behind him, hands locked around his waist.

"Cut, cut, cut!" I yell.

So does everyone else.

Cole tries to turn and slip his elbow between him and his opponent. They stagger toward the edge of the circle. Cole fakes a switch one way, then the other, but the Pioneer wrestler picks him up and dumps him hard to the mat. On his left side, of course.

"Come on, ref, that was a slam!" I shout. "Open your eyes!" The referee glances over, but I don't care. Cole should've been given a penalty point. "You missed that one, ref!"

Cole fights to a base, then to his knees. Now the Pioneer wrestler attacks Cole's injured left wrist. The wrestler side of me thinks that's exactly what he should do; the sister side of me is appalled. I let my objections be known, loud and directly.

"That's bush league!"

"Out of bounds," the referee says, as Cole and his opponent go outside the circle. But before he directs them back to the center for a re-start, he walks directly toward me. "Young lady," the referee says. "Fans have to stay in the stands."

Young lady? What's up with that?

"Hey!" I snap.

The referee looks over his shoulder.

"I'm on the team." I want to finish it with "idiot" or "jerk."

The referee seems confused, then simply shakes his head and continues to the center of the circle. There, he motions for Cole to get set in the bottom position. Cole gingerly touches his left hand down. The Pioneer wrestler is directed on top. Twenty-one seconds left.

Rope be damned. I'm practically stepping over it, screaming for my brother to find a way to escape and tie the match. But his Pioneer opponent is ruthless, now clamping down on his left hand and dropping Cole back to the mat whenever he gets to his feet.

"Explode, explode!" I yell.

And my brother does, getting to his feet one more time, with both hands free. Ten seconds left...

Nine...

Eight...

Cole tries to pull away from his opponent.

"Stalling, ref!" I shout. "Stalling!"

Five...

Four...

Then, in one last burst of strength, the Pioneer wrestler lifts Cole high off the mat, then back down again, just outside the circle.

I hear the clock buzzer go off and Cole howl in pain.

The ride home is dead silent.

After the match, Dad drove us to Uncle Neil's office in Ashton. He's not a real uncle but a close friend of our family. He's an orthopedist and, apparently, a good one. He looked at Cole's wrist, took X-rays, and concluded it wasn't broken but sprained. That's positive news.

I know Cole doesn't see it that way.

He started the day expecting to bring home a gold medal but, instead, has his wrist wrapped in a bandage—

and no medal—to show for his efforts. I don't even think about looking toward the backseat. I can *feel* Cole's anger. I know my brother. He needs time alone to forget what happened. It might take tonight and tomorrow. Or maybe a few more days after that.

Soon, we round the corner and Dad pulls the car into our driveway. The lights are on in the living room and above the garage. I can see our Christmas tree through the bay window. Our family usually waits until the winter break is over before taking everything down. The three of us get out of the car.

"Get your running shoes on," Cole says.

It takes me a moment to figure out that he's talking to me. "Huh?"

"Put on your running shoes."

"Why?"

"Because we're going running."

"Now?"

"Yes, now."

I follow him up the walkway to our front door. "But you—" I start to say, wondering if he's just BS-ing me. "You hurt yourself. And you lost."

"Don't tell me I lost," he says. "I know I lost."

"A big match," I say.

He stops. "Mel, I *know* I lost a big match. I *know* I got injured. But it was my wrist," he says. "Not my leg, my foot, or my ankle. Those are all fine. Those are ready to go running."

Cole continues toward the house. I watch him, as I stand in my tracks. Then Dad passes me. I don't even waste my breath pleading with him for a reprieve. It's useless. I don't want to go running. I'd rather be on the phone with Stewart (even hearing about golf again), or telling Jade how I pissed off the ref today. Or just lying on my bed with Owings, checking out the latest *In Style* magazine. Anything but running.

But I'm going.

Chapter 13

For practices during Christmas break, Coach Hillman starts our warm-ups at eight a.m. Sharp. Then he locks the door. Those who are there on time, practice; those who aren't, don't.

Coach Hillman paces the wrestling room. Everyone is quiet and moving slowly. I hear the rustle of athletic shorts, cotton T-shirts, and heavy sweatshirts. Every half minute or so, Trey or Cole tells the team to change from one stretching position to another. In their normal voices. No yelling. No barking out commands.

"Because of the tournament yesterday," Coach Hillman says, clearing his throat, "I didn't get a chance to ask if each of you got what you wanted for the holidays." He sounds pleasant enough, but I get the feeling it's not going to last long. "I hope so," Coach Hillman says. "I hope you got exactly what you wanted. Every one of you."

Stopping at the center of the runners-up mat, Coach Hillman flashes a smile that's more like a sneer. "It's nice to get what you want, right?" He's only a few feet from me, but I don't dare look at him. "You want this, you want that... I understand. We all want something." His voice just got a little louder. "We all want to win. We all want to wrestle well, right?"

I glance over at Brook. His head is down, too.

"But what you *want*," Coach Hillman says, then coughs, "and what you *earn* may not be the same things. Right?"

He starts toward the front of the room again.

"Bellinger," Coach Hillman barks at the team's 132-pounder. "Did you want to win your weight class yesterday?"

"Uh...yeah, Coach," Max says.

"Did you earn it?" Coach Hillman says, but continues before Max can open his mouth again. "No, you earned third place. What about you, Stadler?"

Joshua, our starter at 145 answers, "I earned crap."

Coach Hillman stands at the top of the champions mat, facing the entire team. "And Radford..."

My brother looks up.

"Did you want to take a first yesterday?"

Cole nods.

"Injury or no injury, did you earn a first, or a fourth?" Coach Hillman says, coughing long and loud. "I could go up and down this lineup and ask each of you if you earned a championship. Only a couple of you can say yes." Now his voice is filling the practice room. "This team may have *wanted* to win the Ann Arbor tournament, but it only placed fourth in the team standings. You get what you *earn*, Ashton. Nothing more, nothing less."

Coach Hillman stares out across the two mats. "Coach Geiger made a good suggestion to me, so we're going to do something a little different to start our practices. Our balance was pitiful yesterday—on our feet, when we were on top, when we were defending against the takedown." He looks at Cole. "We need to change that immediately." He then grabs a box and, from it, spills dozens of tennis balls onto the mats.

Coach Geiger steps up. "This is something my high school team used to do," he says. "There's a ball for each of you. Find some space where you're not going to bump into a teammate."

We're all a little confused. I know I am. But I pick up a tennis ball and find a corner of the runners-up mat.

"Stand with your feet slightly apart," Coach Geiger instructs us. "Reach down in front of you, balancing on your left leg and raising your right leg behind you. Place the tennis ball *gently* on the mat."

Thanks to two years of ballet when I was a kid, this is easy. I'm back in an upright position quickly enough to see most of the guys losing their balance or unable to keep their legs and arms anywhere near straight.

"Now pick the ball up, balancing on your right leg and raising your left leg behind you," Coach Geiger says.

And, again, I'm done before anyone else in the room. As I look around, it occurs to me that wrestling can be a very graceful sport, but wrestlers aren't always.

"Good, Mel," Coach Geiger says to me.

He has us do dozens of reps, each time moving the ball a little farther to our left side, then to our right side. I don't have to think about how my body should move, it just does. Effortlessly. One rep after the other.

My mind starts to wander...

Thoughts of Stewart fill my head...

Last night, we talked for an hour and fourteen minutes (not that I keep track of such things). He's so nice. We talked about school. About my family. And his. Stewart has an older sister finishing med school at UCLA. He told me that because of their age difference, they've never been really close. I guess I'm lucky Cole's only two years older than me. Or maybe not. Maybe I'd be better off if he were much older than me so I could go through Ashton High as the only Radford. Stewart also asked about my younger sister, the one with the British accent. I laughed and told him the truth. He laughed, too.

"What are your friends like?" I asked.

"You ask a lot of questions," he said.

"Well, I wanna know about you."

I heard him take a deep breath. "Truth is," he said, "I'm kind of a loner."

"What do you mean?"

"I don't have a lot of friends."

"Really?"

"Yeah."

"What about at school?"

"I'm not a loser, if that's what you're thinking," he says.

"I wasn't," I said, though it did seem odd to me.

"It's just the way it is, I guess. I spend a lot of time working at the club. When I have free time I'm usually out on the golf course. I have to be. Not too many guys want to hang out with me while I hit a couple hundred bunker shots. But, look, I promised you I wouldn't bring up golf."

"I don't mind," I said.

The truth was I liked hearing how passionate he was about the sport, and how much he wanted to be as good as his dad—

"Stand up straight, Ashton," Coach Geiger's voice snaps me back. "Bend one leg so that the sole of your shoe rests on the inside of your quad. Now bounce the tennis ball. Under control. Without missing it. Without falling to the side. Without embarrassing yourself."

Over the next half hour, we move from one similar position to another, finishing with our feet together, squatting down like we're sitting in chairs, tossing the ball from one outstretched arm to the other. My thighs start to ache. From the sounds around me, everyone else is feeling it, too.

Last night, Stewart asked me why I wrestle. I told him it's because of times just like this, odd as that might seem, pushing myself to the point where I'm sure in the next moment I'm going to quit, but then sometimes finding the tiniest bit of guts to go a little longer. Geez, I sounded just like Cole. Of course, *he* would never had said "sometimes."

My thighs are quivering, and I can feel sweat trickle along my temples, and it's almost impossible to concentrate on catching the ball. I just want to scream, "Enough!" But my teammates are all gutting it out, too. Brook is. Even Georgie. And my brother is over on the champions mat. And I'm sure Coach Hillman is just waiting to see who's going to quit first...and last. And while I may not end up being last, I promise myself I won't be the first.

After another thirty seconds, Coach Geiger says, "You can relax."

I hunch over for a few moments to catch my breath. When I look up, he's standing in front of me.

"I'll bet you can do a heck of a handstand," he says.

"I think so."

Then he addresses the team. "Mel's going to demonstrate the next position. It'd be nice if any of you had the balance she does."

"She's a chick," Georgie says.

Coach Geiger's glare brings an immediate quiet to the room. Then he nods to me. I reach down to the floor with my arms locked, then kick my legs into the air.

"You see it," Coach Geiger says. "Now *do* it."

Even upside down, the sight is humorous. Guys are tumbling and flopping all over the place. A few are able to keep their legs up, but not for much more than a second or two. I wonder if Stewart has to do anything like this during golf practice. I'll ask him the next time we talk. I'm betting he thinks handstands, ballet poses, and tennis balls are a weird mix.

Soon, my arms start to shake. I hold the handstand as long as I can, then let my legs fall back to the floor so I can land on my feet.

"Do it again," Coach Geiger says.

So I do.

When my arms give out, I do it again.

And I keep pushing myself. As I do during our drills and live wrestling. Until, eventually, practice ends, and I can collapse.

Chapter 14

I open my eyes. My grandmother is staring at me in an unnerving kind of way. Guess her generation never got the memo about knocking before entering a person's bedroom.

"Hi, Grandma," I say.

She shoos away Owings, then sits down next to me. "Nice nap?"

"It *was*," I say.

"I'd like to talk to you."

Uh-oh, I get the distinct feeling this is going to be another *serious* conversation. So I reach out and give her a hug. It seems to disarm her, if only momentarily. Then I notice something at her feet. Something leather. And dark. With handles. My grandmother lifts it onto the bed. It's a business tote. Black. Full-grain leather. With my initials, M.D.R., engraved on the front.

"I know Christmas has passed, but I wanted you to have this," she says. "It's very professional. It'll fit you well."

"Uh...thanks," I say, reluctantly.

I mean, it *is* beautiful—that's not my concern. My

concern with a business tote bag is, well, that it's got to be used for business. It's definitely not something that would ever be found, or needed, at Happy Holidaze.

"Tomorrow your mother is going to drop you off at DDI," my grandmother says, matter-of-factly.

"To visit?"

"To work."

"Work? But I thought you were kidding. I'm still on vacation, and I have wrestling practice tomorrow and a tournament the next day," I whine. And, yeah, it was a whine.

"Afterwards."

"After *practice*?"

"I understand wrestling practice starts at eight and should be finished by ten," she says. "That leaves you more than enough time to come home, shower and dress, and get to my office by eleven."

"Eleven?"

"Yes, eleven."

I shake my head. "Guess everything's all figured out."

"This will be good for you."

"I'm sure you think so."

"I do."

"Glad one of us does."

"You're making it sound like punishment," my grandmother says. "It's not. It's an opportunity."

"So..." I say, with a long pause and frowning for effect. "What will I be doing?"

"See, now that's the enthusiasm I expected to hear," she says.

But enthusiastically isn't even remotely close to how I asked her.

Chapter 15

I'm holding the phone in one hand and buttoning my blouse with the other. Jade's been giving me a last-second pep talk.

"...this is it, Mel," she says. "You know your grandma, she can be a smart, scary lady. She can get you to agree to practically anything. That's why you gotta remember what we talked about."

"Goldilocks or something," I say.

"Don't joke around," Jade says. "It's gotta be subtle. You do *not* want your grandma making this a permanent, or even a semipermanent thing."

I look in the mirror. My hair's still damp from my shower, but there isn't much I can do about it now. It's almost ten forty.

"So, basically, I'm taking a dive," I say.

"A dive?"

"Yeah."

"I have no idea what that means," Jade says. "Anyway, be wary of the other people in the office. They're going to be real nice to you. But, trust me, it's all just a ploy to make you feel comfortable so that you work harder than you should."

"Where do you come up with this stuff?"

"I'm well read," she says, with a fake air of snootiness.

I wedge my feet into a pair of black suede flats. "You read *chick* magazines."

"Mel, do you honestly think you're the only teenage girl in the world with an overbearing grandmother trying to push her into the business world way before she has any desire to be pushed?"

Oddly adult, coming from Jade.

But that's kind of how our conversation ends. Mom calls from the kitchen to remind me of the time, so Jade tells me to phone her if I start to doubt the plan. I tell her not to worry, then we say goodbye.

"Be strong," she says, just before we hang up.

It's a familiar drive to DDI. And yet I'm nervous. Kind of like how I feel before a match. But that seems silly. I mean, I've been to my grandmother's office many times before. Mostly when Cole and I were little, but even recently a few times. Of course, then I was the adorable granddaughter. Now, I'm the slave-granddaughter who's coming to work.

"When're you picking me up?" I ask my mom.

"I'm not," she says.

I look at her. "Who is?"

"Your grandmother will drive you home at the end of the day."

Wonderful...just wonderful.

Soon, Mom turns into the DDI driveway and stops the car in front of the main entrance of the building. I step out and shut the door behind me. Then I hear the passenger-side window lower.

"Forgot to give me a kiss," Mom says.

I turn around and lean into the car. "Sorry," I say, giving her an air-kiss.

"Try to enjoy yourself," she says. "You look very grown up."

Of course I look grown up. I'm wearing a cream-colored blouse under a navy blue Ralph Lauren suit, with the tote firmly in my grasp. On the outside, I look like I belong here. But inside—what in the world am I *doing* here?

"It's almost eleven," Mom says.

"You can go now...please."

I take a deep breath, then start up the sidewalk. Inside the reception area, I'm greeted by a young woman who I've never seen in the office before. I notice she's wearing a charcoal skirted-suit and a turquoise blouse. Vera Wang, if I had to guess. She has a pleasant expression and asks me to have a seat, while she takes a call.

Whoa, this really does feel weird.

I mean, this is my *grandmother's* company, and I've been in this waiting area and seen this receptionist's desk plenty of times before. I've admired the dozens of framed business magazines that have her photo on the cover. I've napped on both couches, and I'm pretty sure I stuck a big wad of chewing gum under one of these chairs. Or maybe under one of the chairs that were here before these chairs. I'm not sure. Actually, I'm not too sure about anything at the moment.

The woman hangs up the phone and comes around from behind the desk. She extends her hand. "You must be Melinda. I'm Rachel. It's very nice to meet you. Your grandmother is waiting for you in her office."

I follow Rachel, and as we walk down the hallway, it occurs to me that I've never needed an escort to my grandmother's office before. Offices, which were closed other times I visited, are now brightly lit and busy with people staring at computer screens, talking on phones, and shuffling papers. When I pass by, I get the same reaction— one of those smiles that tells me they know who I am.

Oh, geez, I hope Grandma didn't made a big deal out of this, like some kind of warped take-your-granddaughter-to-work day...

As we approach the end of the hall and the double doors to my grandmother's office, a tall man with thick eyebrows and a potent smell of nasty cologne greets me.

"You must be Melinda," he says. "I understand you'll be joining us from time to time."

Time to time?

"Well, that's just fantastic..." He tells me his name, but I forget it as quickly as I hear it. "...I believe you'll be inputting information on a few hundred potential customers into our contact software for our in-house sales reps to cold call..."

Inputting information?

Contact software?

Sales reps?

Cold call?

Huh!?!

"...we have an open office that you can use," the man continues. "Now I know Gloria—your grandmother—is eager to see you, so don't let me hold you up any longer. When you're done, Rachel will set you up at your desk, and I'll give you some easy instructions. We're assuming, if all goes well, you'll get about 200 in the system today. How's that sound? Great. Glad to have you here."

And I still haven't opened my mouth to say a word.

I look up at the clock.

It's almost one, nearly two hours into my employee-for-a-day time at DDI. I pull out the cheese and cucumber sandwich Mom made me and a Diet Coke from the business tote (the only two things I had in there). Rachel asks if I want to eat in the company's lunch room, but I say no thanks and stay at my desk instead. Though I'm pretty hungry, I take as much time as possible to finish the sandwich.

When Cole and I were young and we'd get in trouble, Dad would tell us we were "in the penalty box"—like in hockey—which meant we had to sit down, shut up, and wait out the time until he was confident we'd learned the error of our ways. Cole was a frequent visitor to the penalty box. I wasn't, but I wasn't entirely unfamiliar with it, either. Today, I feel like I'm back in.

Earlier, when I first walked into my grandmother's office, she was on the phone.

"It's an important conference call," she whispered to me, after she waved me over for a kiss. "I'll be a while."

Then Rachel immediately led me to this room, giving me a couple of pens, a computer login, and a ridiculously long list of companies that the man (whose name I still don't remember) gave me the briefest of instructions for inputting.

Yeah, that's what I'm doing—inputting. Into something called a sales contact program. For DDI salespeople, apparently. For cold calls. I haven't even bothered to ask what those are.

This is ridiculous—wrestling practice, then work. What am I, like, an *adult?*

Fortunately, what I'm doing isn't exactly brain surgery. All I do is check the list of companies with current customers, type the address information in when one isn't there, then mark it off. Every once in a while, someone passes by my office. (Oh, geez, did I just call it *my* office?) The people here are friendly enough, I guess, smiling or saying hello or asking if I need anything. God, it's annoying.

"Yes, I need to be home, lying on my bed with my cat, Owings, thinking about an important wrestling tournament I have this weekend."

It's what I'd like to say.

Nothing, is what I actually say.

Slowly—very slowly—the clock passes two o'clock…
Then three o'clock…
Four…

"How's it going in here?"

I nearly jump out of my seat.

Rachel looks at me curiously from the doorway. "You all right?"

My eyes dart from Rachel to the computer screen, then back. "I'm cool," I say. "I mean...I'm quite well."

"Sorry to startle you."

"Oh, no," I say. "I was just, uh, really focused on inputting these companies."

I wasn't. I was thinking about Stewart. And hearing his voice. Of course, wrestling should be the only thing on my mind. I've been working on the hi-crotch in practice, but it's the front headlock that's become my best takedown. It's a good move for me because my weight is on my opponent instead of visa versa, and I can use my quickness to spin behind, which is something that I kind of recently discovered. In fact, this morning Brook shot in for a takedown and I sprawled, then spun to the side before he could recover. I didn't get the takedown— because time ran out—but I did get a pat on the shoulder.

"... glad to see you catch on so well," Rachel says to me. "Anyway, the phone's for you, extension eleven. A woman by the name of Joy O. Somer."

Not now...

"Thanks," I say, then pick up the receiver and press the button marked "11." "Hello, Ms. Somer." After Rachel steps away, I say, in a forced hush, "Jade, why are you calling?"

"Mel, I needed to make sure you're staying strong," she says.

"Staying strong?" I say. "I'm just trying to stay awake."

"How's it going?"

"As good as can be expected," I say. "I'm tired and haven't even spoken to my grandma yet. They have me inputting account information."

"How many do you have to do?" Jade asks.

"200," I say.

"So, don't put in as many," Jade says. "Do 150."

"150?"

"Yes."

"That's not enough," I say.

"150 and not one more than that."

"Look, I gotta go," I say, against her continued objections. Then someone passes by my office. "Thank you, Ms. Somer..." I say, into the phone. "I appreciate you calling. Yes, you have a pleasant day, too."

Then I hang up.

At five forty, I hear people in the office beginning to leave. Nearly everyone stops at my door again to see how the day went, if I enjoyed myself, and say goodbye. Their friendliness seems kind of patronizing, since I'm sure they'd rush by without a word, if I was anyone other than the owner's granddaughter. But I put on a believable smile, as they ask me inane questions about school and the holidays and where I'm planning on going to college.

College? I'm just trying to get through this weekend, people.

Just as I'm about to check the number of accounts

that I've inputted, the same man from earlier stands at the door. "Melinda, great having you here today, really super," he says, way too enthusiastically. "I've gotta run, my daughter's starting on her JV basketball team for the first time tonight. But thanks for working hard."

How does he know I worked hard?

"I understand we may see you again soon," he says, just before he steps away. "Great, just great to hear."

No, no, no, I do not like the sound of that...

I look at the computer screen and realize I've inputted 222 new names.

"Oh, damn..."

Then, down the hall, I hear my grandmother come out of her office, talking to Rachel.

My finger touches the delete button...

I couldn't do this work for one more day. No way. And there's no way in the world I'd make it through an entire summer. Inputting this. Inputting that. I'd go postal.

Then I think for a moment. Can I really just erase what I've been working on? At my grandmother's company?

I raise my finger.

But if I don't I know Jade'll be calling me up during the day in July and August just to tell me how awesome it is in the mall and how she met guys at Sport Mart, and the video game store, and Music Barn, and how they're all hanging out during lunch at the back of the mall parking lot, and...

I hear Grandma coming down the hall, and I press my finger down. I watch my work disappear on the computer screen. When I take my finger off, the count is 197.

I press the delete button once again. When I lift my finger, the count is 153.

My grandmother steps into the office. "Melinda, how's everything?"

Oh, God, does she know what I just did?

I shrug. "Uh...okay."

"I'm sorry I didn't have any time to spend with you," Grandma says. "It's been a long, long day. Let's go, I'm taking you to dinner."

"You don't have to do that, Grandma," I say.

"You earned it," she says.

I quickly close down the computer. Then I grab my business tote, my coat, and follow her down the hall to the reception area. I shake hands and say good night to Rachel. She, too, thanks me for working hard and points out to my grandmother how little supervision I needed.

"Good," Grandma says, as we walk out the front door of the building. "Self-sufficiency—that's a very important quality."

Chapter 16

Dad and Cole went to the Pistons' game tonight, which is wonderful because, one, I hate basketball, and two, Cole makes me super nervous the night before I wrestle.

He constantly asks how my weight is, even though he knows I hardly have to worry about making 113. Or he bugs me about whether I've been "visualizing moves" in my mind, which he does lying on his bed with the lights out and the sounds of relaxation—waves crashing on a beach and seagulls squawking in the distance—playing in the background. I like to ease my mind by giving Owings a nice brushing. I'll do that later.

So, for a few glorious hours, Mom and I are alone, finishing a spaghetti and seafood sauce dinner she put together just for the two of us. Mom makes a killer lasagna and is pretty good at most pasta dinners, but not much beyond that. "Cooking litigants is my specialty," she always tells me.

"Had enough to eat?" she asks.

I nod, though I didn't have much.

"Nervous?" she says.

"Very."

"How do you think you'll do?"

"We'll see."

Mom begins wiping down the counter. "I spoke with your grandmother earlier."

Uh oh...

"She always enjoys having you at the office," Mom says, turning toward me.

"That's nice," I say.

"And you enjoyed being there, of course."

"Of course."

"Your grandmother's no-nonsense when it comes to business."

"Gee, ya think?" I say, smartly.

Mom gives me a look.

"Well, you should've seen how she was when I was your age. If I wasn't going to work at DDI—and I wasn't—your grandmother insisted I work at her colleague's accounting firm every summer, every vacation, even Saturdays during high school. Work and school came before anything else. You should be thankful *I'm* your mom."

"Oh, I'm thankful," I say. "Grandma would have me do slave labor if she could get away with it."

"Mel, you're so dramatic."

"No, I'm serious."

"Your grandmother gave you work and expected it to be done well," Mom says. "You should be proud of yourself."

"Yeah."

"Because you worked hard, right?"

"Sure."

"Good," she says. "As long as you're satisfied."

"I am," I say. "I mean, for my first time working in an office, I was pretty good."

"But?"

I look at her. "But what?"

"But you could've done better?"

"I guess. Wait, maybe… I don't know… I mean, it was kind of harder than I thought. But it doesn't matter anyway, because the me-working-at-DDI experiment has come to an end, thankyouverymuch."

Mom shakes her head. "Not exactly," she says. "You're going to work there more often. You have a day off from school coming up at the end of January, and another in February. Then, starting the end of June—"

"The end of *June?*" I say, straightening up. "That's when school ends."

"Correct."

"It's the summer."

"Correct again."

Then it occurs to me. "Hey! It's *my* summer. You two have been making decisions about *my* summer without consulting me?"

"Relax, Mel," Mom says. "All we did was talk about what would be best for you."

"How do you two know what's best for me?"

"Your grandmother's very serious about you getting strong work experience. I think it's a good idea. Your dad does, too."

"Dad's in on this, too? I have a good idea for the three of you: Go try this with Cole." I let out a frustrated laugh.

"Yeah, see how well that goes over with him. All he does is wrestle and lift weights and run and be a rotten brother and pretend to be a lifeguard at the town pool when he's really just hitting on girls. Me, I have a job. A *real* job. A job I *like*."

"At Happy Holidaze," Mom says.

"Yes," I say. "At Happy Holidaze."

"And you think you're learning there?"

"*Learning?* Why do I have to be learning? It's the summer. Can't I just *be?*"

"Be what?" Mom asks, entirely too cynically.

"Be hanging out with Jade and Annie. Be having fun. Be enjoying my summer."

Mom stares at me for a few moments. But she doesn't seem angry, maybe just realizing a little that I might be right. Okay, that's probably wishful thinking on my part.

"You should consider this very seriously," Mom says.

"I don't think I need to," I say.

"You do," she says.

"Yeah, well..."

And then I don't really know what to say. My mind's kind of discombobulated. I'm suddenly very anxious about wrestling tomorrow, how it's my first in-season tournament, and stupid stuff like where they're going to stick me to get dressed, and if any guy in my weight class will forfeit instead of wrestle me, and now my mom and grandmother throw all this crap at me about whether I'm going to be allowed to work at Happy Holidaze or if I'm going to spend a miserable summer in an office at DDI, doing stuff I don't give a damn about—

"Mel?"

I look at my mom.

"Everything okay?" she asks.

"No," I say. "Not at all."

She puts the dishes in the dishwasher, then turns it on.

"I thought..." I start to say. "I just thought we were going to have a nice dinner. Just you and me."

Mom knows me pretty well, so our discussion about where I may or may not work this summer ends. She and I do the last of the straightening in the kitchen, then she pulls a pint of ice cream out of the freezer and carves a spoonful. "Crème brulé," she says.

I put it in my mouth.

Although I'm still frustrated, I manage to gush, "Incredible..."

She digs out a spoonful for herself. We share the pint together. Then Mom puts her hand on mine. "Mel," she says, "you worked as hard as you could've yesterday?"

I look at her. "Uh...yeah."

"You sure?"

"Definitely," I say. "It was complicated, and not the easiest stuff. And I've never done that kind of work before."

"Your grandmother thinks you should've been able to input more companies," Mom says. "About 230 or so."

I think my face must be turning white because I feel all the blood draining from it. Now I'm in deep. "230?" I say. "No one could do that many."

"No one?"

"Well, I guess someone could," I say. "But not me."

Mom nods. Halfheartedly, it seems. "Okay, I'll take your word for it."

I sit there for a moment.

"Why?" I ask, eventually. "What'd Grandma say?"

"She's disappointed."

Oh, great...

"She thought you were more capable than that," Mom says. "Don't get me wrong, I understand where you're coming from. I was your age once, not taking things seriously, avoiding challenges, even sabotaging my own abilities." Geez, there's that word. "But look at me now. I'm a lawyer. And a very successful one. And look around you. This house, our family, everything we have and can do... A good part of it is because of how your grandmother pushed me when I was your age."

"Mom..."

"It's the truth, Mel," she says.

Then she goes on to tell me how much she hated working at the accounting firm. One time she accidentally threw away a client's file, and it was completely her fault because she was always flirting with this guy her age in the office. She was almost fired. The firm's owner, Mr. Levin, had an ugly vein on his bald head that turned blue whenever he got mad. That day, she said, it looked like a squirming worm ready to burst.

"Your grandma wasn't too happy with me, either. We had a big argument. It continued through high school and college. She was always pushing me to do more, and do it better. Then, in law school, it ended. By that point, there wasn't much for her to complain about."

"So how do *I* get her to stop pushing?"

Mom gives me a thoughtful look. "I'll talk to her."

"Ma, please."

"I'll see what we can come up with," she says. "Okay?"

I'm not sure if that sounds promising, but I'm too tired to argue.

"...yeah, Jade, your little Goldilocks scheme didn't work so well," I say. She doesn't say anything, but I'm pretty sure I can hear through the phone thoughts rattling around in her head. "And don't even try to come up with another one."

"I wasn't," she says.

"Yeah, you were."

"Okay, I was...I mean, I am," she says. "But it's only because you're my best friend and I want to help."

"Uh...I think your help has done quite enough."

"Wait a second," she says. "Don't blame me. You *can't* blame me."

"Who should I blame?"

"I don't know," she says. "Your grandma, I guess. She outsmarted us."

"And you're going to be able to change that?" I say.

"Well, I'll try."

"That sounds promising," I say, sarcastically.

"Fine, then just give up," Jade says. "I'll have my summer; you'll have yours. I'll have fun, you won't. I'll—"

"Okay, okay," I interrupt, before she gets on a roll. "You keep working on another plan. I gotta get to sleep."

"Hey," Jade says. "Sorry I can't be at the tournament."

"It's okay."

"I can't believe my dad picks tomorrow to have a father-daughter day," Jade says. "That's totally queer, isn't it?"

I don't answer.

"Heard there's a party tomorrow night on the ridge," she says. "Let's go. We'll have a blast."

"The ridge?" I say. "When did you start hearing about parties at the ridge?"

"I don't know, I just heard about it."

"Parties at the ridge are for seniors, Jade," I say, "and we're not seniors. Besides, I can't. I'm going to be with Stewart."

"What are you two doing?"

"Going to the movies."

"The movies?" Jade says. "That's it?"

"I'm sure we'll get something to eat, I guess," I say.

"Gonna fool around?"

"No."

"Yeah, sure," Jade says.

"I'm serious," I say. "I'll let you know how everything goes after I get home."

"Yeah, you do that."

I hang up the phone. Owings hops up on the bed by my feet, then pads his way up toward my pillows. Soon he's in a ball behind my head. I pull up the bed covers, then wonder, almost out of nowhere: Is Jade jealous?

Chapter 17

"Warmed up?" Odessa asks.

"Yeah," I say, shaking out my arms.

We're standing at the side of the bleachers in the Southfield-Lathrup High gymnasium, keeping an eye on the match before mine. There are four mats laid out in an L shape for the tournament. I'd hoped to be scheduled on the mat in the corner, away from most of the crowd. No such luck. I'm on mat one. Front and center. With no place to hide.

I know people are staring at me. I could sense it the moment I walked in with the Ashton JVs, dressed in my team warm-ups, equipment bag slung over my shoulder, headgear in my hand. People might've figured I was the team manager. I doubt any of them have seen a girl in a singlet. Well, like it or not, today they're going to see a girl in a singlet wrestle.

"The guy you're going against is from Howell, right?" Odessa says.

I nod.

She gestures. "Behind the scorer's table."

I see a wrestler in a blue singlet with a large "H" on the front. He seems about my weight. He looks strong, then again, every opponent looks strong to me. They always are. Nothing I can do about that. My plan is to be quicker and execute my moves better. That, or pray he's so freaked out about having to wrestle a girl—and the mocking he'll get from friends and teammates if he loses—that he freezes up.

Sometimes that happens, but not often. More likely, the guy will storm out onto the mat pissed that he has to go up against a girl—one, because he believes only guys have a God-given right to be on a wrestling mat and, two, the horror of losing is all the motivation he needs to make sure there's not the smallest chance of that happening.

"I'm nervous," I say to Odessa.

And I am. I don't even want to lift my arms because I'm pretty sure there's a bit of a stink coming from my underarms. I put on deodorant this morning, but at times like this, it doesn't make a difference.

"Just make it through the first minute," she says. "Guys come out all crazy. When they get that they can't push you around, the match settles."

I nod.

"Thanks for coming," I say.

I wasn't sure she'd be able to make it, but, fortunately for me, the Royal Oak varsity practice this morning ended early. Odessa understands what I'm going through because she's been there many times before. I don't think Cole—or our coaches, for that matter—understands that

I feel like an outsider on my own team sometimes. And not just because I have to get ready in a school bathroom, while the rest of the wrestlers prepare in the gym's locker rooms.

"...Now wrestling on mat four, in the 113-pound weight class"—the PA system booms—"Brook Evans, from Ashton, and Greg Stillwell, from Gross Pointe..."

Shortly after, Georgie's match is called on-deck for mat three.

The crowd suddenly reacts; I look toward mat one where a wrestler has the other trapped in a tight cradle. The ref drops to his hands and knees, counting off back points and watching for the moment the wrestler's shoulders are flat. The struggle ends quickly, with the ref slapping the mat, indicating a pin.

"Here we go, Mel," Odessa says. "Ready?"

"Pretty much."

"Go get him."

I nod, slap my headgear, and make my way to the scorer's table. The referee confirms the Howell wrestler's name, then gives me a curious look. "Radford, Mel."

"Melinda," I say.

"Melinda?" he repeats. "Okay."

I get a green band to put around my ankle; the Howell wrestler gets the red one. I walk to the corner of the mat to hear final instructions from Coach Geiger. But I notice him look past me toward the opposite side. I glance over my shoulder and see the ref and the Howell coach talking. Soon the ref comes over.

"I gotta check her hair and nails," he says.

"Did you check *his?*" Coach Geiger says.

"Give me a break, Coach."

I turn my head so he can see how I tied my ponytail, then put out my hands, palms down. My nails are way short. Manly, but necessary.

"Looks fine," the ref says. "Let's get this match going."

Coach Geiger and I shake hands. "Shoot your singles, Mel," he says. "And don't back up."

"Okay," I say.

I nod to Odessa at the side of the mat, then walk to the center circle where the Howell wrestler is waiting.

"Ready?" the ref says to us.

I crouch down, left foot forward, hands out. My opponent, on the other hand, looks like he's ready to run me over.

The whistle blows.

And that's kind of what happens. Before I have time to think, the Howell wrestler drives me to the edge of the outside circle, then dives at my feet in an awful attempt at a double-leg takedown. I fall straight back, beyond the mat, hitting my head—with a thud—on the gymnasium floor.

I hear a gasp from the crowd, but nothing else, and the only thought making its way through my discombobulated brain is whether people reacted that way because it looked and sounded as bad as the back of my skull feels.

I sit up...

Then stand...

But, with all the grace of a size-20 ballerina, my foot gets caught on the edge of the mat and I stumble.

Another gasp.

Suddenly, the ref is holding me up by my elbow; Coach Geiger is on the other. I say that I'm fine, but they walk me to our corner so I can sit down on a folding chair. Now I can hear their voices, and they're coming at me one after the other.

"You okay, Ashton?" the ref asks.

I nod.

Coach Geiger unsnaps my headgear. "How's your head?"

"Okay," I say.

"Start injury time now," the ref announces.

Coach Geiger nods, then looks at me. "Heck of a fall."

"I'm fine," I say.

"I'm sure you are."

I try to stand, but he puts his hand on my shoulder. "Just sit for the full injury time."

Out of the corner of my eye, I see that my dad has come down from the stands. Odessa's next to him. She's calling out to me, but I don't want to look. I want them to think I'm okay. Even if I'm not.

Coach Geiger kneels down in front of the chair. "Hey, Mel," he says, kind of solemnly. "How about we just call this one?"

Before I answer, I hear—or, at least, I think I hear—someone say, not in a particularly malicious way but just so damn matter-of-factly, "She's going to quit." I look up at Coach Geiger, wondering if he heard the same thing.

"There'll be other tournaments," he says.

"What?" I say.

"No need to risk something more serious."

"You want me to *default?*"

"It's a holiday tournament," Coach Geiger says, in a rational way that pisses me off even more. "If you bang your head again and *really* hurt yourself, then you could miss some of the season."

I lift myself up. "I'm ready to go."

"Whoa, whoa…" Coach Geiger says. "You don't have to prove anything."

"I know."

"To anyone."

"I just want to wrestle," I say.

I straighten my headgear and adjust the straps of my sports bra. Coach Geiger calls over the ref to tell him the match will continue. Then he turns to me. "Okay, then," he says. "Don't let this guy push you around."

The ref waves the Howell wrestler and me back to the center circle. "The score's still zero-zero," he says. "Neutral."

As I get into my stance, it occurs to me that maybe my brain's not quite as ready as I'd thought. I'm not nauseous, but I'm definitely dizzy.

The ref steps between us—too late now, I guess—and blows the whistle.

The Howell wrestler is all over me, again, but this time his double-leg shot isn't nearly as clumsy. He takes me down easily and covers, then wallops me with a cross-face. I guess he's one of those guys who hates wrestling against a—

Stop thinking, Mel!

Too late. In an instant, I'm looking up at the ceiling. I arch my back, *really* arch my back. I can hear my opponent grunting. He shifts all of his weight on top of my chest, so much so, I'm not sure I can breathe much longer.

I know I can't…

But a half second before I'm about to give up the pin, the buzzer goes off.

"Time!" the ref shouts. "End of the first period."

I get up and look toward Coach Geiger. I'm not sure what I expect from him, but it's certainly not the clapping and fist pump he gives me.

"Good job, Mel, good job!"

I'm confused. I glance at the scoreboard. It does say that I'm *losing*, 5–0.

"Ashton," the ref says. "Your choice."

I choose neutral.

"Wrestle smart," Coach Geiger says. "You know what's coming."

For the third time, my opponent and I are on our feet. And for the third time, the moment the ref's whistle goes off, the Howell wrestler charges at me. I've got to buck the trend. So, when he reaches for me, I lower my level and shoot a sweep single, catching his leg, then dumping him to the mat.

"Takedown, green," I hear the ref call out. "Two points!"

Suddenly, my brain's working better, and I'm getting a second wind. I grab my opponent's ankle, lift, and break him down to his stomach. I want so badly to smack *him* with a cross-face, but a sweeter revenge would be to beat him on the scoreboard. So I force in the half and scoot to the side.

The Howell wrestler gets to his knees, then tries to stand. I drag him back down. He tries again. And again I control him to the mat. I can hear myself breathing hard. This guy just won't stop. I try to buy myself a few seconds by settling back with an ankle ride.

"Come on, green," the ref says. "You have to work for a pin."

Easy to say from where he is. I come off the ankle, keeping one arm around my opponent's waist and the other trying to trap an arm. I see a cradle—but it's too late. He gets to his feet. I drive him to the edge of the circle, but he stays inbounds and keeps his feet moving.

End the period! End the period!

I hang on, scrambling to stay with him, my arms locked around his waist.

Then slip lower...

Then my grip comes apart...

"Escape, red," the ref calls out, just before the buzzer sounds.

I fall to my knees.

"That's okay," Coach Geiger says to me. "Two more minutes."

I nod, stand up, and shake out my arms, then look toward the scoreboard. I'm down 6–2.

The Howell wrestler chooses top position to start the third period. I guess he thinks he can put me to my back again. I follow the ref's instructions to assume the bottom position. He then directs my opponent to settle on top.

"Wrestle!"

I'm a half second too slow. The Howell wrestler pulls in my arm and drops his weight on me. His technique is so sloppy, so awkward. I try getting back to a base, but his forearm smacks my face again, then reaches for a cradle. If he gets it, I'm finished. It's what he'd expect from a girl.

I brace. Really hard. And kick my leg back. Really hard. And when he leans even further over me to bring his hands together, I stand. Really hard. And he slips off of me.

"Green, escape," the ref says.

"Fifty seconds left," Coach Geiger shouts. "You need a takedown!"

This time, the Howell wrestler isn't so eager to charge me. We stalk each other, head-to-head, me pushing forward, then him. He's breathing hard. Maybe he's waiting for his second wind. I can't let that happen.

I shoot.

It's a good single. I'm in deep, head on the inside, arms wrapped tight around his leg. He tries to put in a wizzer to hold me off, but I stand up. I know we're near the edge of the circle. He wants to get out of bounds for a restart; I do not. So I lift his leg higher and sweep out the leg he's balancing on. He crashes to the mat like a ton of bricks, and I cover.

"Takedown, green," the ref calls out.

For just a moment, I look over at Coach Geiger.

"Twenty seconds left, Mel! Gotta put him on his back!"

I force in a half.

"Go with it! Go with it!" Coach Geiger yells.

I put all of my weight into this guy and drive with all of the strength in my legs. He's grunting. I'm pretty sure I am, too. The half gets deeper—almost elbow deep—and I feel him turning. Can't be much time left. I dig my toes in the mat and push hard, until his back is perpendicular to the mat.

Just a little more...

But the buzzer goes off.

"No back points," the ref says.

I look up at the scoreboard.

6–5.

I lost.

I unsnap my headgear, pull myself to my feet, and wait at the center circle for the ref to raise the Howell wrestler's hand in victory. The crowd's clapping is loud. And continues to get louder as I walk to Coach Geiger at the corner of the mat. He puts his arm around me.

"All you needed were a few more seconds," he says.

I step off the mat and get a hug from my dad, then one from Odessa. "You're one tough girl," she says.

It doesn't soothe the painful sting of a loss, but it's nice to hear.

Chapter 18

The Ashton Loews is crowded, mostly with college kids still on Christmas break. Stewart and I find a seat dead center, a few rows from the front. He says he likes watching a movie from here because it feels like the screen is surrounding him. I smile and nod. I don't bother telling him my neck is still really sore from my earlier match.

The lights begin to dim.

Stewart opens a box of Sno-Caps—I call them nonpareils, and they're my absolute favorite—and shakes some into my hand. I put them in my mouth, then let my other hand slide down to the side of my chair. It grazes Stewart's, and our fingers interlock.

For a moment, the theater is dark, then a wall of sound shakes the room and the screen explodes with, well... explosions. "In a world where good and evil are locked in an eternal struggle..." rumbles a man's ridiculously deep voice.

Oh, great, the trailer's for another in the latest trend of nuclear annihilation movies, this one pitting Middle Eastern cyborg sheep farmers against a class of French Lit students from Nebraska unwittingly snatched from their semester abroad and thrust into the frontline of a global confrontation.

I'll pass.

I have other, more immediate, interests. Out of the corner of my eye, I watch the screen illuminate Stewart's face. He's even hotter than I remembered. He's got high cheekbones, thick eyebrows, and just the right amount of stubble on his chin. Dare I say, he's a whole lot of *rugged*. And I love his mussed-up hair. He doesn't look like any golfer I've ever seen. When I told him that on the drive over, he said, "You don't look like any wrestler I've ever seen, either."

But I *am* a wrestler. After today's tournament, a wrestler who lost—but a wrestler, nevertheless.

I'd like to put the tournament out of my mind and just enjoy being with Stewart. But now that I'm thinking about it, I can't stop myself. I guess my brother isn't the only Radford who can be obsessive....

After Dad and I got home from the tournament, he told Mom about my match, except for the falling-backward-and-banging-my-head part. I don't think she would have been too upset, though. It's not like she sees me as her China-doll daughter. He went on, saying how proud he was that I didn't give up, and that even though I'd lost, it was a well-earned moral victory. Mom smothered me in a hug and promised that work wouldn't keep her from my next match. Maybe she'd get Grandma to come to that one, too. All things considered, I left the kitchen feeling pretty good.

But it only lasted until I got to the top of the stairs. There, Cole stood, lips pursed, forehead wrinkled, shaking his head.

"What's your problem?" I said, side-stepping him on my way into my bedroom.

"You lost," he said.

"I wrestled well."

"You lost."

"Heard you the first time."

I noticed Owings' head poking out from under my bed. I put down my equipment bag and walked over, lifting him into my arms. In my vanity mirror, I could see Cole was still at my door.

"Do you mind?" I said. "I'd like some privacy."

"Why didn't you win?"

"Because I didn't."

"Don't be a wiseass," Cole said. "When you lose, there's a reason for it. You need to identify the reason and fix it."

I didn't need him trying to be a coach right then. I only had an hour before Stewart was going to pick me up. It would be our first date. Just thinking about that made my heart thump.

He was taking me to see *Dead Horizon,* the hottest movie out right now. I had to shower. Blow out my hair. Pick an outfit to wear. Borrow Mom's silver necklace. And give Jade a quick call to quell my last-minute jitters. On top of all that, I had a scratch on my forehead to conceal, a slightly puffy lip to worry about, and a pounding headache.

I walked to my bedroom door and said, "Buh-bye," then swung it closed. Cole, however, put his foot in the way so that it bounced back open.

"Dad!" I shouted, then said to Cole, "I don't care what you think. I tried hard. Dad said it was—"

"A *moral* victory," Cole mocked.

"Shut up."

My brother shook his head again. "Mel, there are no moral victories. You win or you lose. That's it. One or the other."

"Dad!"

Footsteps came down the hallway from the kitchen. "Cole, leave your sister alone," Dad said, from the bottom of the stairs. "You always need time to yourself after your matches."

Cole stepped back from the doorway. "She lost," he said. "And she doesn't even care."

I cared.

I cared enough...

Another on-screen explosion brings me back to the movie theater, though I can't even remember what the other trailers were about. They sort of passed over my eyes in a blur. So did the beginning of *Dead Horizon*. My body was there in the seat, but my mind was back in the Southfield-Lathrup gym...

Bouncing on my toes. Shaking out my arms. Worried about how tough my opponent looks. Breathing in deep to calm myself. Taking instructions from Odessa. Keep circling and stay tough, she tells me. Nodding my head.

But I didn't do that, did I? I let the Howell wrestler push me all over the mat—even *off* it. Did too much thinking, not enough reacting. I practically gave him that five-point lead early in the match. Geez, I've got *so* much to learn. Too much, maybe. I should've circled, then sprawled. I should've had my strategy ready long before I stepped out—

"Melinda..."

My eyes focus, and I turn my head.

"Want some more?" Stewart whispers, leaning in toward me.

I cup my hand. He shakes out more nonpareils.

"Thanks," I say.

Stewart smells good. Really good. Like cinnamon. I'm usually not around guys who smell too nice (except for Brook). And I don't mind at all missing *Dead Horizon* because I'm watching Stewart watch the movie, noticing his eyes widen at the good parts or his lips move just the tiniest bit, like he's telling the guy on the screen what to do next. He blinks slowly, too. I don't know why he does, and I don't know why I find it adorable, but I do.

And yet I can't focus on Stewart for very long.

Call it disappointment. A nagging, disappointment. Throw in regret—persistent regret.

Again, I'm back on mat one, turning the match around in the second and third periods. Using technique and speed against my opponent's strength. Wrestling tough.

But for all the good that I did in the match, especially after being taken down and put to my back early, when I look up at the scoreboard after time runs out, the score remains the same.

6–5.

Damn... Much as I hate to admit this, Cole was right. I *didn't* win. I lost. There was no moral victory, no you'll-get-him-next-time satisfaction. There certainly was a lot of I-should've-done-this and if-only-I'd-stopped-him-from-doing-that. It'll stay with me a while, I'm sure.

"Having fun?" I hear.

"Fun?"

"Enjoying the movie?" Stewart asks, but he says it in such a way that he seems to have his doubts.

I smile. My neck doesn't hurt so much anymore. "Yeah, it's pretty good," I say. Then I lean into him, close enough that our shoulders touch.

Stewart parks his car at the end of my driveway. A light over the front door is on, but we're far enough away from the house that I don't think my parents can see us inside. Stewart turns the heater on high, but I still pull my coat tight against my body to keep out the cold.

"You didn't like the movie, did you?"

"It was okay," I say. "Definitely, okay."

Stewart smiles. "Okay means you didn't really like it, but you don't want to hurt my feelings. Next time you get to pick."

I shrug and tease, "That's if I give you a next time."

"You might not?"

"Well…"

Suddenly, Stewart leans over the console and puts his lips against mine. Oh…My…God… We're kissing… My hands hold him off, slightly. I don't necessarily mean to, but my body and brain need a moment to take in what's happening.

He pulls back. "This all right?"

I nod. "Uh…yeah."

He leans into me again, but this time my hands give way. Geez, wait until I tell Jade. Stewart's lips are warm and soft and taste good. Like nonpareils.

Some time later, when we come up for air, I look out toward the house, but the windows are fogged up. It's the longest I've ever made out with a guy, and all I want to do is keep going, letting him kiss my neck, my earlobes…

"I like you, Mel," Stewart says, softly.

"I like you, too."

I feel his hand slip through my open coat and touch my breasts, over my shirt. A sensation swirls in my belly. And lower. Gently, he squeezes my left breast. I can feel his breath on my skin. Something inside me wants more, but it's almost too much already. Then, Stewart lifts my shirt and runs his fingers inside my bra, grazing my nipple.

Whoa, that's *way* too much.

"No need to rush," I say, putting my hand on his.

"A little more?"

"Not yet. Later."

"Later when?"

"Next time," I say.

"Next time?" he says. "Not now?"

But my hand isn't giving way. I can't let it. And Stewart realizes this. He nods, but it seems, from the expression on his face, that he's disappointed. He pulls his hand out and gives me a kiss.

Was that out of obligation, so we don't end the night in this uncomfortable place of unrequited desire?

(Did I just really think that?)

Or, did he kiss me with the hope that a few more moments of the thrill in my belly will change my mind?

(Stop! Why am I asking all these questions?)

Jade's going to tell me I'm so weird, making the uncomplicated complicated, and undoubtedly leaving him with what she'll say is "a major case of blue balls."

"I gotta go," I say. "It's late."

He rests his forehead against mine and whispers, "I understand."

I know I'll spend the rest of the night thinking about whether he's mad or if he really gets it. But for right now, I have to get inside.

"Want me to walk you to your front door?" he asks.

"I'll be fine." I kiss him on the cheek, wrap myself in my coat, and open the car door. "Bye," I say, then close it.

Halfway up the driveway, I do a little spin and wave, hoping Stewart can see me through the fogged windows.

Geez, I hope that didn't look too goofy.

Chapter 19

"You really like this guy, don't you?" Jade says to me as we make our way down the school hallway, trying to get to our Psych I class before the bell rings.

"I don't know," I say, trying to hold back a blush. "Maybe."

"Yeah, right." Jade grins. "I know you've been on the phone with him every night since Sunday. And the reason I know this is because you haven't been on the phone with *me*."

"Sorry," I say.

We rush into the classroom and slide into our seats just before our teacher, Mrs. Filgrace, walks in.

Jade nudges my arm. I look over. On her notebook, she's written, *Was he good?*

I roll my eyes.

Jade taps her pen on the paper.

I shrug.

Then Jade underlines *good* three times.

If I don't give her something, she's going to bug me all day. So I mouth the words, "At what?"

In what I can only describe as one of the stranger things (of many) I've seen Jade do, she ducks behind Derek, who's sitting in front of her, turns to me, and French kisses the air—lips flared, tongue swirling, and all.

My attempt to stifle a laugh is made even more difficult when Mrs. Filgrace, having noticed, marches up the aisle to our desks. She looks at Jade with an expression of profound confusion.

"Excuse me," Mrs. Filgrace says.

Jade opens her eyes.

"*Who*, may I ask, are you pretending to kiss?"

Everyone in the class turns. The guys seem particularly interested in the answer, or maybe in catching a glimpse of her technique.

"Uh..." Shockingly, Jade is at a loss for words.

"Well?" Mrs. Filgrace asks, looking around the room. "It appears we'd all like to know."

The girls seem totally annoyed that, with a single air-kiss, Jade has monopolized the attention of all the guys, who themselves are being more attentive than they've ever been in this (or, undoubtedly, any other) class. And still, Mrs. Filgrace looms large, hands on her mega-sized hips, perfecting the disciplinary air that makes her nickname, "Warden Filgrace," an understatement.

I want to reach out to Jade and shake her from her stupor, since I'm as curious as everyone else as to what her answer will be. So we wait. The guys. The girls. Mrs. Filgrace.

"Melinda!"

What?

But it isn't Jade who said my name. All at once, the class and Mrs. Filgrace turn to the front of the room.

There, Georgie bursts out laughing, loud and obnoxiously, pointing at me. Or Jade. Or both of us.

A few others start to laugh, too.

Then a bunch more.

Then practically everyone.

"Jade's gonna join the wrestling team," Georgie says, doubled over, "so her and Melinda can *practice* on each other."

If the sudden shade of Jade's face is any indication, she is not a happy camper.

Neither am I.

Ha, ha, ha...the lone girl on the wrestling team is a lesbian. How cliché. Like I haven't heard that a thousand times. Girl wrestles because she wants to be a guy, or she wants to roll around with guys on a mat. Either she's a self-hating chick who really wishes she had testicles, or she's a slut who wants guys' hands all over her body.

While the entire class has one big laugh at our expense, I remember Odessa telling me the sorts of things she went through early on in wrestling. When she was on her middle school team, a teammate took her down and covered on top, then reached inside her shorts and grabbed her crotch. The instant she reacted, he threw in a half and pinned her. Later, she talked to her coach, but he was clueless about what to do. It was never brought up again, even though the guy put his hand in the same place a few more times that season. Fortunately, the next year, he quit wrestling to play basketball. In the end, Odessa told me, she learned to deal with those situations in her own way. By winning. That forced guys (and everyone else) to give her respect.

I look over at Georgie. Once again, he's got that stupid grin on his face. I spend the entire class staring at him. Forty-eight minutes to let my anger stew. Relishing the idea that I'll get a chance to teach him a lesson today at practice. And tomorrow. And the next practice. And the one after that. Until I decide I'm done teaching him a lesson.

"Come on, Ashton, the holidays are over!" Coach Geiger shouts from across the runners-up mat. "I'll remind you there's a two-pound allowance in place through the rest of the season. That should help some of you who're tight with your weight. Now, let's start getting serious."

It's been a long practice, but I'm not complaining. In fact, I'm considering asking Georgie to embarrass me in Psych class every day. I've kicked his butt all over the mat when we've drilled together or wrestled live. And I've held my own against Brook, too

As it nears five o'clock, Coach Geiger has the team working "situational wrestling" on our feet, with one wrestler in deep with a double-leg. On the whistle, that wrestler tries to finish the takedown while the other defends. Thankfully, I'm paired with Georgie again.

He doesn't seem as pleased.

"Let's go," I say, standing in front of him.

He says nothing but gets into position, head on my hip, arms around my legs, hands cupped behind the backs of my knees. He's leaning into me already. *Always trying to get an edge, right, Georgie?*

Coach Geiger surveys the room, then blows his whistle.

I sprawl back hard and push Georgie's head down. It's a good start. He moves toward me, trying to re-penetrate into position. Then my anger switches on, and I start reacting instead of thinking.

Cross-face.

I nearly separate Georgie's head from the rest of his body, spin behind, and steal the takedown from him.

"Should've done that at the tournament," Coach Geiger says.

He's right. But it was nice to do now. Especially against Georgie.

Chapter 20

A heavy snow's been falling all day.

The pavement feels soft, and the sounds of the few cars still out on the roads are pleasantly muffled. Cole and I are running at my pace, not his—and it's not even Christmas morning. I'm guessing he wants to talk about something. Most likely it's Stewart. Usually, I'd dread this, but tonight I'm feeling pretty good.

Soon enough, Cole says, "What's the deal with the golfer?"

I knew it. "*Stewart,*" I say.

"And?"

"And what?"

"Look, if you don't wanna talk," Cole says, "I'm fine just running."

And we do run, for a while, in silence. But then I change my mind.

"He's smart," I say. "And nice, and…"

I give my brother a little bit more, but most things I keep to myself. Unfortunately, Stewart and I don't get to see each other often. I have practice every night, of course, and JV matches once or twice during the week and each

Saturday. And I go to every varsity match, which are mostly held after the JV matches. So, the best we can do is talk on the phone at night and get together on Sundays.

Cole and I continue down Algonquin Avenue. "So golf's his only sport?"

"Yeah," I say. "Apparently, he's really good at it."

"But it's still just golf," my brother says.

I ignore that comment.

"He's gonna teach me how to hit a ball," I say.

My brother gestures toward the next corner. "Turn left here."

We start up Nokomis Trail, a switchback road that climbs the biggest hills in Ashton, passing through Blue Rock Reservation. This is a new route for us, and soon we're beyond any streetlights. I'm struggling big time. Cole is, too. Normally, that would be surprising, but tonight he is "running with weight," as he calls it. Last season, he took a wool jacket Dad used to wear on hunting trips and sewed pockets in the lining (I helped him, since my brother is spastic with a needle and thread) so that it could hold a dozen or so small bags of sand. He claims, proudly, that the jacket now weighs an extra twenty-five pounds.

As my tiring calves plow through snow, I say, between breaths, "What...about...you and Jennie Fox?"

"Nothing there," Cole says, even though I've seen the two of them together in the hallways a bunch of times.

"Samantha Ricks?"

"Nah."

Having named two senior cheerleaders, I try another grade.

"Lisbeth Hersh?"

A rumor's going around that my brother's an item with that scrawny brunette who sits across from me in biology lab. She's obviously trying to make a name for herself.

"We *had* a thing," he says.

Well, that confirms it; my brother's a guy slut. Not that I'm surprised. Being co-captain of the varsity wrestling team at Ashton High is a golden ticket for hooking up. Of course, since wrestling is the first, second, and third most important things in his life, I know none of his conquests will turn serious. I almost feel sorry for the girls.

Then, after a long silence, Cole says, "Jade's my newest."

We run a little longer before what he's said registers. "What?"

"She's cool."

"Who?"

"Jade."

"*My* Jade?"

Cole looks toward me. "I like to think of her as *my* Jade."

"*Your* Jade?"

How in the world did this happen? My best friend and my brother? When? Sure, they flirt whenever she comes over to the house...and at school...and sometimes after varsity matches...

Suddenly, even in the frigid cold, I feel the heat of anger rise from my chest. Damn it. I'll bet anything they get together on Sundays when I'm out with Stewart. An entire high school to choose from, but they can't find other people?

"Mel…" Cole says.

"What?" I snap.

I don't want to hear about how they make out in the school stairwell, or in the practice room when no one's around. And there's definitely no way I'm going to be able to handle hearing them giggle down the hall from my bedroom without spewing my guts.

"I'm only kidding," Cole says.

Keep your cool, Mel. Pretend you knew he was joking all along. No big deal, even if it had been true, right?

But now my concentration is shot, and my energy is practically gone. We've been running for twenty-five minutes—after we finished wrestling practice only an hour ago—so I didn't have a whole lot left anyway. I'm sure Cole's going to get mad at me if I ask him to stop. I'll just let him go on. It's a long walk back home, but I'll be fine. After his little joke, it'd even be nice to be alone.

"I gotta stop," I say.

But instead of saying anything, Cole stops, too. I hunch over, seeing my running shoes, ankles, and most of my calves hidden in the snow. Cole, his breath visible in the night, stands with his hands at his hips, tilting his face at the slashing flurry. He rolls one ankle, then the other. It's hard to tell how much injuries really bother my brother. He never complains. Even a twisted ankle in last week's 3–1 win over a tough opponent from Pontiac High goes unmentioned. When you're the co-captain of an undefeated, state-ranked team, there's no time to show weakness, I suppose.

Cole looks over at me. "You know Grandma called earlier."

I don't say anything.

"You're duckin' her, aren't you?" he says.

"She wants me at DDI again. Next time we have a day off from practice. Mom and Dad agree with her."

Cole laughs.

Then he turns and starts back down Nokomis Trail. I follow him. For a moment I let my mind wander, imagining we're the only two people alive in the world (not that I'd *ever* want to be stuck with my older brother), making our way through a Michigan snowfall without streetlights, car headlights, or porch lights.

"Cole?"

"What?" he says.

"Just for the record," I say. "You and Jade, I didn't believe it for a second."

Chapter 21

"Watch me a few times," Stewart says. "Then you can give it a try."

I never thought I'd be caught dead at a place like this. But here I am at an outdoor driving range in Plymouth called Fore Seasons because, as Stewart says, "Golf doesn't quit for the winter." He told me to dress warmly and comfortably, which I totally didn't. But there was no way in the world I was going to waste the chance to put on my Uterqüe sweater, Ralph Lauren jeans, and matching boots. Well, at least the heaters are on high.

"You see, Mel," Stewart says. "Golf is about concentration and precision, and doing the same swing over and over."

Then he takes on an odd kind of demeanor, as if he's completely alone. No cold. No other golfers. No me. And, like a switch turned on, he swings—*thwak!*—sending the ball high and far out into the range. After a few seconds, it comes down just in front of a large target indicating a distance of 250 yards.

Though I don't care a bit about golf, I am impressed. I mean, he really smacked the snot out of the ball.

Stewart does it again. Then a few more times after that. And each time his motion is exactly the same, as if he's done the swing a thousand times before. When I tell him that, he seems to think about it for a moment.

"Probably been about ten thousand," he says, putting another ball on the plastic tee and pulling out a different club from his bag. "This should be about your size. I used it as a kid."

I take the club. It feels funny in my hands and, for some reason, all I want to do is whack the ball. But golf, apparently, doesn't work that way.

Stewart moves behind me. He has to reach down to put his hands on my hips and though he's not super muscular like most wrestlers I know, he sure does hold me firmly.

"It all happens here," he says.

I giggle. "Hey, now, who said you could just put your hands there?"

"You mean this?" he asks, holding me even tighter.

"Yes," I say. "That."

"You must be used to it," he says.

I turn. "What does that mean?"

"Don't guys put they're hands all over you in practice?" he asks.

"No," I say.

"They don't?"

"Well, yes, but..."

"But what?"

"It's part of wrestling," I say. "And it's not like I enjoy it. In fact, I try to keep their hands *off* of me."

"Okay, okay," he says. "So, can I put my hands here?"

"Yes, *you* can," I say, then turning back toward the ball, "and your hands should never be on any hips but mine."

"Fair enough."

"Good," I say.

Suddenly, Stewart gives me a kiss on my earlobe. It sends a shiver through me that has nothing to do with the cold.

"Mel, get serious for a moment," he says, close to my ear. "A golf swing is nothing without proper hip rotation."

I wonder if the other golfers are stealing glances at us. Not that I would mind the attention.

Stewart instructs me to bring the club back over my right shoulder. "Notice your left knee bends inward slightly," he says. "And your hips shift." I don't really get it, but I love the attention. "As the club comes down from the top of the swing, your hips shift back toward the opposite direction." He explains that the club should pass through the hitting zone and continue all the way over my left shoulder. "Understand?"

"Can I try it?"

Stewart steps back. "You're on your own."

"Here goes," I say.

The first few times I swing, I miss the ball completely. Then twice I hit the plastic green mat instead of the tee; the final time, the impact hurts my hands so much that I lose my grip on the club and it sails out into the range.

"Oh, crap!" I say, then cover my mouth.

A few golfers look over. I can't help but burst into laughter. I turn to Stewart.

"I was almost getting the hang of it," I say.

"Sure," he says. "The club went a good long way."

"Real funny," I say.

Later, on the way home from the driving range, I tell Stewart I'd like to introduce him to wrestling and show him some of my favorite moves. He grins, mischievously.

"You can show me in your bedroom any time," he teases. "Or in my bedroom. Either one."

"Oh, that's such a guy thing to say." I roll my eyes.

"I'm only kidding."

"That's even more of a guy thing to say."

"What?"

"Playing it off as a joke, when the girl isn't dumb enough to fall for the line."

"No, I swear," Stewart says.

It's okay, though, because I don't think he was completely serious. And, actually, I'd like for him to experience a double-leg takedown or a headlock hip throw. Have him hit the floor, pull himself to his feet, then have it done again. Just a little taste of what I do on a mat. Afterward, I'd comfort him with an ice pack.

And a kiss, or two.

Chapter 22

"It's only the Ashton High *Tablet*..." I whisper to myself. "It's not the *Livingston County Daily Press & Argus* or—God forbid—the *Detroit News* or *Detroit Free Press*. Just our rinky-dink school newspaper..."

And barely even a newspaper. It only comes out three times during the school year. And no one reads it, really. Everyone knows it's only published for the sake of Mrs. Scholtzer, the head of the English department, who was supposedly a big journalist years ago but isn't anymore. In fact, if the *Tablet* didn't have a color cover or wasn't printed on glossy paper, it'd probably be mistaken for one of those throwaway ad booklets for the Ashton Village shopping center. Most kids at school use it as an umbrella on rainy or snowy days anyway.

The same'll be true with this issue, I'm hoping.

Maybe I'm making too much of this. No one's said anything yet. Of course, no one could, since I've spent the morning alone in the auditorium balcony.

I open to the newspaper's main article again. I can't help myself. "Going to the Mat with Coach Hillman," it reads.

It's no surprise that the *Tablet* interviewed him. He's been at the school since forever and is a coaching legend. He's the reason Ashton is near the top of Michigan high school records for dual meet victories, team tournament championships and state titles, and individual state place-winners and champions. He's the reason why guys like my brother join the wrestling program as little kids, in the hope that they'll have him as a coach when they get to the varsity. And he is the reason why people who know Michigan wrestling give that nod of recognition when our town is mentioned. Coach Hillman and Ashton Wrestling are one and the same, and pretty much the centerpiece of our school's athletics.

So, for anyone who bothers to read the article, they'll learn where Coach Hillman grew up, how he got started in wrestling, what his hobbies are, that he and his wife, Margie, have three kids, and the names of his dogs. Regular stuff. No big deal, right? If the article ended there, sure.

But it didn't.

Instead, Darlene McAdams—major wench and yellow journalist, who couldn't write a decent birthday card greeting to save her life—poses the question whether girls in wrestling is "a passing fad, or a legitimate sports trend borne from feminist idealism that girls can be all they want to be?" She actually wrote that—*feminist idealism.* Like she has any idea what it means. *I* don't even know what it means. (Besides the fact that women's wrestling is in the Olympics.)

I wouldn't be sitting in the balcony, with a lump in my throat, if Darlene had instead asked a mundane question to end the article. Or better, if Coach Hillman had offered one of those milquetoast clichés about the quality of an athlete being a function of his or her heart, not gender. Or best, if Coach Hillman had simply said, "I think that's enough questions."

But he didn't.

Instead, he said—and I quote:

> "In the forty-one years I've been in wrestling, girls' participation has been the biggest change, even though it's not as widespread in Michigan as it is in some states," Coach Hillman said, in a thinly veiled reference to sophomore JV member Melinda Radford, younger sister of the team's co-captain. "Our school needs to balance offering sports opportunities to all students, with my interests as the coach to make sure all members of the team are comfortable in the practice room and in competition, and that each feels a part of the team." Then Coach Hillman added, "There are a few instances in other high school sports where boys and girls compete on the same JV and varsity teams together. Now wrestling. I don't know if that's a good thing. Girls should compete against girls, and boys against boys."

I read the article over and over, and each time I do, my stomach knots just a little tighter. I'm not sure what bothers me more, Coach Hillman saying, "I don't know if that's a good thing," or Darlene including a quote from an unnamed varsity wrestler questioning if I "wouldn't be better off playing girls' basketball instead."

"Mel?"

I wipe my eyes and see Jade coming down the balcony aisle.

"You missed class," Jade says.

"So?"

"So?" she says. "What's up with that?"

I shake my head.

"You're crying?"

"No."

Jade glances back toward the door, then shuffles down the row to me. I hand her the *Tablet*. She gives me a look.

I point to the article. "Read it."

Jade sits down, then says with a laugh, "Me reading the *Tablet*, now that's a first."

I'd always wondered if the only reason I was given permission by the school to wrestle was because my brother was one of the best wrestlers on the team. I guess I'd been right all along. When I first petitioned Ashton's athletic director, Mr. Williamson, I had to convince him and Coach Hillman that joining the team was something I really wanted. I stuttered and stumbled over my words a lot. It wasn't my best moment. So Mr. Williamson had me write a page-long essay explaining what I thought I'd accomplish by wrestling. It took me three nights. I wasn't even sure what to write. I still have a copy of that essay folded in my journal, which I keep hidden inside the cover of Owings' bed. Looking back, it seems wrong that I had to justify my interest in wrestling. I never told anyone about the meeting (except Jade, of course). Or the essay. Not my parents. Not Cole. It was my deal to handle. Alone.

"So, what's the problem?" Jade asks.

I glare at her.

"Okay, okay," she says. "I understand."

"You better."

"I guess Coach Hillman still isn't too thrilled about girl wrestlers."

"Gee, ya think?"

"But you've been part of the team for two seasons," she says.

"Jade, he's the head coach," I say, exasperated. "And what about that quote from one of the varsity guys? Girls' basketball? Are you kidding me?"

The bell rings for the next period. I can't miss another class.

"Let's go," I say.

Jade and I walk out of the balcony and into the crowded second-floor hallway. Soon, I notice her staring at someone. I look ahead. There's Darlene, coming right toward us.

When she gets close, Jade sneers, "Skank."

"Drop dead," Darlene hisses back.

Jade starts to cut across the hallway, but before anything can happen I steer her into the girls' bathroom.

"Mel, what'd you do that for?" Jade says.

"One—I don't want you getting in trouble," I say. "And—two—a fighter, you're not."

We take our places in front of the mirrors. Jade pulls out lip gloss, while I begin to work on my bloodshot eyes.

"Hey, for all we know, Darlene misquoted Coach Hillman," she says. "Let's face it, she's had it in for the Radfords ever since Cole dumped her fat ass last year."

But I'm pretty sure Coach Hillman meant every word. He made it perfectly clear in that first meeting I had with him and Mr. Williamson. He used high-falutin' phrases like, "protecting the program's integrity and cohesiveness," and questioning my "intestinal fortitude for a rigorous sport like wrestling." It would've been a joke, if it hadn't been so damn serious.

I turn to Jade. "How do I look?"

She wets the tip of her finger. "Just a tiny smudge here," she says, touching below my bottom eyelid.

"My eyes still red?"

"Hardly," she says, but I can tell she's just trying to make me feel better. "Come on, let's go."

"Hey, Jade," I say. "Thanks."

She shrugs her shoulders. "My dear, Mel, it's what I do. I'm just a caring, loving, great best friend forever. Need I say more?"

I can't concentrate.

And wrestling is definitely a sport that has to have 110 percent of your attention. If it doesn't—*bam!*—this happens. I'm on my back, with Brook on my chest. I turn hard, trying to keep my shoulder blades off the mat. But I can't focus. And I can't fight it anymore. I don't want to fight it anymore. I can't believe it, I'm actually going to give up and go flat.

"Let's start again," I say to Brook.

He eases up, then looks at me funny.

"Nice trip," I say.

But Brook knows it wasn't that good a move. It was sloppy. On any other day, I would've defended the trip easily and we would've continued in a tie-up, fighting for position on our feet. On any other day.

I haven't even glanced at Coach Hillman all practice. I don't know if he's looked toward me either. He certainly hasn't come over and said anything. He has to know the *Tablet* came out today. By the end of the day, a few people asked me what I thought, and if I was mad. I brushed aside their questions by saying, "I'm on the team." As if that was enough of an answer.

"Mel," Brook says. "You ready?"

I look at him. "Uh...yeah."

We slap hands and circle each other. I could shoot in, but my mind's not completely into this. And if my mind's not completely into this, then my body certainly isn't. Before I can react, Brook shoots in deep with a double-leg. In an instant, he lifts, cuts out my legs, and crashes me to the mat, then covers for the takedown. Now, *that* was a nice move.

Of course, it helped that I was a total fish.

We're only an hour into practice, but I'm fried mentally. Before Brook and I start on our feet again, I wave him off, unsnap my headgear, and walk over to Coach Geiger.

"What's the matter?" he says to me.

"I feel lousy."

"What is it?"

"Cramps."

It's not cramps, of course. But I know whenever I mention the word "cramps" guys back off. Unquestioningly. Works like kryptonite.

Coach Geiger nods. "I understand."

Do you really, Coach?

I walk to the door, but give one last look toward the champions mat, wondering who Darlene quoted, then make my way down the hallway to the girls' locker room. Inside, I take a seat on one of the benches. Leaving practice may have been a chicken thing to do, but I sure feel better being alone with my thoughts than out on the mats letting those thoughts get my ass kicked.

"Can you turn up the heat?" I ask Cole.

But he ignores me.

We're in his car, on our way home. I'm sitting in the front seat, staring out into the darkness. The sweat on my body has long dried, but I'm starting to feel chills. And I'm kind of hungry. Think about something good, I tell myself. So I think about Stewart. I can't wait until we're together this Sunday. I hope he calls me later. I know he has a calc test tomorrow, but he can't possibly study *all* night.

"So why'd you quit practice?" Cole asks.

"I didn't quit."

"You left. That's quitting."

I'm in no mood to argue with him. "I have cramps."

"Cramps," he says, but I can tell he doubts me.

"Want to see the tampon when I'm done?" I ask. Great, I've become as disgusting as my brother.

"Tempting, but I'll pass." Then, he says, "I know what has your panties all in a bunch. I read the *Tablet*."

I don't say anything.

"Look," he says. "Coach *did* let you on the team, so don't make a thing about it now."

If my brother only knew. I could tell him about the meetings, and the essay. I'd like to know if he had to go through the same crap. Or if he would've. But instead, I keep my mouth shut. I just want to get home.

"He's a great wrestling coach, one of the best," Cole says, turning onto our street. "I'm not saying he's right or wrong about whether girls should wrestle—"

I interrupt him. "Wait, Cole, you think he might be right?"

"Wouldn't you rather wrestle against girls?" my brother asks.

"Answer my question," I say.

He shrugs so nonchalantly that I have to believe he's acting this way just to get me angrier.

"Cole?"

"All I know is I wouldn't want to wrestle a girl," he says. Then he turns and, with a big smile, adds, "Unless she had smokin' tits."

"Don't make a joke about this," I say.

"Come on, you know the deal," Cole says, in a semi-serious kind of way. "If a guy wrestles a girl and beats her, it's no big deal because he's supposed to. And if he wrestles her and loses"—he shakes his head—"his life would be over. Done. He'd be called a pussy or fag forever. He'd never be able to live it down."

"Oh, that's ridiculous," I say.

"It is what it is," Cole says. "And you know I'm right."

The next morning, there aren't hordes of feminists swarming the school to protest Coach Hillman's interview in the *Tablet*.

Actually, *nothing* happens. Not that day. Or the one after. No one else asks me about it either. And I certainly never bring it up with my mom or dad.

When I'm alone and I've got some time to think, I wonder what I expected to happen. Maybe Jade was right, and I've been reading way more into what Coach Hillman said than I should have. Besides, did I really expect anyone to rush to my side? I'm just a JV wrestler. A backup at that.

Still, I've got this nagging, frustrated feeling that the *Tablet* thing is still just wrong. I can't totally put my finger on it. I feel angry, but I'm unsure exactly why, or where my anger should be directed.

The first few times I pass Darlene in the hallway, I give her nasty looks. Soon enough, I stop doing even that. I tell Jade to stop, too. This is my battle (if it's one at all), and I'll fight it myself.

Then things return to the way they were before. Actually, I'm not sure they were ever different. I continue going to practice, preparing for the JV matches and praying that our opponent has a second-stringer at my weight class willing to wrestle a girl, and promising my grandmother (but not meaning it) that I'll be at DDI the next time we have a day off from practice. And, of course, talking on the phone, and spending as much time as I can with Stewart.

In the end, I guess, Coach Hillman's interview never was that big a deal.

Chapter 23

"We are...the Ashton Eagles! We are...the Ashton Eagles!"

The gymnasium is packed to the rafters, with our home crowd going wild—so much so that Stewart and I can hardly hear each other. That's okay, though, it just means we have to lean in real close whenever we talk.

"Is it always like this?" His breath tickles my ear.

"Pretty crazy."

"You mean you don't get this in golf?"

He smiles and shakes his head.

Deerfield High came into the match as the next best team in the county, with two state-ranked wrestlers at 145- and 152-pounds. But we've built up a big lead before those weight classes have competed, so our varsity is well on its way to upping its record to 14–1.

Jade is sitting on the other side of me. As always, we're in the last row of the stands, surrounded by my JV teammates. I notice some of them glance back at Stewart, probably wondering who he is. Even Brook does. I'm relishing it. Unfortunately, though, I didn't get to wrestle tonight. The Deerfield JV coach claimed his team didn't have anyone around my weight. But it sure seemed like they had extra guys who could've wrestled me in an exhibition match.

Even though I'm used to that kind of stuff, tonight I'm more than disappointed. I'm really annoyed. I wanted Stewart to see me wrestle. I wanted to show him my sport and what I'm able to do. I guess I'm going to have to bust my ass to break into the JV lineup, so that teams can't avoid me without making it look completely obvious. And, of course, Stewart's going to have to keep coming to all of our matches.

Jade taps me with her shoe. I look over. She leans in and says, "He's a good guy."

"He is, isn't he?"

"And cute."

"Thanks," I say. "Next time I'll make sure he brings a friend."

Jade starts clapping her hands and stomping her feet with the rest of the Ashton fans, willing our 138-pounder to pin his opponent. "Nah, I wouldn't want to get distracted," she says, with a wink.

For the briefest of moments, I think that maybe she means she doesn't want to be distracted from watching the wrestling. I should've known better. Her eyes are fixed on something else.

"I love these outfits," she says. "What're they called again?"

"Singlets," I say, even though I know she knows perfectly well what they're called.

"Yes, I love singlets!" Jade says, loudly, but it's lost in

the noise as our 138-pounder does, in fact, stick the pin. She and I jump to our feet, high-fiving the guys in the row in front of us, then yelling our favorite cheer. "We don't just want a win... We want a pin, pin, PIN!" I glance at Stewart, who's still sitting, looking up at me with a kind of bemused expression on his face.

I can hear my breaths, shallow but quick. I lick my lips—they're dry and cool. Then I feel that familiar warm swirl below my belly. I want to give in and let go, but a part of me resists. The feeling makes me anxious and embarrassed and exhilarated—all at the same time.

I open my eyes. The windows are fogged up (again), and there's a layer of newly fallen snow covering the car. Along with the hum of the heater, it feels like our own little cocoon.

Stewart's staring at me. He's got that serious look on his face again. Or maybe it's just the dark shadows. He's so good looking that I could almost forget that his hand's inside my shirt, under my bra, cupping my naked breast.

"Is this cold?" he asks, gently rubbing his thumb over my nipple.

I shake my head slightly.

"Sorry if it is," he says.

I nod. I'm not sure why. I'm not sure of anything at the moment. I'm feeling things I've never felt before. I'm losing control...of my thoughts...and my body...

Stewart leans in to kiss me. My mouth opens. His lips are moist and warm, and his tongue begins to touch mine. He tastes like the Reese's Pieces we shared earlier. He presses against me some more, caressing my earlobe with one hand, the other touching me in all the right ways. *How is it*, I'm thinking, *that he's so good at this?*

I pull back from him.

He stops. "You okay?"

"Yeah..." I say.

"What's the matter?"

"Nothing."

His thumb rubs my nipple again.

"Wait," I say. "I just need to...um...catch my breath."

In the back of my mind, I'm wondering how I got here. I mean, of course, I know how Stewart and I ended up in his car parked at the end of our driveway with the lights off. For the purpose of explaining to my parents, he's dropping me off after the match. But we've been out here a while, and I know it's only a matter of time before my mom and dad get suspicious—if they haven't already. I suppose we could've sat in our den and watched TV with the lights on and my parents within earshot. But then there'd be no way for us to have *any* privacy. So if we want to be alone at all, we've got to be out here and go along with the charade of pretending we're just "saying good night" to each other. I mean, I'm sure they know we're out here doing something more than talking. And, who knows, maybe one of them (Mom, probably) is putting on boots and a coat right this very moment to come out and knock on the window.

"I've never gone this—" I start to say.

"Ever?"

Stewart says it, not in a surprised way, but almost

appreciative. And for some reason that makes me feel funny, like, by allowing him to touch me, I've made some big decision that I didn't really know was such a big decision. I don't think I like that kind of responsibility.

"You have a great body," Stewart says. It sounds like such a guy's line, yet I'm sure I hear sincerity in his voice.

"Thanks," I say.

"I want you to feel good."

"I do."

"Even more," he says.

I ease my hand off of his. He takes it as a sign and moves his hand to my other breast, his fingers drawing circles around that nipple. I press back into the car seat, anticipating the warmth that's, again, about to flood to my stomach...

And it does.

I wrap my arms around Stewart as he nuzzles my neck. I'm not sure what to do exactly, so I rub his back through his shirt and tilt my head, letting him run his lips along my neck and under my ear.

My breath is quick, again; my mouth dry. Before I realize it, Stewart has dropped his head and lifted my shirt. With a hand on one breast, he puts his mouth on the other.

Oh, God... This feels good... Better than good... Amazingly, incredibly good...

And it's just *way* too much.

"Stop," I whisper.

Stewart looks up at me. "What?"

"Please," I say.

"Stop?"

"Yeah."

"Now?"

"Please."

Stewart looks like he's about to say something more, then he just sits back. I pull my shirt down. I ask him if it's okay that we stopped. He nods as if he understands, but I'm not sure he does. God, a part of me just wants to rewind the last few moments and let him continue what he was—what *we*—were enjoying. But where would that lead? I don't know. Actually, I do. Maybe that's why it's good that my parents would never in a million years let Stewart come up to my bedroom. I can't think about that. I just want to make sure he's okay with this. It won't be this way forever, just for now.

"I'm going to turn on the radio," Stewart says. He presses the car stereo button. "That all right?"

"Yeah."

"Want the heat on more?"

"Okay," I say. I guess we'll just go on pretending nothing happened ten seconds ago.

For a while longer, we talk about the next match. When it is and who it's against. Whether the snow's going to continue all night. And what's going on at school. And we listen to music. He likes country mostly; I don't. But we both know the words to the latest hit on Kiss-FM. He has more candy that we share (thankfully, I don't have to worry about my weight).

On the surface, it seems like everything's fine. But underneath, it's not. I mean, maybe I should be explaining why I stopped him. And he should be honest about whether it bothers him. Instead, we act like nothing ever happened. I guess that's the way it is. I mean, something's changed, I think. There's definitely an awkwardness between us, like we just realized we might not really know each other as well as we thought.

Whoa, that was *way* too adult for me.

Chapter 24

The kitchen is bright from the noon sun. I walk in, tired and hungry, still feeling a kind of buzz from having Stewart on my mind all night. Mom's standing by the window above the sink, with a coffee mug in her hand, looking out over our backyard.

"A lot of snow out there," she says, almost to herself. "Pretty, though."

"Morning," I say, opening the refrigerator and grabbing a bottle of flavored water and an orange.

"That was a long goodbye last night," Mom says.

Uh oh...

"Really?" I say, trying to play it cool.

She turns. "Yes, it was. But I think you know that."

Geez, this is not a conversation I want to have right now. I need to make a quick exit.

"Where are you going?" Mom asks, before I'm out of the kitchen.

"Upstairs."

"Why don't you sit down with me for a few minutes?" But she's telling more than asking me.

I hesitate, but then take a seat at the table. "We're the only ones up?"

"Your father had to go into the office this morning," she says. "He'll be back later. Cole's door is closed; he's probably still sleeping."

I should be, too.

"What were you doing in the car all that time?" she says, in an accusatory way.

"Back to that," I say, more snidely than I meant.

Mom's eyes narrow. "Melinda..."

"Sorry," I say, sheepishly. Then, more convincingly, I say, "We were just talking, and listening to music. You know, stuff."

"Stuff?" Mom says.

"Yeah."

"You couldn't have done *stuff* in the house?"

"With you and Dad in the next room?" I say. "Might as well have a spotlight on us. We'd have no privacy."

"And why would you need privacy?"

I frown. "I'm just saying. It'd be nice every once in a while to have some."

"For?" Mom pushes.

"Talking."

"And?"

"Nothing else."

"And?" she says, more forcefully.

I roll my eyes and let out a deep, frustrated sigh. "Kissing, okay? Yes, we kissed. Nothing else, just kissed. Geez, Mom, weren't you ever a teenager?"

My mother gets up from the table to fill her mug. I watch as she pours some coffee, adds a spoonful of sugar and a little skim milk, then stirs. "Yes, of course, I was a teenager," she says. "And I know what can happen when you sit in a boy's car for as long as you did last night."

"So, you *do* know," I say, to lighten the mood.

"Mel, stop playing games," she says. "This is not about me, it's about you."

"You don't trust me?"

"It's not *you* I need to trust."

"Nothing happened, Mom," I say. "I mean, nothing happened that you should be worried about."

She sits back down at the table and reaches her hand out to mine. Then she nods. I don't know if it's because she believes me. I hope she does. It's *mostly* true. Mom takes a few more sips from her mug, while I peel the orange. We share the wedges.

"I'm going back up to my room," I say. "Anything else you need to talk to me about?"

"You tell me."

I roll my eyes. "There's nothing."

We're quiet for a while, then Mom says, "Mel, let's not make this a habit."

I nod.

"Oh, and your grandmother called while you were sleeping. She said she's going to call back a little later."

I guess I can't avoid her forever. "Do you know what she wants?" I ask.

It's an odd question, I know, even a stupid one, if Mom's face is any indication.

"To talk to her granddaughter," she says. "She probably wants to ask about last night's match."

"Not much to say."

"It's a shame you didn't get to compete."

"It is."

"These boys shouldn't be allowed to avoid you," she says, with a comforting smile. "They should realize you're on a high school team just like they are, practicing and learning just like any of them."

"You'd think."

"Telephone's for you," Mom calls from the first floor.

I raise my head from my pillow. Damn... I was hoping my grandmother might've forgotten. I'm too tired to argue anymore about this working at DDI stuff. Why's it so important to her anyway? Didn't my first day there prove DDI's not for me, and I'm not good for them?

"Mel..." Mom says.

"I got it."

I slide off my bed and walk over to my vanity, then I pick up the receiver. "Yes, Grandma?"

"Uh, excuse me..." It's a woman's voice. One I don't recognize. "I'm calling for Melinda Radford."

"Who's this?"

"Hi, Melinda, this—"

"I didn't say it was Melinda."

"But it is, right?"

"Who wants to know?"

"But you *are* Melinda Radford, correct?" the woman says.

"Yeah," I say, slightly annoyed. "Who are you?"

"I have a good idea. How about we start over?" the woman says in a friendly tone. "I didn't mean to intrude on your Sunday afternoon. My name is Jessica Shepherd and I'm a freelance writer finishing up a piece about high school girls competing on boys' sports teams. I wanted to get your perspective."

I want to stop the woman, but she's not slowing down for anything.

"I received a copy of the Ashton *Tablet*," she continues. "I was interested in some of the comments that Coach Hillman made about females in high school wrestling. You're familiar with the interview in the *Tablet*, right?"

"Well—"

"Exactly," the woman says. "I spoke with Ms. Darlene McAdams, who gave me your phone number so we could discuss this further."

"Darlene gave you my number?"

"Yes, is that all right?"

"No, it's not all right."

"Melinda, please understand—"

"What's there to understand? It's a stupid article in our school paper written by a loser. You know Darlene's a total loser, right? Her article means nothing. I've already forgotten all about it."

"Maybe you have."

"I *have*."

"To be honest, it doesn't sound like you have," the woman says. "And, if that's the case, I wouldn't blame you one bit."

I'm about to scream at this woman, when I hear a knock at my door. "Hold on," I say into the phone.

Mom leans in. "Everything okay?"

I nod. "Just on the phone."

"With your grandmother?"

"Someone from school," I say. "It's fine." I wave Mom away, then wait a few moments until she closes my bedroom door. "Look, I don't know why you're calling," I say to the woman, "but I don't really want to talk to you about this. I'm on the high school wrestling team. The guys in the practice room are my teammates."

"And you all get along?" she says.

"Yeah, mostly."

"Some have a problem?"

"I didn't say that."

"Well, at least one does."

"We don't have to like each other," I say. "We just have to be willing to make each other better on the mats. Now, look, I'm going to hang up because I don't really like answering your questions."

But the woman won't give up. "Your coach is an older man, from a different generation. Do you think he just doesn't get it?"

"Get what?"

"The rights of a girl to play any sport she wants."

"Why're you asking me? Ask him."

"But it's obvious your head coach has misgivings about girls—*you*—on the team."

"I don't know."

"It's in the *Tablet*."

"Maybe he was misquoted," I say. "I wouldn't trust Darlene to get anything right. I've got to go. If you try to keep talking to me I'm going to hang up. I don't want to be rude but—"

"One last question," the woman says.

"One?"

"Promise."

"What?"

"Would you prefer if someone else were coach?" she says. "Do you think then you'd get a fair shake?"

I take a deep breath. "Coach Hillman is the varsity coach. As far as a 'fair shake,' I don't know what that means. I'm treated just like everyone else. I keep going to practice every day, trying to improve myself as a wrestler. I drill hard. I wrestle hard. That's what I care about. Now I'm hanging up."

"But, Melinda, there's—" I hear right before I click off the phone, then toss it on my bed.

Why are people always trying to stir up garbage?

I need to get the phone call out of my mind, so I put on a couple of long-sleeved shirts, then a pair of heavy sweatpants and a sweatshirt. Down in the laundry room, I lace up my running shoes. I'll bet that woman's a friend of Darlene's family. That's how she got a copy of the *Tablet*. Otherwise, how would she?

It doesn't matter. It's over.

"I'm going running," I yell to no one in particular, then close the laundry room door behind me and step out into the cold.

Chapter 25

"Mel!" Jade shrieks, her voice echoing in the empty auditorium.

I try to shush her, but Jade will have none of it.

"You. Are. Such. A. Prude," she says, emphasizing each word, with particular delight on "prude."

I glance over my shoulder toward the balcony exit, then give her a firm look. "Will you be quiet?"

"Well, you *are*."

"I'm not."

"You are."

"I'm..." I say, then get totally lost thinking of the right word. I mean, I'm not a prude, I don't think. I'm just... Then it comes to me. "Deliberate."

Jade stares at me like I've just spoken German, or Japanese, or in tongue. "Deliberate? What's that even mean?"

I shrug. "I'm letting things build up."

"Build up?" she says. "What is this, a science project?"

I ignore her. "Jade, you should've seen us," I say, staring up at the ornate ceiling. "It was *sooo* passionate. We were just driving each other crazy. You practically couldn't see out the windows, they were steamed up so much. Imagine what it'll be like in a few weeks, or a month."

"It'll be, like, *over*," Jade says.

"Over?" I look at her.

"Guys don't care about the build-up."

"Of course they do."

"No, they don't."

"What do you mean?"

"Guys... don't... care... about... the... build-up..." she says, emphatically.

"Why not?"

"It's nature," Jade says, as if an innocent like me wouldn't know this. "Guys like the moment right *after* the build-up. That's what they care about."

"You mean?"

She nods. "Yeah."

"How do you know?"

"I just know."

"How?"

"Mel, while you're rolling around on a sweaty wrestling mat, what do you think I'm doing? I'll tell you. I'm reading *Cosmo, W, Glamour*." She puts her finger to her temple. "Collecting *knowledge*."

"Knowledge?"

"Guy knowledge," she says, nodding her head.

I don't know if what she knows is right, and I don't care. I just have to trust Jade about this kind of stuff. After all, she's had more boyfriends than me.

"So," I say. "What do I do?"

She wrinkles her forehead as if she's giving this considerable thought. Then she says, "You let him touch a boob?"

"Both," I answer.

"Under your bra?"

"Yeah."

"Anything lower?"

"No," I say, in such a way that "of course not" is more than implied.

"So, not even that," Jade says. "What about him?"

"What about him?"

She rolls her eyes. "Mel, did you put your hand on... you know?"

"Uh, hello?" I say. "Whaddya think I'm a slut like—"

We look at each other and chime together, "Darlene!" When we stop laughing, Jade says, "Okay, so you didn't want to break our two-month rule. But, after that, you're going to have to do *something* with him. You don't want to lose him. There are probably lots of girls at Grand Hills willing to do stuff. It *is* a slutty school."

"Stewart is willing to wait," I say.

"Seems like he's already waited," Jade says.

And, for some reason, that kind of hits me. Not Stewart. He's totally willing to wait. Patiently. He likes being with me—and not *that* kind of "being with me," but the kind that means spending time talking and joking and laughing. And, yes, some kissing and touching. But we're about more than just that, I'm positive.

✦ ✦ ✦ ✦ ✦

I hear Stewart yawn through the phone. His voice's been soft and slightly strained.

"Tired?" I ask. I really don't want to hang up.

He says he's been working a lot of hours at Crystal Fog, helping out in the maintenance area after school, then filling in as a valet at night. The transmission in his car is slipping (whatever that means), so he's trying to make the money to get it replaced before it's completely shot.

"Work's killing me," he says.

"Sounds it," I say.

Of course, dragging my butt around a wrestling mat for two hours, after a day of school, then studying all night (or at least staring at the same page in my marketing textbook), isn't a picnic either. But I keep that to myself.

"Want to hang up?" I say.

"Not yet."

I hesitate. "Thought about you during class today."

"Which one?"

"All of them."

He kind of laughs.

"And Jade thought you were really nice," I say. "She hardly likes anyone. Of course, not everyone likes her, either."

"She's weird," he says. "But in a good way."

Then we're quiet for a few moments, which is unusual because, lately, we're never at a loss for words. Especially me. I mean, on the phone I can talk anyone's ears off. Stewart, even more so. But the silence continues. I wonder if it's from him being tired, or because we won't be able to get together this weekend. There's a varsity match on Friday night, and Stewart's having dinner with his dad. The next day, I'm going to a wrestling clinic for girls at Eastern Michigan University. On Sunday, Stewart's working all day at Crystal Fog.

"The clinic's all afternoon?" he asks.

"Most of it," I say. "I'm pretty excited because I don't get to wrestle girls very often." But my enthusiasm doesn't seem to mean much.

"Maybe you can come over Saturday night," he says. "You've never been to my house. I should be done with work and stuff by, like, six or seven."

"Stewart, you know my parents won't let me." I'm *so* embarrassed to say that.

"You can ask," he says.

"I already know the answer."

"You sure?"

"Yeah," I say.

Silence again.

Finally, I say, "But you can come over here. We'll have to hang out in the den." Lights on. Parents in the next room. Brother upstairs. "But it won't be so bad," I say, trying to convince us both.

"I guess so."

Something in the way he says it reminds me of all the stuff Jade told me in the auditorium. That I'm a prude. That Grand Hills is full of slutty girls allowed to go over to boys' houses. That, because of both, I could lose him.

So I blurt out, "I'll make it worth your while."

"Worth my while?" he says. I can hear him grinning over the phone. "How?"

It's an obvious question to which I don't have an obvious answer. So I kind of giggle. I have no idea why. I never giggle.

"It'll be a surprise," I say.

"A surprise?"

And I can tell from the sudden life in his voice that he thinks it'll be something of the after-the-build-up kind. Or at least he hopes. Oh, geez, the two-month rule isn't up for another week and a half and, now, I've committed myself to something I'm not sure I want to do (or can do, hanging out in our den) just yet.

"You go to sleep with that little mystery," I say, teasingly. I have no idea where that came from. It's like I momentarily channeled Jade.

"I will," he says.

"Sleep tight."

We hang up the phone.

Uh-oh...

Chapter 26

I woke up queasy.

And still feel that way.

I'm going to get my period soon—this time for real. But it's way more than that. I didn't study last night for my marketing concepts quiz. I mean, I tried. Sort of. I don't really like the class that much, but Dad thinks marketing's important to learn. So does my grandmother. She says it's very useful in the business world. Of course, they're not the ones who have to deal with the tests and quizzes.

Annie passes me in the hallway. "Mel," she says, cheerfully, "don't forget your four P's."

Four P's?

I stare at her over my shoulder. "Annie, wait—" And then I slam right into Trey coming the other way.

"Watch yourself," he says.

I step to the side. I know that as the team's other captain there's a lot of pressure on Trey, but that sure wasn't very pleasant. When he passes, I continue down the hallway, searching every nook and cranny of my brain for any P's, let alone four of them.

Suddenly, it hits me.

Duh... The four P's of marketing.

Except, I can only name price and product—the two that even the biggest idiot in class would know. What the hell are the other two? I mean, if I can't remember something as basic as this, those cramps better arrive in a big way in about eleven minutes.

Price...

Product...

It's still as far as I get.

Honestly, though, this isn't completely my fault. I had every intention of studying last night. But when I went over my class notes, my eyes glazed. Then Stewart called. After our conversation, I spent the rest of the night, and into the early morning, staring at the four walls of my bedroom wondering how I was going to "make it worth his while." What was I going to—?

Suddenly, someone grabs me hard.

"Hey!" I yell.

Then I realize *my brother* is dragging me out of the hallway, down the stairwell, and through a school side door. When we're outside, he lets go.

"What's your problem, Cole?"

"Mel, you really fucked up this time."

Whoa, he's pissed. Majorly pissed. "What are you talking about?"

He slaps something into my hands. "Look." It's a folded newspaper. The *Detroit News*. Today's, apparently. "Open it," Cole snaps.

Reluctantly, I do.

He points to an article with a headline that seems to grow bigger and bolder as my eyes stay on it: GIRL'S RIGHTS TO WRESTLE, BODY SLAMMED

Oh, damn...this *can't* be good.

The queasy feeling in my stomach spreads to the rest of my body. I glance up at Cole, then back at the article.

"You've gotten yourself in a world of shit," Cole says. "We're in the middle of the season, with all these huge matches coming up, and you go and do something galactically stupid like this."

"Do what?"

"Why'd you say that crap?"

"I don't know what you're talking about."

"Come off it."

"No," I say. "I really don't know."

Cole shakes his head. "Read it then."

He turns and stalks away.

"The guys are pissed, Mel. Really pissed," he adds as the school door closes behind him. I'm left alone. I realize it's freezing out here, but I don't want to go in. I sit down on a nearby bench and start reading.

I'm going to throw up. No joke. Just barf up whatever's in my stomach all over the ground. My name is in the newspaper—the *Detroit News*. And I'm *quoted*.

"When Ms. Radford was asked about how she gets along with the boys on the wrestling team, she said, 'We don't have to like each other.'"

I didn't say *that*.

A little further, I'm quoted again.

"Ms. Radford seemed reluctant to indicate whether she felt she was being treated equitably, or whether she would welcome someone else guiding the team. 'Coach Hillman is the varsity coach,' she said. 'As far as a "fair shake," I don't know what that means.'"

Those weren't my words. I was careful about what I said... Wasn't I?

But there it is in black and white.

This is not happening. This is not happening to me.

I gotta find Jade.

"You can't just not go to practice," Jade says, as we walk out the school back entrance.

Neither of us wants to be outside, but the auditorium is being used for a ninth-grade assembly and our backup secret place—the bottom of the staircase near the janitors' closet at the far end of the school—has been under renovation for the past two weeks. There's just no place for privacy in this damn school.

"It's *coooold,*" Jade says, shrinking into her wool coat.

For some reason, I hardly notice.

"Hey, how'd your quiz go?" she asks.

"Uh...can we please stick to one disaster at a time?"

"I already told you," Jade says. "You gotta go to practice."

"I don't have to."

"Yeah, you do."

"Why?"

"One, you're on the team," she says. "Two, you gotta go on principle."

"You mean this whole 'do it for the female species' thing?"

"More like," Jade says, "if you don't go, you're 'a quitter' thing."

I turn to her. "I am *not* a quitter."

As we continue up the school driveway, Jade hooks my arm and pulls me in for warmth. "I know you're not. I do. Of course, Melinda Radford does not quit. But if you don't go, well...what would *you* think?"

"I don't know," I say, sharply. "Maybe that this Melinda person needs a break. That's reasonable."

"You're right," Jade says.

"Of course, I'm right."

"I know, I just said so."

"Good."

"Yes, good."

I look at Jade and frown. "You're patronizing me, aren't you?"

"Noooo," she says, with pretend earnestness.

"You are."

"I just have one thing to ask you," Jade says. "And I'm heart attack-serious about this."

"What?"

"What would your *grandma* tell you to do?"

"Oh, geez, you're pulling the grandma card."

"Not the grandma card," Jade says. "I'm pulling the *your* grandma card." Then her lips curl into a grin.

Maybe she's right. Who knows? I have no idea. I'm not thinking too straight, and I'm still pissed that Cole got so mad without hearing my side of the story. I'm not even sure what my side of the story is. I didn't say the stuff that was written in the article. Or maybe I did. Who knows? It's not what I meant.

I look up and notice Danielle Schwartz, Chloe Wasserman, and another senior girl walking down the sidewalk toward us. Jade and I quickly move out of their way. As they pass by, Danielle says, in my direction, "Hey, don't you get enough attention?"

"Huh?"

"I said," Danielle snaps, "don't you already get enough attention being the dyke on the team?"

There's that nauseous feeling again. Jade and I continue straight ahead, without looking back.

"Ignore them," she whispers.

"Yeah, keep running," Chloe yells.

Great, now senior girls are my enemies. Doesn't anyone understand all I want to do is wrestle? All I've *ever* wanted to do is wrestle. I just want to be on the mats. And compete. And, I think, none of this garbage, now or before, would've happened if I was a guy.

And that totally sucks.

"Hey..." Jade says, tugging on my coat to get me out of my head.

"Yeah?"

"Let's head over to Wheeler's," Jade says, nodding toward the party store across Broadmore Avenue. "I'll get a diet pop and some gum. But we gotta get back. I can't

180

miss any more classes because of you. You're lucky I'm such a good friend."

And I know that Jade says it in a teasing way, but I also know that we're pretty even in the who's-been-there-for-who kind of thing. Whether it's her dealing with guy stuff or the times she and her dad get into insane arguments, I'm there for her, calming her, comforting her, rebuilding her.

"I'll buy," I say.

Jade turns and laughs. "Of course you're going to buy," she says. "God, I'm freeeezing!"

Then we start running in the shop's direction.

I feel like I'm losing it. My mind. My emotions. Right here in the girls' locker room. I'm dressed for practice, but nervous shivers keep coming. They just won't stop. Not even when I throw on a sweatshirt and slide down the bench so that I'm directly under the ceiling heating vent.

On the floor, crumpled in a ball, is the newspaper article. Someone tacked it on the locker room corkboard and wrote "Quit Now Bitch!!!" over it in a black marker. I tore it down, but that doesn't change a thing. Who put it up? And why would they write such a mean thing?

I can't seem to lift myself to my feet. And if I could, I'm not sure whether it'd be to walk down the hall to the wrestling room or to take a right and leave the school. I feel tears welling up from where the thick knot in my stomach is, rising up into my chest, squeezing through my neck and throat, and, finally, pressing against the back of my eyes.

No, no, no... I can *not* cry.

On the shakiest of legs, I struggle to stand and take a deep, deep breath. It seems enough to hold off the shivers. Momentarily. I push the locker room door open and head down the hallway. A few wrestlers are ahead of me. I can turn right and get the hell out of here...

But I don't.

Instead, I follow them into the practice room.

All eyes are on me, it seems, twisting the knot in my stomach even more. No one says hello. I find a spot on the runners-up mat and sit down, then begin stretching my legs, mostly so I have something to do instead of looking at any of the guys. I pull off my sweatshirt. A faint but not particularly pleasant smell drifts up from my underarms.

As discreetly as possible, I pretend to use the sweatshirt to brush sweat off my forearm, then take a quick swipe of my underarms. I do the same with the other side. I pray that helps and toss the sweatshirt to the corner. Another sniff. Not any better. I don't want to suddenly leave the practice room, everyone will think it has something to do with the article. But if I don't get to a bathroom for some soap and water, the smell is definitely going to get worse after we start drilling.

I notice Brook warming up to my left. *Please don't come near me.* Thankfully, he doesn't. Neither does anyone else.

Where's Cole? And where are the coaches? Suddenly, it occurs to me that maybe the reason Coach Hillman isn't at practice is because this whole crap storm has gotten him in trouble with our principal, or even with the Board of Ed. That's all I need. Another headline in tomorrow's newspaper: ASHTON SOPHOMORE MELINDA RADFORD GETS LEGENDARY COACH FIRED.

The practice room door opens.

Coach Geiger walks in, stone-faced. Cole and Trey follow right behind. When I see my brother's expression, my stomach sinks. He's concerned. Or still pissed. Or maybe both.

"Bring it in," Coach Geiger says. "On the champions mat." The team gathers in front of him, but when it takes too long for Coach Geiger's liking, he shouts, "Take a goddamn seat right here, right now."

Everyone scrambles to sit down. I do, too, behind the other wrestlers.

"Guys, I need to talk to you about something," Coach Geiger says. "We're going to be without Coach Hillman for a while."

Oh, no, what did I do?

But then Coach Geiger says something none of us expected, certainly not me. "As I'm sure you guessed from his absences, Coach hasn't been well. He's taking time off from wrestling."

"What's the matter with him?" asks Connor, our varsity 106-pounder.

"There's nothing to worry about," Coach Geiger says. "Coach is getting excellent care. He could be back at practice in a few weeks."

I hang my head. No one else seems to believe that either.

"I'm sure you have a lot of questions," Coach Geiger

continues. "But right now we need to keep our heads on straight, go back to practicing hard and winning matches just like we've done all season. This is an important time. Less than a month until the post-season tournaments. We have to focus." Coach Geiger repeats it, "Focus."

The room is silent for a few moments, then someone says, "Stop talking to newspapers." It's Lionel, our 285-pounder.

Some of the team looks at him; the rest toward me.

"Shut your mouth," I hear. My brother's voice is sharp.

"She shouldn't be talking to newspapers," Lionel says.

I don't know why I open my mouth (and I certainly wish I hadn't), but I do. "I didn't say that stuff, I swear—"

"Mel," Cole snaps, cutting me off. Then he turns to Lionel and says, angrily, "It's none of your damn business."

"The team *is* my business," Lionel says. "It is for every guy in this room."

Cole's about to blow a major fuse and, oddly, in the back of my mind, I'm wondering why Coach Geiger hasn't stopped this.

"You worry about yourself," Cole says.

"Stop protecting her," Lionel says.

"Say another word, and we're going at it."

"Yeah, that's the answer."

Cole snickers. "Just what I thought, you're a pussy."

Lionel starts to stand up. Cole's already there.

"Sit down!" Coach Geiger yells. "Sit down, now!" And when Cole doesn't, Coach Geiger says, "Both of you sit down or I'll suspend you for the next match," in a voice that leaves little doubt that's exactly what he'll do.

Then he looks over the team.

"Break into pairs. Let's warm up by working our takedowns. Good stances, good setups, sharp drop-steps, then finish them off."

I walk back to the runners-up mat, wondering if anyone's going to go with me. My brain's messed up, I stink, and I'm not sure I even want to practice right now. Georgie and I bump into each other. It's obvious from his look that he doesn't want to drill with me; I definitely don't want to deal with him either. So we ignore each other.

Then I see Brook. "Us?" I say, reluctantly.

He answers with a shrug.

I put on my headgear.

"Let's go, Ashton," Coach Geiger barks. "Takedowns!"

Brook and I get in our stances, knees bent, head up, hands out in front. Brook pulls my head down, lowers his level, and shoots in for a single. He picks up my leg, his head in my chest, and runs the pike, sweeping me down to the mat.

Then it's my turn.

Back and forth we go, taking each other down. Singles, doubles, hi-crotches, duck-unders...

I've given up being worried about my underarms. I just focus on fighting for inside position, changing levels, exploding with my drop-step. It's like, for a short time, I have a reprieve from all the crap that's gone on today.

Then, with Brook's leg up in the air and me about to

sweep his leg, I trip on a seam between the mat sections and we tumble awkwardly. I get to one knee and shake my head, frustrated and embarrassed.

Brook says, "Mel, why'd you say that stuff?"

"Huh?"

"In the newspaper. Why'd you say it?"

I open my mouth, but before I can say anything, Coach Geiger shouts, "Grab someone new to drill with."

I look at Brook, but he doesn't really want an answer, I can tell. He's already back on his feet, finding a new partner.

A bad, bad day has just gotten worse.

Chapter 27

I huddle over my dinner plate, pushing the food around with my fork. I'm not hungry at all, but I want to stay at the kitchen table with my parents for a while. I'll talk to Stewart later, maybe, but right now I feel better not sitting alone in my bedroom. And I'm definitely ignoring the phone. If it rings, Cole or my parents can answer.

"How was school?" Dad says to me. He then passes a platter of sirloin strips to my mom.

"You're kidding, right?" I say.

"Did something interesting happen?" he asks.

I roll my eyes. "Interesting...that's not exactly how I'd describe it. I can think of a few more descriptive adjectives instead. Nightmarish. Horrible. Crappy. Yeah, crappy's a good one."

"I think you can find a better word," he says.

"No, I really don't think so."

He looks at me. "So, what happened?"

Why bother going into it? Dad won't understand. I've kept stuff to myself in the past anyway. Like the essay Mr. Williamson had me write. And being alone in the girls' locker room, instead of the guys'. And sometimes wishing Cole wasn't on the team.

"Never mind," I say.

"Mel," Dad says, "tell us what happened."

"I was quoted in the *Detroit News*." It disgusts me to even say the newspaper's name.

"The *News*?" He nods, pleased.

"Yes, the *News*," I say. "It's not a good thing, Dad, so stop acting like it is. I'm in a bunch of trouble. The thing is, I didn't even say the stuff the article says I did. I mean, maybe I did. But I don't think I did. And even if I did, I didn't mean it like it was written."

Without any concern for my dilemma, Dad says, rather cavalierly, "Mel, how bad could it have been?"

Frowning, I shake my head. "Never mind... Just never mind..."

Mom and Dad exchange platters of food. He hands her a dish of fried red peppers, while she passes him roasted eggplant. I'm entirely aggravated by their nonchalance.

"Forget I ever brought it up," I say.

"Now, hold on," Dad says. "Let me take a guess at what you might've said."

"Just drop it, Dad."

But he doesn't. Instead, he cocks his head and raises his eyes, then rubs his chin as if giving scholarly thought. "Knowing my daughter for the past fifteen years," he says, "she said something to the effect of..." There's a long pause, long enough to get me even madder. "'As far as a fair shake, I don't know what a fair shake is.'" He looks at me with one of those fatherly, know-it-all grins.

"How'd I do?"

It hits me. "You read the article," I practically shout.

"Someone in the office showed it to me this morning," he says, pulling a newspaper out of his briefcase. "Then a few of my clients recognized your name and called me. We were all talking about it. I'm going to have the article framed. This is the first time my little girl's been quoted in the *News*."

"Don't let him joke about this," I say to my mom. "Do you two have any idea how awful today was?"

"Well, I'm proud of you," Dad says.

I want to explode. "*Proud* of me?"

"Yes," he says. "Very."

"Proud of me?" I repeat, and turn back to my mom. "He's proud of me. Great. Are you proud of me, too?"

"Of course," she says, spooning garlic mushrooms onto her plate.

I'm nearly at a loss for coherent words. "Don't you— I mean, do you get how—" I stop myself and start yet again. "Do you understand people at school think what was in the newspaper had something to do with Coach Hillman being out today? Do you know how many people at school hate me now? Do you?"

"Like who?" Mom asks.

"All the guys on the wrestling team for starters," I say. "Which is a pretty big deal since they're my *teammates*. I'm also quoted saying that me and the guys don't have to like each other—which I totally don't think at all."

"They'll get over it," Dad says.

"Then some senior girls yelled at me, calling me names," I say. "That wouldn't be as much of a problem if I was a senior, too. But I'm a *sophomore*. That kinda stuff isn't good for the life of a sophomore."

Mom shrugs. "Girls being girls," she says. "They'll move on to some other gossip soon enough."

I throw my hands up in frustration. "You two have *no* idea what it's like to be part of a sports team."

Mom laughs and shakes her head. "Of course, we don't."

In the confusion of my frazzled brain, I suddenly remember that Mom captained the Hillsdale College varsity softball team, and Dad once set a record for points in a game for his high school basketball team. Geez, I've looked through their scrapbooks a zillion times, which makes what I said sound even more stupid.

"How is Coach Hillman?" Mom asks. "Cole didn't say anything."

I shrug. "We weren't told much. We were all kind of stunned. And because of this newspaper thing, Cole almost got into a fight with Lionel protecting me. Not that I asked him to. I didn't at all. But he was really pissed at Lionel."

"Language, Mel," Mom says.

"Oh, and Cole's mad at me, too," I say. "Did he tell you about that?"

"I'm sure he's a little more worried about Coach Hillman," Dad says.

"Yeah, well...I guess so."

My parents continue eating. Not a word or glance in my direction. I stare back and forth at them, waiting for some kind of response. Again, with remarkable nonchalance, Dad nods his head and says, "Yes, he did voice his anger."

"And?"

My dad looks at me. "And what?"

"Did you tell him I was sorry?"

"Are you sorry?"

"Yeah, of course."

"You shouldn't be," Dad says. "Your mom and I didn't raise you to keep your mouth closed if you feel strongly about something."

"Mom, are you listening to this?" I say to her.

"Your dad's right," she says.

"Oh, this is crazy," I say. "I didn't even say those things in the *News*. I was misquoted. And I think it was on purpose. To stir up controversy at my expense."

"Yes, it's all a big conspiracy," Mom says, with a wink. "Actually it's a good lesson: Be careful how you speak to a reporter."

"Ma!"

"Mel, let me ask you a question," Dad says. "Does every guy on the team treat you fairly? Wait, here's a better question. If you weren't Cole's sister, do you think you'd be treated fairly by everyone on the team?"

I purse my lips and answer, grudgingly, "I don't know. Probably not."

"And do you think Coach Hillman's been fair with you since the first day you joined?"

"Maybe."

"Will he let you wrestle varsity?"

"I haven't earned it," I say.

"But if you did?"

I shrug.

"What if, for whatever reason," Dad says, "you were the only one in your weight class on the team. Do you think he'd let you wrestle in a varsity match? I remember you telling us that you didn't think he would. Has that changed?"

I don't answer.

"So, because you're a girl, you're not treated exactly like the rest of the team," Dad says. "That doesn't seem fair to me."

I remain at the kitchen table, my face in my hands. Mom puts a hand on my shoulder and gives me a kiss on my head. I know they mean well, but they just don't get it. I don't want to be a social leper at school. I just want to fit in, wrestle on the team, and go to class. Just another face in the crowd.

The first floor of our house is dark. I can hear the clothes dryer in the laundry room humming and my parents up in their bedroom watching television. I walk down the stairs from the kitchen to the basement. Cole has the wrestling mat rolled out on the floor, with a portable heater on full-blast at each corner. With his earbuds in and his sweatshirt hood up, he's burning drop-steps across the mat.

For a while, he doesn't notice I'm there. Then when he does, he just stares.

"Can we talk?" I say.

After a hesitation, he pulls out his earbuds.

"Sucks about Coach Hillman," I say.

Cole sort of nods.

"What do you think's wrong?"

He shakes his head, continuing to glide across the mat with one drop-step after another. I don't get to watch him during practice that much, and I sometimes forget how good he is.

"Can we talk about today?" I ask. I've got to make sure he knows the truth.

"What's there to talk about? You caused a shit storm."

Cole gets into bottom position, then explodes to his feet, mimics having wrist control, and cuts to free himself for an escape. Then he drops down and does the same thing again. And again.

"The stuff in the newspaper, I swear I didn't say any of it," I plead.

Cole stops drilling and paces around the mat. "Then how'd it get in there?"

I sigh. "I don't know. I mean, I did talk to this woman—she called totally out of the blue, I didn't even know who she was."

"The varsity doesn't need this kind of distraction."

"I know."

"This is my last season," he says. "You have two more. I don't."

There's an unexpected emotion to Cole's words, a kind of...urgency. I begin to realize just how much he has at stake in the upcoming weeks. I hope someday I get to feel that way, too. Like he said, I have two more seasons after this one to make my mark, if I'm ever going to make one. As obvious as that is, it never really occurred to me.

"I need to keep going," Cole said.

I nod. I know he wants me to leave him alone. But before I do, I say, "Thanks for sticking up for me."

"Lionel," Cole says, with a mocking laugh, "should keep his big mouth shut. He barely has a winning record."

I start to climb the stairs to the kitchen.

"And, Mel, don't for a second think I did it for you," Cole says, his words piercing whatever silly notion of sibling love I was feeling. "I wanted to keep the guys from obsessing about Coach. It's screwing with everyone's head. I had to find a way to smack them out of it. I think it worked."

"Sure," is all I'm able to say.

I leave my brother alone in the basement, hearing behind me the sound of his wrestling shoes shuffling along the mat. I feel empty. It's been a long day, the longest of my life, I think. I can hardly remember what I did this morning. I wish I could take a do-over on the quiz—and everything else. Obviously, I can't. I've got to hug Owings, then try to fall asleep. I'll return Stewart's call tomorrow night. Jade'll have to wait, too.

Chapter 28

The next morning, Jade's waiting for me at the front steps of the high school. She smiles, awkwardly, and I notice something tucked inside her jacket. The uneasy feeling in my stomach immediately gets worse.

"Now what?" I say.

Her eyes widen. "You didn't see?"

"See what?"

She pulls out a folded newspaper. I stop in my tracks and hang my head. I think I feel ill. No, I *know* I feel ill. She hands the newspaper to me; reluctantly, I take it. I look back to see if Cole's around, but he's already gone through a side door.

I think I hear Jade make a noise. Was it a *giggle?*

"Mel," she says. "You're so serious. Too serious. You gotta lighten up."

I stare at her and want to scream.

Jade rolls her eyes. "Just open it."

So I do.

But instead of reading a headline like, NEW TOTALLY INCRIMINATING QUOTES FROM MELINDA RADFORD—MUCH WORSE THAN YESTERDAY, I see car ads and the classifieds.

Jade, best friend for oh-so-many years, shoulder to cry on, who's shed plenty of tears on mine, has handed me the advertisements section as a joke.

"Think this is funny?"

My eyes start welling. My lips quiver, then I suck in a halted breath. And, as I hold the moment, I see Jade fully understand that I don't find this the least bit humorous.

"Oh, no," she mutters. "I'm sorry, I swear I'm really sorry. I thought you were over what happened yesterday. I figured that's why you didn't call last night because it was no big deal...I guess not."

I turn my head and start toward the school entrance. *Jade, my dear comedienne, I'll just let you go on a bit longer.*

"Okay, okay," she says, in a plaintive voice. "It was a rotten joke, I mean almost as bad as when we convinced Annie that the wart on her palm was an STD. But once we apologized she got over it, right? And, now that I'm apologizing, you'll get over this really quickly, right?"

I'm a step or two ahead of her, and she's trying to catch up. I look over my shoulder and let just enough of a grin cross my lips.

"Hey, wait," she says. "You're—you're not smiling, are you? Tell me you're not." She puts a hand on my arm. "You are!" she says. "Wonderful. You let me go on spilling my guts and you weren't even upset... Were you?"

I smile a bit more.

"Okay, Mel, you got me," she says, throwing up her hands. "You totally got me. We're even, okay?"

I stop at the top of the school's front steps and say, "Come on, Jade, let's get to homeroom."

And, in an instant, things are (almost) back to normal between her and me. And I'm glad because I don't know what today has in store, and whether this whole newspaper quote thing is (literally and figuratively) yesterday's news. Our varsity has matches tomorrow night and Saturday afternoon, so hopefully that's all the guys on the team will be thinking about.

"Hey, I forgot to tell you," I say to Jade. "Guess who Cole was talking to on his cell phone the other night?"

"Who?"

"Lisbeth Hersh."

"Her?" Jade says, with definite concern in her voice. "Why?"

"Duh," I say. "They're probably gonna start seeing each other."

"Lisbeth and Cole?" Jade says.

"Heard them talking."

"Lisbeth?"

"Hersh."

And, just like that, Jade isn't such a happy camper. I open the school door and let her go through first. She doesn't look at me, doesn't say thanks. We get to the second set of doors. She swings the door open, marches through, then starts down the hallway toward her first class. I veer off down the other hallway. I think I hear Jade mumble goodbye. That's when I call out to her.

"Hey," I say.

She looks over at me, totally pissed. "Yeah?"

"Now we're even," I say.

✦ ✦ ✦ ✦ ✦

I lift my head up from my desk.

Everyone in the class is staring at me, including my Spanish II teacher, Mrs. Rios, and the school secretary, Ms. LaFleur, standing next to her at the front of the room.

"Señorita Radford," Mrs. Rios says. "Ven aqui, por favor."

"Me?"

"Si."

I stand up to a chorus of "Ooh, Mel's in trouble...," then grab my books and handbag and make my way nervously up the aisle of desks.

"Mr. Williamson wants to see you," Ms. LaFleur says loudly enough for everyone to hear.

"Mr. Williamson?" I ask. "Now?"

"He asked that I come get you," Ms. LaFleur says.

Oh crap... This has to be about my quotes in the *News*.

Mr. Williamson's office isn't very far down the hallway, so the short walk doesn't give me a whole lot of time to think about what I'm going to be facing—and Ms. LaFleur is yapping away with chitchat that isn't even registering in my brain. "Please shut up," I want to say.

Ms. LaFleur and I enter the office, and the first thing I see is the newspaper spread out on Mr. WIlliamson's desk. But unlike Jade's little joke this morning, I can see the *News* article I'm quoted in front and center.

Oh, this is not *going to be a pleasant experience...*

"Thank you, Ms. LaFleur," he says, then to me, "Have a seat, Melinda."

I do, which I'm almost thankful for because my legs are

weak and my heart is thumping, and I'm suddenly feeling very tired.

"Something wrong, Mr. Williamson?" I ask.

His eyes narrow. Then he sits back, picks up the newspaper, and reads, "'As far as a "fair shake," I don't know what that means.'"

"It's not what I meant," I say.

"Don't talk; just listen," Mr. Williamson says. "I remember our first meeting. You had asked permission to join the wrestling team. I didn't like the idea. I still don't. I think you know that. Ashton High has never had a female play on a male team. But with Cole on the team, Coach Hillman and I decided, reluctantly, that you wouldn't be as much of a distraction. Frankly, I went against my personal feelings and what I thought would be best for the wrestling program. This," he says, pointing to the article, "is making me regret that decision more than any other I've made as athletic director."

My eyes begin to well up, but I fight it.

"And this couldn't come at a worse time," he continues. "Coach Hillman is not well, as you've heard. Not well at all." Then Mr. Williamson stops himself. I can tell he's getting more and more angry. He throws down the newspaper and says, "Melinda, I thought you were going to take wrestling seriously. I thought you were in it for the sport. I believed that essay I had you write. I trusted that you were being truthful. Was that all for show?"

I hold off the tears, feeling the heat of my anger rise up in my body.

"Were you trying to make a name for yourself?" Mr.

Williamson says to me. "It's what all the kids try to do these days. Say something outrageous. Say something without any consideration for how it might affect other people. Well, I'll tell you something, you've made Coach Hillman and Ashton High look bad. There are reputations at stake. Reputations that are years in the making."

I neither move nor say anything, but look him straight in the eye.

"I'm not going to remove you from the team, Mel. I'd like to, I really do, but I don't want to make the situation any worse than it already is. I hope you learn from this."

But then before Mr. Williamson says another word, my mouth opens. "What I've learned is that you're not fair at all. Blaming me isn't right. You've made up your mind without even hearing my side of the story. And I'm telling you it wasn't my fault."

"Whose was it?"

"I didn't say those things the way they were written. How many times do I have to tell people in this *damn* school?"

"Excuse me, young lady."

I'm about to continue, but I stop. I can tell by Mr. Williamson's expression that whatever I say will mean nothing.

"I expected a lot from you, Melinda. I still do." Mr. Williamson looks at the clock on the wall, then says, "You should get to your next class."

Jade's at our usual cafeteria table, head down, writing in a notebook. She looks up, then pushes aside her books and handbag, giving me room to sit down. We don't say anything right away. There's a sandwich sitting in front of her, but it doesn't look like she's touched it. I pull out a peach yogurt I brought from home and offer it to her. But she shakes her head.

We're silent a while longer, then Jade asks, "Where were you?"

"Balcony," I say.

"All morning?"

I nod.

"Heard you were called into Mr. Williamson's office," she says.

"Crappy news travels fast."

"That bad?"

"Worse."

"But you're still on the team, right?"

"Does it matter?"

"We can talk about it later, if you want," Jade says. "And if you don't want to, that's fine also."

I nod. "I'm sorry about this morning," I say.

Jade nods. "Me, too."

"Lisbeth and Cole never talked on the phone."

"I figured," she says.

She puts her left hand up. I put my right hand up to mirror hers. We're about to put our hands together when we both look at each other.

"Kinda queer," I say.

"Very," Jade says.

"Let's not hurt each other ever again, okay?"

She nods.

Chapter 29

The next two days don't go particularly well. I lie low in school, going to class, hiding in the balcony when I can, and just getting by in practice. There are still a few guys to drill with, but plenty of others continue to give me the cold shoulder. I'd like to complain, but I can't. And no one would listen to me anyway. Except Jade and Annie. And Odessa, of course. She totally gets it. She calls to tell me to hang in there, that someday dealing with all this stuff will have been worth it—hard as that is for me to believe right now.

"Let's go," Cole says to me.

He's waiting at the end of the hallway with a Styrofoam cup in his hand. His weight is tight; it's always tight. I know he's going to ask me for gum, so I pull out a pack from my equipment bag and hand it to him. He unwraps four or five pieces and stuffs them into his mouth. Soon, he's spitting. It's gross, but necessary. If the day ever comes that I need to lose weight that badly, it certainly won't be by filling a cup with saliva. I'm way too civilized for that. But for my brother, it's perfectly okay.

I follow Cole out of the school exit. As we pass under one of the building's outdoor lights, someone calls my name. It takes me a moment to figure out where the voice is coming from, and another to recognize whose it is. When I turn, I see the silhouette of a guy standing against a car.

"Stewart?" I say, awkwardly, but I'm not sure whether it's because my brother is nearby, or because Stewart is here, at my school, after my wrestling practice.

"Hey," he says.

"Hey to you," I say. "What're you doing here?"

I walk up to him, wanting to give him the biggest kiss, but I fight the urge. At least, for the moment. I look back at Cole, which kind of annoys me because I know I don't need his approval to have my boyfriend—yeah, I said it—meet me, anytime, anywhere.

"I'm off from Crystal Fog tonight," Stewart says. Oh, geez, he did not just mention Crystal Fog, did he? I don't want anyone in my family to know where he works. My ears pique to hear if Cole has any reaction. "So I thought I'd stop by," Stewart continues.

"That's cool," I say, trying my best to act the same. But the truth is he's like my valiant knight stealing me away from the prison that has become Ashton High. I take a deep breath. I guess my hesitation is longer than I thought because Stewart jumps right in to introduce himself.

"I'm Stewart," he says to Cole. "How's it going?"

"What's up?" my brother says.

"Yeah, this is my brother, Cole." And to Cole, I say, "Stewart's my, uh...friend."

"Heard you got a big match on Friday," Stewart says.

"Yeah," Cole says, then spits a wad into his Styrofoam cup. "Real big."

I'd be more disgusted with my brother, but I know this is just guy interaction and I'm sure it doesn't bother Stewart at all.

"Good luck," Stewart says.

Cole nods, looks in my direction, shooting me a serious stare, then continues to his car. When I think he's out of earshot, I say to Stewart, in my sweetest voice, "This is a nice surprise."

"Good," Stewart says. "You were on my mind today."

"Yeah?"

"Yeah, I was—"

Just then, Cole's voice bellows from the parking lot, "Hey, I wanna get going."

I turn and shout, "Wait!" I let out a frustrated breath, then say to Stewart, "Hang here a sec, okay?"

"I'm not going anywhere."

With that, I run across the sidewalk to the parking lot. Cole's in his car, with the engine running. I knock on the driver's side window. It lowers.

"Let's go," Cole says. "I want to get home and run."

"I need some of that gum," I say.

"Time. To. Go," my brother says.

I hold out my hand. "Just give me some gum. I *never* get to see him during the week."

Cole shakes his head but tosses me a small piece. "I'm not waiting."

I put it in my mouth. "I don't want you to."

"The golfer'll get you home?"

"Yeah."

"You'll have to deal with Mom and Dad."

"I know."

"Later," Cole says, and the window raises shut.

I walk slowly back to Stewart, watching Cole turn out of the parking lot, then speed down Broadmore Avenue. I've chewed the heck out of the gum, so I'm pretty sure my breath's decent. Discreetly, I drop it to the ground.

"I'm going to need a ride home," I say. "Know where I can get one?"

"Your *friend*—the chauffeur—awaits," Stewart answers, with a sweep of his hand.

"I meant boyfriend," I say sheepishly.

"I know," he says with a smile.

I rush up and throw my arms around him. He wraps me in his overcoat.

"So...I was on your mind?" I say.

"All through English Lit," Stewart says. "My teacher was going on and on about Shakespeare and Marlowe and Donne—and all I could think about was this really hot Ashton girl with a British accent."

"'Ello, Guv'nor," I say.

"Yes, *that* Ashton girl," he says. "I was wondering what class she was in, what she was doing, and I wanted to see her."

I can *feel* the smile on my face.

"That's why I'm here," Stewart says. "I even brought her a present of sorts."

"A present?"

"It's in my pocket."

I roll my eyes.

"I'm serious," he says.

I admit I'm just the slightest bit nervous putting my hand in his pocket, until the moment I realize a box of candy is in there. I pull it out.

"Nonpariels," I say. "You remembered."

"Sweets for my sweet," Stewart says.

"Oh, I am *sooo* looking forward to Saturday night," I say.

"I don't know if I can hold out until then."

"I'm sure you can," I say. "Just think how really nice it'll be."

"Will we kiss?"

"Yeah," I say, looking around to see if anyone's leaving the school. "We can even kiss now."

"Maybe I want to wait until some of your teammates come out," Stewart says, his hands sliding down to my butt. "You know, just to let them know what I get to do with you."

"Oh, they get to do that in practice," I say with a straight face.

Stewart gives me a surprisingly serious look. "You're joking, right?"

"Just kiss me," I say.

So he does... And it's another good one. His lips are warm and moist, while his arms feel strong around my waist. Soon, his hand has slipped underneath my sweatshirt and is on my lower back. It sends a chill up my spine, and part of that is because I'm also aware that the longer we kiss, the more chance there is that someone might see us. God knows, I don't need a reputation around school. But I also don't want to stop. So we kiss a lot more and, before I realize it, Stewart's other hand is on my back, too.

"Wait until Saturday," I say, playfully pushing away. "I have to get home."

"Now?"

I nod.

We get into Stewart's car and, just as he starts to drive away, I see Mr. Williamson and Coach Geiger walking out of the school. Stewart notices me looking.

"Who are they?"

"One's the athletic director, the other's my wrestling coach," I say.

Stewart nods. "The coach you have a problem with?"

"I don't have a problem—" I start to say. "Wait, how do you know I have—I mean, might have—a problem with one of them?"

Stewart gives me a nonchalant shrug. "Lucky guess."

I narrow my eyes. "Lucky guess?" Then it hits me. "Oh, geez, you read the article, too?"

Stewart smiles. "My dad gets the *News* delivered every morning. He pointed out the article. I was surprised he remembered your name, but he's good with names. I gotta say, it was pretty cool seeing my girlfriend quoted in the newspaper. Showed it to a few guys at school."

Wait, did he just say *girlfriend*?

"They said you must be a total b—"

"What?" I interrupt. "A bitch?"

"Badass," Stewart says, driving down Kliedmeir Avenue toward my neighborhood. "A girl who wrestles *and* takes on her coach—whoa, that's a badass girl."

I take in a deep breath and let out one long sigh. "I am not a badass."

"But you *are*," Stewart says, with a laugh.

"I'm not."

"Well...at least you should've told me about the article."

"I was trying to forget it."

A few minutes later, he takes a right, then a quick left, and, soon, we're coming up the street to my house. I wonder if my parents are going to be waiting at the front door. I want to sit in Stewart's car for a while, so I'm going to. If they get mad, they get mad. I don't care. I want to be with my boyfriend.

Stewart pulls into our driveway and turns off the engine. I ask him to leave the headlights on, figuring it'll make my parents less suspicious—but only slightly less so.

And maybe because both of us know our time is limited, we immediately lean toward each other, pressing our mouths and tongues together. Stewart's hand finds its way back under my sweatshirt and on my bra. He's relentless, yet gentle. And maybe because my body is so tired from practice, his touch has excited something even deeper in my belly than any of those other times.

"I'm glad you came by," I whisper, to keep from gasping.

With a snap of his fingers, my bra is unhooked. Whoa, he's getting good at that. His hand squeezes my breast, flicking my nipple with his thumb. I can feel heat rising, filling my sweatshirt, and I know that my body wants him to touch me even more. And Stewart must be reading my mind because his hand moves down, taking a few moments to caress my stomach with his fingertips before sliding under the waistband of my sweatpants and stopping inside the top of my underwear.

I look out the windshield toward my house. "We can't," I whisper, almost out of obligation.

"Why not?" he whispers back. "Doesn't it feel good?"

His fingers edge lower. My heart is thumping, and my legs feel like they're quivering, even if they're not just yet. I bury my face in his neck, letting the heat from my breath and the heat from my sweatshirt wrap around me until my skin becomes ever-so-slightly moist.

I have to stop this.

"I gotta go," I mumble, breathlessly.

"Don't leave," he says. "Let's do more."

"More?"

"It's time, right?" he says. "It's been time."

"Uh...I *really* have to go."

I know he's disappointed—even confused—but I can't go any further. He asks me to promise. Promise what? Promise that I won't let anything hold me back on Saturday night?

"Okay," I say, weakly.

"Sure?"

"I promise," I say, then lean over to give him a kiss on the lips before opening the passenger door and stepping out. I head up the driveway, then the stone path. It's strange to admit, but I feel a little relieved actually.

When I open the front door, my mom is standing in front of me, looking less than pleased—much less. I wonder if she notices how flushed my cheeks are. I wonder if she can tell that excitement is still flowing through my body and my mind, and I can hardly stop it.

"He drove you home?" she asks.

"Yes, Stewart drove me home," I say. "I needed a ride."

"Why didn't you come home with Cole?"

I say nothing. Mom takes my coat and watches me intently as I pull off my hat, then my shoes. "Your face is red," she says.

"It's cold out."

"Didn't he have the heat on in the car?"

"Well, yeah," I say, trying not to say the wrong thing. "The heat was on in his car...*and* it was cold outside."

"The windows seemed fogged," Mom says.

"I didn't notice."

"I'm sure you didn't."

I look at her. How far is she going to push this?

"You do know it's a school night," she says. "And you do know we're not going to make this a habit."

I start to chuckle. "Is this what it's like when you put someone on the witness stand?"

But Mom doesn't see the humor.

"He just gave me a ride," I say. "It was no big deal. Then we parked in the driveway and talked for a few minutes."

And still she's not saying anything.

"Come on, Mom, I hardly ever get to see Stewart. It's not like we snuck around. I was right outside. Talking."

But Mom's not buying any of it. She follows me up the stairs to the second floor, then into my bedroom. She asks for any dirty workout clothes, which I hand to her, then I start to get undressed so I can wash my hair. But the instant I lift the sweatshirt over my head, I realize I'm in trouble.

"Melinda," Mom says. Uh-oh, she used my full first name. "Why is your bra undone?"

"What?"

She gives me that look like she knows damn well that I heard every word of her question.

My mind is suddenly in overdrive, trying to come up with an excuse. But as hard as I try, I can't think of anything reasonable. I've felt this way before, like when I've wrestled someone who is so much better than me that my mind can't keep up with the reality of what's going on, until, finally, I just give in.

"Mom, I'm not a little girl," I say, with all the confidence I can muster. "I know what I'm doing."

"So you *were* doing something," Mom says.

I say nothing.

"That answers that," she says.

"Okay, Stewart and I were in his car," I say. My voice is neither strong nor weak, just stating a fact as if reading it from one of my textbooks. "Kissing. And we did a little more." Then I add, "But not much more, I swear."

Mom raises her eyebrows momentarily, then shakes her head.

"Please don't tell Dad," I plead.

There's a hesitation, then she says, "I won't."

"Thanks," I say. "And I'm sorry. Okay?"

But I'm not really sure what I'm sorry for. Or if I'm sorry at all. It was totally intense kissing Stewart and having his hands touch my body. I wouldn't give up those feelings for anything in the world. On Saturday, it'll be a million times better. We'll hang out in the den for a while, then take a walk. Or hang out in his car again. I will have thought about stuff. I'll be ready, I'm sure.

"Actions have consequences, Melinda," Mom says. "That'll be the last time you get to see this young man."

"What?"

"You heard me."

"Wait," I say.

"Excuse me?" she says angrily.

"Can't we discuss this?"

But I can tell from the expression on my mom's face that this conversation has come to an end. Period.

"You're being so unfair!" I say.

She walks out of my bedroom without another word, closing the door behind her.

The first thing I do is call Jade.

"No way," she says. "Your mom said you can't see him? Like *ever*?"

"Yes," I say.

"Just like that?"

"Exactly like that," I say.

There's a hesitation on the phone. Then Jade says, "Okay, I have a plan."

"Oh, no," I say. "I'm not going along with any of your plans. No way."

"I'll just talk to her," Jade says.

"What's that gonna do?"

"Your mom loves me like a daughter," Jade says. Which is true. "I'll just tell her it's really hard to get any guy to go out with our little wrestling girl since they're all so chicken-shit. Now that we've got one who's smitten, we can't just kick him to the curb."

"Oh, yeah, that's bound to work."

"You'll see," Jade says.

Chapter 30

There isn't much traffic on I-94. An airplane leaving Detroit Metro passes noisily above us.

Dad hasn't said much, occasionally sipping from a mug of coffee. I normally hate it being so quiet, but it's the kind of respectful silence that Cole gets before his matches. Even though I'm only going to a wrestling clinic, I guess it's important enough for everyone in the family to take seriously. Mom, who I'm still mad at because of her edict about Stewart (and who wasn't the least bit moved by Jade's plea on my behalf), woke up early to make me breakfast and a sandwich for lunch. Even Cole came down to tell me to "kick some chick ass." It almost seemed like he meant it, too.

We pass a sign for Eastern Michigan University. It starts my heart thumping. I shouldn't be nervous. I practice with guys every day. Working out with girls should be a piece of cake. Then again, the ones going to something like this are probably all like Odessa—girls who wrestle *like* guys.

Odessa mailed me a registration form last September. I didn't know what to think when I read that the clinic was sponsored by the U.S. Girls Wrestling Association, with coaches brought in from the U.S. Olympic Training Center in the Upper Peninsula. I had no idea there even was an Olympic wrestling facility in the UP. Or that there was a USGWA, for that matter. I asked my dad what he thought. He said it was an opportunity that I couldn't pass up. The next day he called Coach Hillman. I'm sure that's the reason I got permission to miss a team practice.

While Dad turns off I 94 onto Hamilton Street, I do a final check of my equipment bag for my singlet, shoes, headgear, lunch, and a bottle of water. Soon, we're at the Eastern campus.

"The clinic's in Bowen Field House," I say, then I take a deep breath. It must've been louder than I thought.

"Excited?" Dad asks.

"Yeah," I say.

Within minutes, we pull up to a building that's much bigger than I expected. I notice a group of girls walking toward the entrance. I wonder if I should be sizing them up.

"I'll be back by three," Dad says. "Make the most of this clinic."

I give him a quick wave, then close the car door behind me.

Inside Bowen Field House, there's a line at the registration table. It gives me a chance to look around. The building is huge, maybe ten times the size of our school auditorium, with an indoor track around the perimeter and three large wrestling mats laid out in the middle (though there's room for many more). Green and white banners celebrating Eastern athletic teams hang from the rafters. I'm amazed at how warm it is in such a large space.

When it's my turn, I step forward. I'm greeted by one of a half-dozen older-looking girls wearing USGWA Coach shirts. They look strong and tough, and have done little to conceal the bruises and marks on their foreheads and cheekbones.

One, with a nametag that reads Katie, asks, "Name?"

"Melinda Radford," I answer.

She quickly finds a folder and thumbs through some papers. "Great, we received your registration, check, and waiver form. Looks like you're all set." Then she pauses. "Radford? From Ashton?"

"Uh...yeah," I say.

Katie calls over a few of the other coaches. "Guess who this is?" she says. "*The* Melinda Radford. From that article I sent you. The hell-raiser. Naomi Wolf in a singlet."

Oh, geez...

Each of the USGWA coaches reaches a hand out to me. "Catch a lot of shit for that?" one of them asks.

"Like you wouldn't believe," I mutter.

"They reprinted the article in my local paper," another says. "I loved it."

"I'm going to keep an eye on you, Radford," Katie says, directing me to a locker room, where the other clinic attendees are changing.

Inside, the first person I see is Odessa with her infectious smile. We give each other a huge hug. She's only a weight class heavier than me, but she seems so much bigger.

"Mel, I'm really glad you're here," she says.

"So am I."

"How's that guy you're dating? You two serious?"

I can't help but grin. "He picked me up after practice the other night," I say. "Totally outta the blue. Said he just wanted to see me."

"Oh, that's so sweet," Odessa says.

"My mom's hassling me about him, big time," I say.

"It's what moms do."

"What about you?"

Odessa shakes her head. "No boyfriends during the season."

She introduces me to a few of the other girls: Sharisse, a freshman on the Royal Oak team; Maggie and Bridget from Ohio; and Gabrielle from Canada. The rest are from different parts of Michigan. They all seem nice. And anxious. Like I am. I wish I was as confident as Odessa. I bet they do, too.

I pick a locker near hers. I take off my sweatshirt and sweatpants, then put on my singlet and wrestling shoes and pull my hair back into a tight ponytail. One of the USGWA coaches leans into the locker room and announces that it's time to warm up.

Odessa smiles at me. "Ready?"

"Yep," I say.

We leave the locker room, toss our headgear to the side, and find a place among the forty or so girls jogging along the edge of the mats.

"Congrats on the season you're having," I say.

"Yeah, you're making your mark, too," Odessa says,

with a knowing laugh. I roll my eyes. "We can talk about it some more later," she adds.

After a few laps, the USGWA coaches instruct us to spread out on the mats, then they lead us through stretching, pushups, and sit-ups, and five minutes of jumping rope, until we're all sweating. Then we're split into two groups: advanced and novices. I suppose I could be in either group, but at Odessa's urging I stay with the experienced girls. Katie and two other coaches get us started with some shadow wrestling and working on our drop-steps.

"Start with a good stance," Katie says. "Move around a little. Change levels. Drive off your back foot when you penetrate."

I'm trying to focus on myself, but I can't help but watch the others. Most are quicker than me. It's impressive. And intimidating.

"Now, work on your defense," Katie says. "Your opponent shoots in deep. You have to use your hands to block. Then, kick the leg that your opponent is shooting for as far back as you can. Finally, circle back up to your feet."

Sprawling has never been my forte. I prefer to attack. I think I got that from Cole, since that's how he wrestles. After years of watching him on the basement mat, telling himself, "Attack, always. Attack, always," I guess it rubbed off on me. So I sprawl kind of clumsily.

"Don't flop to your stomach, Radford," one of the coaches says. "Stay up on your hands or your elbows."

I nod and try it again. This time, I imagine Georgie

shooting in on me. I use my hands to keep his ugly head from getting a solid position, then thrust my legs back so that all my weight is crushing him to the mat, then I circle away, and I'm back to my feet.

"Nicely done," the coach says.

Odessa catches my eye and winks. She's always so upbeat and positive. I thought I was a fairly happy person, but she's off the charts. It's one of the reasons I like her so much. It's too bad she doesn't go to Ashton High.

From drop-steps and sprawls, we move on to stand-ups, sit-outs, and switches—again without partners. Each time, Katie is shouting for us to go faster, hit the move harder, while the other coaches tweak the flaws in our techniques. I've been helped a few times. It doesn't bother me at all.

"Good job," Katie says to the group. "Take a knee."

She and two other coaches, Liz and Patricia, say a few words about their wrestling backgrounds. Katie's on the US national women's freestyle team, and Liz was a silver medalist at the University World Championships two years ago. Patricia's a red-shirt junior on the Oklahoma City University women's team. Their achievements are mind-boggling.

"I'm going to give you my philosophy on winning at the high school level," Katie says. "It's simple: If you can take your opponent down, and not be taken down yourself, then all you need is one escape from the bottom, and you're almost guaranteed to win ninety percent of your matches."

As she walks among us, I notice the black-and-blue

marks on her thighs, tape on her fingers, and mat burns on her knees. *She* is a badass.

"With that in mind, we're going to go over some of our favorite setups to a hi-crotch, single, and double—with a tie-up and without," Katie says. "It's a lot to follow, so ask questions."

Liz and Patricia, who both look to be about 130 pounds, demonstrate the takedowns and, for a moment, I forget that they're girls only a few years older than me. Everything they do, each movement, is done with, as Coach Geiger likes to say, "bad intentions." And I can understand why their faces and bodies are bruised, because they finish off the hi-crotch or single or double as if winning is at stake. There's nothing gentle or feminine about these two when they're on the mats. I'm guessing Katie is even less so.

"Pick a partner around your weight class," Katie says. "Spread out on the mats. Alternate takedowns, using the setups we just showed. You can finish them off."

A girl taps me on the shoulder. "Wanna go?"

"Sure," I say. "I'm Mel."

"I'll go first," she says.

I make a quick assessment: She's got short brown hair, cut shoulders, and walks with her toes kind of pointing out (I forget what that's called). She gets set in her stance; I do the same. Then she tugs my head down, drop-steps into a tight hi-crotch, captures my far leg, and drives me to the mat. In an instant, she's back on her feet, ready to go again.

"Nicely done," I say.

She looks at me, oddly.

So I do an arm-drag to a hi-crotch, switch to a single, then run the pike to finish off the takedown. And, again, she pops back to her feet. Before I'm set, she clears my arms and shoots in for the double-leg, lifts, and drops me to the mat. Wow.

I get up and do the same to her, but I'm a half-second slower, I can tell. I get back to my feet; she's already waiting for me.

Back and forth we go for a few minutes, neither of us saying a word. Then Katie calls, "Switch to someone else."

The girl shakes my hand before quickly moving on to pick another partner. I feel a hand on my arm. It's Odessa.

"Hey, girl," she says. "You and me."

I'm still trying to catch my breath, and I must've looked a bit overwhelmed because Odessa says, "I know we're not the same weight, but I wanted to make sure we drill together at least once."

I nod.

"You first," she says.

I start with a low single, then run the pike to finish.

"Good," Odessa says.

In an instant, she's in on a hi-crotch, lifts, and brings me down to the mat. She's so quick, I'm not sure I could've stopped her shot even knowing it was coming. We alternate, and I marvel (when I have a second to think) at how she's able to set up the takedown by controlling my hands and wrists. It's impressive.

"Two-minute break," Katie calls out, her voice echoing

in the huge gymnasium. "Get some water, if you need it."

I definitely do.

"Good job, Mel," Odessa says, giving me a pat on the back.

As I walk to the water fountain, I think about how comfortable Odessa is on the mats and around so many other wrestlers. She has such confidence. It doesn't seem much different than the way Cole is. That's how I have to become. Confident. Tough. Even a little nasty.

Over the next hour, Katie and the coaches show us the finer points of setting up the takedown using an underhook, overhook, and a Russian tie-up. The time goes quickly, and we switch partners often. Katie says that's important because every wrestler brings something slightly different to each drill, live shot, or practice match.

At least these girls smell okay. One's a little funky, but nothing like a few of the Ashton guys who really need to be introduced to deodorant. And, while some of these girls are totally hardcore, for the most part they're pretty supportive. Of course, right now we're only drilling.

We have lunch in two training rooms. The university has left cases of Gatorade for us, along with Eastern Wrestling plastic water bottles on the side for us to take home. I'm sitting at one of the tables with Odessa, Sharisse, and a dozen others. At first we're all kind of quiet, probably from hunger. So Patricia, the USGWA coach, has us introduce ourselves. Some of the girls are on their high school boys' teams, while others compete for local clubs. Most seem impressed when I say I'm from

Ashton, and that my brother is the varsity co-captain.

"You're not—" one of them starts to say.

I sigh. "If you're going to ask about the *Detroit News*, yeah, it was me."

Odessa chimes in, "My girl Mel has big balls!"

At their goading, I explain that I wasn't trying to make some big gender statement, and insist it was the newspaper reporter's fault—a woman, no less. But it didn't matter, I tell them. Before I knew it, the whole thing snowballed out of control. It's obvious from their expressions that I'm not the only one who's faced this kind of stuff. My situation isn't even close to the worst. One of the girls, Veda, took five forfeits last season because her JV team competed against parochial schools that didn't feel it was "fair or appropriate" for boys and girls to wrestle each other.

"Why are boys so scared to wrestle us?" she asks.

"Not all are," someone answers.

"Yeah, those are the guys that want to kill you."

And, apparently, we'd all felt that, too.

"My parents had to threaten to sue my high school just to get me on the team," Maggie from Ohio says. "Then the coach made my life a living hell. Making me practice with the best guys on the team all the time. I'd get killed. Eventually, all I wanted to do was quit. The coach wanted me to quit. Even the guys on the team did."

"Why didn't you?" I ask.

She shrugs. "I like wrestling too much."

"That's what I like to hear," Patricia says. "Lots of people will tell you why you shouldn't wrestle; listen

223

to the ones who tell you why you should." She stands up from the table. "Another five minutes, then we'll get started again."

Each of us grabs a Gatorade bottle and heads out. "Ya'll got nothing on me," Odessa says. "Once, I was wrestling this guy from Dearborn and he gets, you know... stiff."

"Stiff?" Maggie says. "During the match?"

"Yep."

"Whaddya do?" another girl asks.

"Pinned him," Odessa says. "But I stayed *far* from his boner."

We all laugh.

It's the last laughing we do for the rest of the clinic. Katie runs us ragged. We work on bottom first, sitting out to a stand, then sitting out to a switch. And with each move, they show us some subtle technique, a few of which I've never seen before. I don't know if I'm going to remember all of it, but even if just half manages to get stuck in my brain, I'll definitely be a better wrestler for it.

The girl I'm working with, Sylvia, is not a good technical wrestler, but she is strong. And pretty—even when sweaty and grungy. When Katie calls for a practice match, Sylvia and I remain a pair.

"A two-two-two," Katie says. "We've gone over a lot so far. Now is the time to use these moves and techniques. It does you no good to stall, or hesitate, or be afraid to take a chance. Ready?"

She blows the whistle, starting the first two-minute period.

Sylvia has taken Katie's words to heart. She shoots in on me right away, sucking my right leg in tight. I can feel her strength even more than when we were drilling. I try to push her head away, but she keeps her posture, coming up with the single-leg. I can't tell if she knows how to run the pike, but she's definitely not prepared for the switch. So I hit it hard, bringing both of us down to the mat. I scoot my hips away as she tries to step over, then put pressure on her shoulder until I'm able come up on top, just as we run out of mat space.

"Excellent," Patricia says to us, clapping her hands. "Start again, top and bottom."

The rest of the match goes well for me. Since I'm used to going against guys, I use my speed and flexibility against Sylvia, and by the end of the six minutes, I've beaten her 6–2. Not that I'm keeping score, which, of course, I am.

My second match is with a girl who I haven't spoken to yet. She's definitely gone heavy on the perfume and has a tendency to talk a lot, mostly in a whisper, almost under her breath. And she does this the entire time we're wrestling. I want to tell her to shut up. Or speak louder so I can hear. I beat her, 7–6, but she pisses me off at the end of the match with a cross-face that I'm sure was way beyond legal.

I can taste the blood at the back of my throat.

"Take a one-minute break," Katie says. "Last session coming up."

I'm glad, but I'm not glad. I mean, I'm beat. We all are. Sweat's pouring off my face and my T-shirt's sticking to my skin. But it feels pretty good. I kind of wish I could wrestle girls all the time.

Odessa puts an arm around me. "I'm crazy tired," she says, but she certainly doesn't seem it. "How's it going for you?"

"Kickin' ass," I say.

"Bet you are," Odessa says, before gulping down some Gatorade. "When the season's over, let's spend more time together."

"My parents have a summer cottage on Mackinac Island," I say. "You should come out for a long weekend in July."

"Definitely."

Later, after we've gone over tilts and Turking the leg to pinning combinations, Katie puts us through a few of the exercises that the US women's national team does to finish off its practices: Handstands across the mats, followed by crab walks, cartwheels, and piggyback sprints. Soon enough, my thighs start to give out. My arms follow quickly. With Sharisse on my back, I do my best to push through the pain. All the while, the coaches are shouting out encouragement.

"This is the end. Suck it up, suck it up!"

Finally, Katie blows a whistle. "Give yourselves a hand," she says. We all begin to clap. "Great job today. One of the better clinics we've had."

It's two fifteen. Dad should be here for me soon. In the locker room, I take a seat between Odessa, who's talking about her best varsity matches, and Sharisse. I imagine Odessa's a tough act to follow. On one hand, she's already gone through all the stuff that Sharisse might have to face, and yet her legacy at Royal Oak would be hard for any girl to surpass.

I pass around the energy bars Mom stuffed in my bag. We gobble them down. Soon enough, we're all laughing and telling stories—some about wrestling, but mostly just stuff about boyfriends and hope-to-have boyfriends. I think we're all feeling a sugar rush.

But it's more than that, too. As close as I am to Cole and my mom and dad, I don't know if they fully understand what I go through at Ashton. No matter what anyone says, it's still a little odd to have me, a girl, on the team. Just like it's hard for lots of people to understand how girls could be, or even want to be, involved in a guys' sport like wrestling.

In a week, I'll get my period. I'll still practice. I'll still run to keep my weight down. How can I explain to Cole how much of a pain in the ass that is? And, not that I think any of the Ashton guys do it intentionally (except for idiot Georgie), but how can I be *sure* a guy I'm practicing with, who's put in a tight waist a little high on my chest, did it completely by accident?

These girls understand. And maybe if we were away from this wrestling clinic, like, at a mall checking out guys, we might fall into that typical catty, girl-eat-girl competitiveness—like me, Jade, and Annie sometimes do. But for today, right now, we're just hanging out together, worn-out but loving it, knowing we've spent the morning and afternoon making ourselves better wrestlers.

Chapter 31

It's been a half hour since we left Eastern, and I don't think I've let Dad get in more than a couple of words. I'm still so excited about how everything went today. Seeing Odessa, meeting all those cool girls who wrestle, learning techniques from awesome coaches...and, yes, even getting positive recognition for my newspaper quotes.

"So, you enjoyed yourself?" Dad asks, when my mouth momentarily stops.

"Understatement of the year," I say. "We had the entire field house just for our clinic. Do you know cool that is?"

Dad smiles.

The ride home is flying by, and before I realize it we've passed the airport and turned off I-94 onto 23 North. Dad's head must be spinning. After a match, Cole rarely says a word. Here I am, going on and on about a *clinic*. Who knows what I'll do when I actually win a big match. Bet my jaw muscles will cramp from talking so much.

"So when's the next one?" Dad says.

"I asked the same thing. The USGWA is having another clinic in June, but none of us want to wait that long, so

Odessa's going to find open mats where a bunch of us can practice together after the varsity season. I'm already looking forward to that."

I turn off the faucet and pour in more lavender bath salts. The water is hot, the way I like it. I raise my legs one at a time, noticing that black-and-blue mark on my right thigh still hasn't gone away, though the mat burn on my left knee almost gives it symmetry. I lay my head back in the tub, thinking of Stewart. I still haven't called him to tell him we can't be together tonight—or any other night, for that matter. I don't know what I'm going to say. I'm embarrassed and angry. I want to see him so badly. Especially tonight. We could've gotten something to eat, or seen a movie. I could've told him about the clinic and how great it was. Or just sit in his car. Anything to be together. Alone.

There's a knock on the bathroom door. "Mel," Mom says, "I'm coming in."

The door opens, but I don't say anything.

"Okay, enough with the silent treatment," she says.

"I'm still mad," I say.

"Well, don't be."

As if it's as simple as that. I notice that she's dressed up. "Where are you going?" I ask, cautiously.

"Your dad and I have a seven o'clock dinner party," Mom says. "We're leaving in a few minutes."

My parents are going out?

"Cole's got his music on loud," she says, putting a phone down on the toilet seat, then checking her hair in the mirror. "I doubt he'll hear if it rings." She glances at me. "Your father said the clinic went well."

"It did."

"You can tell me all about it tomorrow."

I sit up in the tub. "Is that the Valentino dress you bought last week?" I ask, then look down at her shoes. "And the Oscar de la Renta's?"

"They are."

"Can I borrow them sometime?"

"Borrow?" Mom says.

"Yes," I answer.

"We'll see."

"What do we have to see about?"

But Mom ignores the question. She reminds me that there's food in the refrigerator and our neighbors, the Houghtons, are on speed dial, in case of an emergency. "We'll be home by midnight. Cole's in charge of the house."

"When do I get to be in charge?" I ask.

"Never. So what're your plans?" she says, in such a way to remind me of her edict.

I want to declare my own edict: Stewart and I *are* going to be together, whether she likes it or not. And I know how. Pretty simple. I'll tell her that I'm going to Jade's house (though I really won't be), and instead have Stewart pick me up around the corner, near the Matuzaks' oak tree.

"I think I'll walk over to—"

"No," Mom says.

"No?"

"You can stay home. Or you can stay home and have Jade come over."

"That's it?"

Mom purses her lips. "I know you want me to allow you to see..."

She keeps talking, but I've closed my eyes and dunked my head under the water. Damn it, I'm definitely old enough to be in charge. And I'm definitely mature enough to be with the guy I'm dating. I'm not a kid. Mom should've seen me today. I'd bet then she'd think differently about whether I'm able to handle things—whatever "things" that might be. I hold my breath for as long as I can, hearing my heartbeat and the soft splash of my legs under the surface. When I come back up, she's gone.

A half hour later, the bubbles have disappeared and the water's cool. I can't believe I've been in the tub so long. Must've nodded off for a few.

A thud on the door startles me.

"What?" I say, annoyed.

"I'm leaving," Cole yells from the other side. "Don't burn the place down."

"You're going out?"

"Did one of those chicks bang your head?" he says. "Yeah, I'm going out."

"Where?"

"Where?" he mocks, with an odd laugh. "I don't have to tell you where I'm going."

"Fine," I say.

I lie in the water for another half minute or so, stunned by my good fortune. I stand up, grab a towel, and step out of the tub. I'm going to be the *only* one home. For hours. I pick up the phone, then notice my reflection in the mirror. I'm smiling in a major way.

I dial Stewart's number.

No answer.

Damn...

So I leave a message. I try my best not to sound concerned. I mean, it's still early. Maybe he thought I wouldn't be back until later. I'm sure I told him the clinic would end at two thirty and I'd be home by three thirty and be ready to go out by seven or so. But Jade says guys hardly ever listen to times and stuff like that. Anyway, I've got a lot to do.

I run into my bedroom, waiting a moment at the top of the stairs to make sure Cole's left the house, then towel off. I smooth lotion over my neck and arms, legs and belly. It stings a little where my skin is raw.

I check the time. And check it again, a few minutes later. But the phone still doesn't ring.

So I start blow-drying my hair, figuring I always look best with side-swept bangs. At least Jade's convinced me of that. She's scoured magazines for the perfect look, picking a Fabergé ad in *Cosmo* with this Ukrainian tennis star, Kalyna, who's like the new "It Girl." She has that kind of hairstyle. I know I probably can't get it exactly like hers, but it's worth trying, even if it takes a while.

Stewart better appreciate all the effort.

I know he will. He's good like that. Considerate and patient. Interested in me, for me. But I know that won't last forever. I mean, he *is* a guy. Guys want stuff. That never changes. I kind of want stuff, too. I think about it. At night, alone. At school, daydreaming. About the only time I don't think about Stewart is when I'm in the wrestling room. He's sexy, and I can tell he's got a hard body. I just melt whenever he takes me into his arms. And his lips...

Oh, his lips...

My belly flutters and a shiver runs through my body. I shouldn't be anxious about tonight. Fate has smiled on me in a major way. My parents go out to a dinner party, which I didn't even know about, then Cole leaves. I've got the house to myself. Tonight, a Saturday night. I can tell Stewart he no longer has to be patient. He can touch me like he wanted to the other night. Like I pretty much wanted him to. I'm not going to stop him this time. Nothing else will either.

I suddenly realize the blow dryer is whirling in my hand, but it's not even pointed toward my hair. In the mirror, I catch my goofy, I'm-thinking-about-my-boyfriend stare, and snap myself back.

It's getting late.

I slide open my closet door. So many tops. And pants. And skirts. So many wonderful possibilities. I pull out an armful and spread them out on my bed. With one eye on the time, and the other figuring out what looks best on me, I settle on the perfect outfit. I slip on a low-cut black sweater over a matching bra and underwear, then my skinny jeans and Uggs. After some eyeliner, mascara, bronzer, and raspberry lip gloss, I put on a few sterling silver bangle bracelets to match my favorite onyx earrings.

It takes some time, but when all the pieces are in place, I step back from the mirror to look myself over.

Hot...

It's the first, second, and last word that comes to mind. I know that's totally egotistical, but it's also totally the truth.

"See, Mom," I say to myself. "Your daughter is all grown up."

Chapter 32

"Relax, Mel," Jade says. She's using that soothing voice that always works when I'm totally stressed. It's definitely being put to the test now.

"But I *can't* relax," I whine into the receiver. "He hasn't answered his cell phone."

"I'm sure he's still busy doing something with his dad," she says. "Don't they both work at the country club?"

"He told me he wasn't working tonight," I say.

"You sure?"

"Of course... I mean, I'm pretty sure."

"Maybe he accidentally turned off his phone," Jade suggests.

I sit down on my bed and stare in the mirror. Flames of jasmine-scented candles on my dresser, vanity, and nightstand flicker in the dark. My clothes are perfect. My hair is perfect. My makeup is perfect—though I doubt my mascara will be much longer, because I can feel my eyes start to well up.

I'm not going to cry. No way.

"He'll call," Jade says, but it seems she's just trying to fill the silence.

I glance at the clock. "It's too late," I say. "Cole could come home early. Or my parents. Tonight was going to be *our* night. We would've been here all alone."

"Mel, there'll be other times."

"No, my mom won't let me see him."

"She'll get over it," Jade insists. "Give her some time. She can't stop *love*, right?"

Who knows if my mom was stopping love, but she was definitely stopping *something*.

"I guess not," I say.

"You do love him, right?"

Jade's jumping the gun a bit. "I know I like him a lot," I say. "I mean, I did."

"Mel, you still do."

"I know." As much as it hurts me to say, it's the truth. "I was going to let him tonight."

"Let him what?"

"You know," I say. "What we always talk about. But more."

"Tonight?"

I hesitate. "Yeah."

"You're ready?"

"I think."

"How come you didn't tell me?"

"I didn't know," I say.

"So, you're just going to ignore the two-month rule?" Jade says.

"We've been going out that long," I insist.

"No, it hasn't even been two," Jade says, mildly scolding me.

"But tonight was going to be special," I say. "I mean, earlier I thought it'd be like the other times we were together, sitting all cramped in his car parked somewhere. Which is okay. I mean, it's what we're used to. But then everything went so good today and I came home feeling really great and then, like a gift out of nowhere, I find out I'm going to be alone in the house. It was like it was meant to happen."

Jade doesn't say anything. I figure she's run out of ways to try to comfort me. When Annie got screwed over by Georgie, Jade and I could see it coming from a mile away. But not this. She's not prepared for proper damage control, and I'm definitely not either.

"Well, maybe it's for the best," Jade says, finally.

"What's that mean?" I say, annoyed.

"I don't know."

"Seems a dumb thing to say."

There's a hesitation, then Jade says, "I'm sorry." She seems kind of distracted.

"Feel like coming over?" I say. I don't mean to be selfish, but if can't get an answer as to why Stewart didn't call back tonight, then I surely deserve having my best friend listen to me bitch about it.

"Now?"

"I kind of don't want to be here alone."

And yet, part of me (actually, a lot of me) is holding out hope that Stewart might still call. How stupid is that? Ridiculously stupid, I guess.

"How about tomorrow?" Jade says. "I'm pretty tired."

Tired? Jade *always* wants to come over. Even when

she's tired. We'd grab a bag of those mini Hershey bars, throw a few extra blankets on my bed, put on a movie, and go to town stuffing our faces. Then we'd spend the next morning at the breakfast table, laughing and going on about how totally bloated we feel.

"Yeah, okay," I say, not quite sure whether I'm mad or relieved. "Talk to you tomorrow."

"But, if you need me..." she starts to say. Half-heartedly, I think.

"No," I say. "I'll be okay."

Chapter 33

Owings is sniffing my ear. It's what wakes me up. I open my eyes, seeing him settle his body against me, hearing him purr. It would be entirely endearing on any other morning. Not today.

"Sorry, boy," I mutter. "I gotta sleep some more."

I turn over and bury my head under my comforter. I stayed awake past two last night, long after hanging up with Jade, long after watching some stupid old-time movie, long after eating two chicken enchiladas with a pile of sour cream and guacamole. And, still, Stewart never called.

It's enough to make me want to barf. Then, and now.

So I close my eyes and hope that I can doze off quickly before I start obsessing again about why Stewart didn't call. But that doesn't work. Did he forget? Did he get in an accident? Did he find someone else? And, if there's even the tiniest, smallest, most miniscule chance at all that he calls today, did I leave the phone ringer on? Am I sure I can hear it from under this comforter? Will I even bother picking it up?

I just want to scream.

"Mel?"

I shutter awake and open my eyes. I look at my clock. It's almost noon.

"You up?" I hear.

I prop myself on my elbows.

"Jade?" I say.

She opens the door. "I told you I'd come over today," she says. "Wow, you were still sleeping. I take it he never called."

I shake my head.

"You all right?"

"I always have Owings," I say, picking him up to hug. He meows, then squirms away from my overbearing arms. "I guess not him either."

Jade walks over to my dresser, picks up one of the candles, and holds it to her nose. "Smells nice." Then she notices the clothes on my chair. I hadn't put them away. "Your skinny jeans with this top? God, you must've looked hot."

"I did."

"I'm sure," she says, putting on her angry face. "Stewart's a jerk. Let's call him up and curse him out."

"Let's not."

"Yeah, you're right," Jade says. "You're too good a person for that."

Still, we think up various creative and devious ways to get back at him, even though we have no intention of doing anything. Besides, he goes to another high school, so I wouldn't even get a chance to make him jealous by

240

flirting with someone at Ashton. It was a case of just a guy being a guy, Jade tells me. Maybe so. It's all so confusing.

I decide if he doesn't call in the next few days, after my anger and disappointment have (hopefully) eased, I'm going to leave him a message asking what went wrong, why he blew me off, and how come he couldn't have ended things in person? Was all that time we spent together just him trying to get in my pants? But I'm not sure I want to hear the answers.

Jade tells me to take a shower and wash away how lousy I feel. It doesn't work. When I'm done drying off, I throw on some sweats and find Jade in Cole's room and they're *tickling* each other.

"Oh, gross," is my reaction.

"Relax, chubby," my brother says.

"Why didn't you just wait in my room?" I ask Jade.

"We were just talking," she says.

I drag her back to my bedroom. Then I close the door.

"So, you're done being empathetic?" I say.

Jade rolls her eyes. "Sorry, didn't know I had to be morose while you were in the shower."

"Morose?" I say. "I'm going to have to take away your dictionary privileges."

"Oh, that's real nice," she says. "And, anyway, your brother's actually kind of funny."

Funny? I don't even know what to say to that. Cole's a pain in the ass, he's obnoxious, he's gross. He's a lot of things, but none of them are "funny."

Chapter 34

It's a gloomy Monday morning. And not just because of how I feel, or the fact that Stewart *still* hasn't called. Seems like the same layer of snow's been on the ground since Christmas, only it's long had that grimy look to it, which matches the gray clouds stretching across the sky. I'm so tired of wearing wool coats, scarves, and boots. I know it's the usual Michigan winter, but I'm beginning to think we may never see the sun again.

Cole pulls his car out of the driveway, then turns in the direction of the high school. With the district tournament in two weeks, he's already getting focused. He's expected to win the districts and regions, and make it to the states. But I know the season'll be a total failure unless he places in the top eight of his weight class.

Me, I'm melancholy. After Jade left yesterday, I locked myself in my bedroom for the rest of the afternoon and fought a constant knot in my stomach, agonizing about whether I should call Stewart, while still holding out the most ridiculous glimmer of hope that he might call me first. It was pitiful, to be honest.

But hope springs eternal (or something queer like that), even on a day like this one. Things can't get any worse, I figure.

After turning onto Broadmore Avenue, Cole says to me, "You going to practice today?"

I look at him, oddly. "Why wouldn't I?"

"Because you're all depressed."

"I'm not depressed," I say. "Why would you think that?"

"Because the golfer dumped your ass."

Damn it! Can't Jade keep her big fat mouth shut about anything? I'm immediately annoyed, feeling my face flush. No way. I'm not going to let my inconsiderate jerk of a brother ruin the day for me.

"He didn't dump me," I snap, hardly noticing that we're almost at the high school.

"What do you call it then?" Cole says.

Now I'm ready to explode. My mouth is quivering, my hands are shaking, and I'm just waiting for the moment when my mind settles enough so that I'm not cursing in gibberish. As we pull up to the school driveway and turn in, I'm about to unleash my fury when I notice something seems wrong...

We pass Carrie Moffett standing on the sidewalk. I wave, but she doesn't wave back. That's odd.

"Me and Stewart are just working things out," I say to my brother, my voice trailing off as I realize Carrie is crying. Bawling, it seems.

Closer to the school entrance, kids are huddled

together. But not like they usually do in the morning, to talk and joke and flirt. This is different. It's like they're consoling each another.

Something's *very* wrong.

"Cole?"

"What the hell's going on?" he says.

I stare out the passenger window as Cole steers the car into the student lot, then parks in the nearest open space. I pick up my equipment bag; he grabs his from the backseat. We both get out of the car.

Trey is walking in our direction. When he gets to Cole, he says, "Did you hear?"

"Hear what?"

"About Coach..." he starts to say, then catches his breath. "Coach Hillman died last night."

Died?

I think I feel sick. And, as my mind starts to shudder, I catch a glimpse of my brother. His mouth is open, his eyes searching for something—I don't know what. He slumps against the car. Trey puts a hand on his shoulder. They don't say another word.

Our homeroom teacher, Mrs. Portman, tries to maintain her composure, even as she dabs her reddened eyes with a balled-up tissue.

"Boys and girls," she says, in a strained voice, "please settle down for today's announcements."

I hear some whispering, but mostly everyone is quiet. The news has gotten around the school. I wonder how my brother's doing. He looked so confused, so distraught. I've never seen him like that. I hope never to again.

The PA system comes on with a crackle. Then, after a long pause, instead of Ms. LaFleur's voice, it's our principal, Mr. Newsome.

"Good morning, Ashton High..." he says. "It is with a heavy heart that I deliver sad news this morning. Late last night, I received a phone call that Coach Hillman had passed away..."

Someone gasps.

"As most of you know, Coach Hillman taught history at our school for over thirty years. And led the wrestling team for the past twenty-eight... He has been a fixture at Ashton for the past three decades... He will be profoundly missed..."

There's another pause, this time longer.

"The school will have a grief counselor in the health office all day," Mr. Newsome continues. "I urge any student who would like to come in, to do so... And now, let's all observe a few moments of silence..."

I don't know how long we're supposed to be silent. Maybe a half minute, maybe longer. I glance around the room. Some people are really broken up, while others simply seem at a loss. I'm not sure how I feel. I've never personally known anyone who's died. I guess now I do. That's a weird thought.

The bell rings.

Slowly, we get up to go to our first-period classes.

"I'm available if anyone wants to discuss their

feelings," Mrs. Portman says. But no one stops. Instead, we file quietly into the hallway.

Jade's the first person I see. With tears in her eyes, she gives me a hug. "I can't believe what happened," she says. "I saw Cole. He's really upset. What about you? You okay?"

"Yeah," I answer.

And I am. I'm handling the news well, I think. Actually, why am I *not* crying?

"Mel, it's just so sad."

And it's the way that Jade says it that I suddenly wonder if maybe I'm not okay. I mean, I'm not devastated by Coach Hillman's death. I should be, right? Everyone else seems to be, even people who didn't have him as a teacher or coach. He's been *my* coach for the past two seasons, and I knew who he was long before that because of Cole.

"It is sad," I say, but maybe without the emotion Jade expects.

She takes her arms from around me and looks into my eyes. "I know you and him had that little problem," she says, "but I don't think it was personal. Don't feel guilty."

Guilty?

Should I be feeling guilty?

Dressed in our street clothes, with backpacks and equipment bags at our feet, we wait in silence in the practice room. It's probably the first time that anybody has stepped onto the Ashton mats wearing something other than wrestling shoes. But I suppose this is a time like no other.

Coach Geiger opens the door and walks in. He looks kind of weary.

"Take a knee, fellas," he says. "We won't be practicing today. I think it's important that each of us gets time to ourselves this afternoon. And I'm not sure any of us has the desire to make it through a few hours of drilling."

He pauses, rubbing his eyes.

"As you know, this is my first year at Ashton, but in the time that I've spent with Coach Hillman I've grown to appreciate all he's meant to this school, to this wrestling program, to you wrestlers. He cared about each one of you very much."

I can hear muffled crying, but I don't dare look to see who it might be.

"Coach knew his illness was serious for some time, but he didn't want to say anything because he thought it would distract the team from focusing on the season. He wanted each of you to have the best chance to get your name on a plaque on one of these walls."

There's more sobbing. It's all around me. Coach Geiger, too, seems to be having trouble. He coughs, then takes a deep breath. He asks us to leave equipment bags and backpacks on the mat and stand up.

"Hands in," he says.

We crowd together, pushing in as tight as we can, reaching our hands to the center. I hear sniffles and coughs and halted breaths.

"Today, we grieve. We have to," Coach Geiger says. "Tomorrow, we come back and practice, just as we will on Wednesday and Thursday. The varsity match against West Bloomfield is rescheduled for Saturday, and we wrestle Livonia next Tuesday night. Then it's the district tournament. Every minute, every second we're in this room or competing in a match, we give everything we have as individuals, and as a team, to honor Coach Hillman."

Coach Geiger looks at us.

"Ready?" he says, with a surge in his voice. "One, two, three. This is—"

"ASHTON WRESTLING!" we shout.

Sort of.

Chapter 35

I'm lying in bed with earphones on, but have no desire to press the "play" button. It seems every time I feel like hearing a certain song, my mind gets jumbled up with thoughts about Coach Hillman. I don't get this "dead" thing. I mean, I get it...but I don't. How can someone be here one minute, then gone the next? For eternity. Forever.

I think about that for a while.

And for some incredibly disturbing reason, I think about what it would be like if my mom were suddenly gone. Or my dad. Or my grandmother. Or Cole. Or Owings. And I feel myself getting choked up, even though I know they're all still alive. I don't think I could handle any of them dying. Ever.

And, though I never met her, I think about how Mrs. Hillman must be feeling. How can she deal with her husband being gone...for eternity...forever?

Why's it have to happen?

I hear a soft knock. Mom opens my bedroom door, momentarily letting in the hallway light, then closes it. I watch her silhouette as she walks over to my bed and sits down.

"How're you feeling?" she asks.

Maybe it's the comfort of darkness, but I answer more honestly than I thought I would. "Confused," I say.

Mom seems to wait to respond. "About death?"

I stare at her, though I doubt she can see my eyes.

"It's frightening and sad," she says.

"It is," I say.

Mom puts her hand on mine. I don't know how she found it in the dark.

"But it's part of life," she adds.

I get the feeling that someday that's going to be clear to me, maybe even reassuring, but right now it's not. Death can't be part of life. Death is death; life is life.

"I spoke with someone at the school this afternoon," Mom says. "There'll be a special service in the gymnasium on Wednesday. All the wrestlers are going to be part of the ceremony."

I don't say anything.

"Both you and Cole."

Still, I say nothing.

"Mel?" Mom asks. "Are you uncomfortable with that?"

And then it's like my mind suddenly clears.

"Mom, this thing...this problem me and Coach Hillman had..." I choke up. "It happened while he was sick." My eyes flood with tears. "While he was *dying*." I sit up and bury my head in my mom's arms, my chest heaving and collapsing in sobbing fits.

"Oh, Mel," Mom says, hugging me tightly. "You can't think about that."

"It was *my* name in that article," I manage to say. "And my name with those quotes. No one else's..."

"From what I've been told, Coach Hillman had been sick a long time," Mom says. "You didn't make it worse."

"What gave me the right to say those things?"

Mom doesn't answer and, for a while, I cry in her arms. I guess she doesn't have any magical words to offer. Then again, maybe I'm *not* supposed to feel better. Maybe I'm supposed to feel regretful, and mad at myself, and sad that I never had a chance to apologize and to explain that what was in the newspaper article wasn't how I felt at all.

Eventually, Mom whispers, "You're a good person, Mel. Coach Hillman knew that. And I'm sure he appreciated having you on the team."

"How do you know?"

"I just do," Mom says.

How can she?

"I know you don't believe me," she says. "And that's fine. I think you want to defend yourself. You don't need to. But if you feel strongly about it, then make sure you're part of Wednesday's ceremony. Show everyone just how much you respected your coach. Okay?"

"Sure, Mom," I say.

I suppose it's the only thing I can do.

As Mom leaves my bedroom, she says, "Annie called earlier." Then she adds, sounding as if she debated whether to tell me, "And that boy you've been spending time with."

"Stewart?"

"Yes," she says, then closes my bedroom door.

A big part of me should be excited. This is what I wanted, right? For him to call and explain himself, then to apologize profusely and repeatedly. And yet, I don't feel any excitement. Nothing like before Saturday night when I'd feel my stomach flutter just being around him, or hearing his voice on the other end of the phone. And I'm not all that interested in finding out what his excuse is for blowing me off. Or how he thought he was going to make it up to me. We can't see each other anyway, so what's the point?

I walk over to the window and stare outside. A half-moon hangs in the sky. Nothing is moving. No cars passing by. No wind swaying tree branches. No neighbors taking a late-night walk.

Just stillness.

Is this what life is about? I wonder. *Monumental things happening when you least expect them?*

Chapter 36

The practice room is silent.

I don't know if I'm ready for this. I don't know if I even deserve to be a part of it. But I'm here nevertheless. Dressed in JV match warm-ups, with my wrestling shoes on and hood up, waiting with the rest of the team.

It's strange. In some ways the last forty-eight hours seem like they've passed in a blur. In other ways, it's like time's standing still. Tuesday wasn't much different than Monday; and today, just like Tuesday. People in school are still broken up, and the hallway, even between periods, remains subdued. I can't remember what we've done in any of my classes and, thankfully, all of my teachers have put off homework and quizzes until next week. Yesterday, Coach Geiger worked us hard, or at least tried to. I think he did that on purpose, to get us back on track by distracting us from Coach Hillman's death, if only for a couple of hours. I'm not sure it worked. I mean, Coach Hillman is all around us. His name is on dozens of the plaques in the practice room, just as his face is in nearly all of the photos hanging on the walls.

The *Detroit News* had an article highlighting Coach Hillman's career. I read it. Alone in my room. I didn't totally want to. But something inside me wanted, or needed, to know more about him. His life was impressive. He'd been a decorated US Marine, been married to his wife for thirty-seven years, and had two sons and a daughter. All three live in Michigan. The *News* listed his coaching accomplishments, the team titles, the individual champion wrestlers, the respectful quotes from other head coaches, and declared him one of the most important contributors to the sport of high school wrestling in the state's history.

Had it ended there, all would have been fine. Instead, the *News* saw it necessary to include one small line, which might as well have been set in bold: "...a gold-plated career slightly tarnished only by a recent controversy regarding remarks about female participation in his wrestling program..."

I'm that female.

I'm going to be linked to Coach Hillman forever. In a terrible way. I wonder how many of my teammates also read this? And, now, here I am with those very same guys about to honor the man.

"Mel—"

It's my brother.

Then he says, in a strained voice, to the rest of the team, "Ashton, get in weight-class order; varsity on the right, JVs on the left. Hoods up."

We put our hoods over our heads, then follow my brother and Trey out of the practice room. We walk in silence down the hallway, then around the corner, until we reach the gymnasium.

Cole holds up his hand. "Varsity lines up on the home side of the mat," he says. "JVs on the away side. No talking. And don't screw this up."

I can feel my heart thumping. Cole opens the gymnasium door a crack, and we can hear the murmur from the crowded stands. My heartbeat quickens.

Then the gymnasium lights shut off one by one until a single lamp shines down on the wrestling mat. A snare drum, in a slow, solemn cadence, begins.

Brrump... Brrump... Brrump, brrump, brrump... Brrump... Brrump... Brrump, brrump, brrump...

Cole lowers his hand and the team begins walking into the gymnasium, varsity and JV, shoulder to shoulder. I'm not even sure who's next to me because I don't dare look to the side. My head is facing forward, my eyes looking down, just making sure I don't trip Brook, who's in line in front of me. We come up the side of the stands, then veer toward the center of the gymnasium. At the wrestling mat, the varsity line splits to one side, the JV to the other. Then we turn and face each other.

The drumming stops, and an American flag is lowered from the ceiling. Below it, at the top edge of the mat, is a microphone stand. Out of the corner of my eye, I can see beyond the light that the darkened stands are filled, though I can't make out any single face.

Then Mr. Newsome steps up to the microphone, his dress shoes clicking on the hardwood gymnasium floors.

"These have been incredibly difficult days for our school, and our community," he says. "I have seen the profound sadness in the faces of students, teachers, administrators, and alumni..."

He pauses.

"It is not an easy thing, dealing with the death of a loved one, finding meaning, making sense of our Creator's decisions. And, perhaps, it is our Creator's purpose that answers, if there are any at all, are well beyond our grasp. What I do know is Coach Hillman was a loving husband and father, a tireless teacher and coach, a loyal friend and colleague..." For a moment, Mr. Newsome's voice breaks. "He was an exceptional man, but human, like all of us... I am reminded of a quote from our twenty-sixth president, Theodore Roosevelt."

Mr. Newsome reaches into the breast pocket of his suit and pulls out a note card.

"'It is not the critic who counts,'" he begins reading. "'Not the man who points out how the strong man stumbles, or where the doer of deeds could have done them better. The credit belongs to the man who is actually in the arena, whose face is marred by dust and sweat and blood, who strives valiantly; who errs and comes short again and again; because there is not effort without error and shortcomings; but who does actually strive to do the deed; who knows the great enthusiasm, the great devotion, who spends himself in a worthy cause, who at the best knows in the end the triumph of high achievement and who at the worst, if he fails, at least he fails while daring greatly. So that his place shall never be with those cold and timid souls who know neither victory nor defeat.'"

Mr. Newsome slips the note card back in his pocket and steps to the side. Out of the shadows, Mr. Williamson walks to the microphone.

"As we all know, Coach Hillman was not a timid man." He offers a small grin, and I can hear a smattering of weak laughter. "His arena was a wrestling mat. As such, I am proud to announce that as of last night, having been approved by the Ashton Board of Education and the School Superintendent, the team practice room will, from this day forward, be known as The Robert J. Hillman Wrestling Room."

A cheer goes up from the crowd. I see the varsity wrestlers clapping, so I clap myself.

"Ashton High," Mr. Williamson says, "please join me in welcoming Coach Hillman's wife, Jean, his daughter, Isabella, and sons, Roger and Benjamin."

Now the cheering is much louder. I wonder if this is appropriate for such an occasion. I don't feel like cheering. Rather, I feel a lump in my throat and in my gut.

An older woman walks up, a young woman at her side, and two men who seem to be the same age as my dad, one holding a pair of wrestling shoes. Mr. Newsome shakes hands with each of them and steps back.

Wearing a black dress, a gold pin, and an air of dignity, Mrs. Hillman smiles, momentarily. "My husband," she says into the microphone. "My husband was so proud to be a part of this school. He called it his second home. And he relished every day that he could come here to teach. And to coach. He considered each of you part of his second family. The past few days have been hard—very hard—on our family. But they've been just a little bit easier to get through knowing there are so many students and teachers and friends who loved my husband. I can't thank Principal Newsome and Mr. Williamson enough for this ceremony today. And, of course, for naming the wrestling room in his honor."

Mrs. Hillman clears her throat. And, for a few moments, she seems nearly unable to continue. Her daughter reaches out a hand, which Mrs. Hillman clasps.

"I understand, in the sport of wrestling, placing your shoes at the center circle of a wrestling mat symbolizes your retirement from competition." She tilts her head skyward. "My husband will always be looking down on the Ashton High wrestling team. But it's time for another man—and you have a very fine one in Coach Geiger—to guide this team, and the program, to even greater success. My oldest son, Benjamin, will do the honors."

Benjamin Hillman, head bowed, with the wrestling shoes held in his palms, moves across the wrestling mat to the center circle. He bends down and places the pair of shoes on the mat, then walks back to his family.

Across from me, under his hooded warm-ups, I can see my brother fighting back tears. So is Trey. So are the other varsity wrestlers.

Then, among the quiet sobs, someone in the stands yells, "We love you, Coach Hillman!"

"We'll miss you!" another person shouts.

And another. "Rest in peace, Coach!"

I turn to look, and though I can't make out anyone in particular, I can see people in the stands are on their feet. Shouting. And clapping. And stomping. And somehow, almost spontaneously, the stands sound no different than they do when our varsity team is defeating one of our rivals, with a kind of thrilling excitement filling the gymnasium.

"Coach Hillman," a few people shout.

Then more. "Coach Hillman!"

Until the gymnasium is reverberating. "COACH HILLMAN... COACH HILLMAN... COACH HILLMAN..."

And as this continues, Mrs. Hillman walks down the row of varsity wrestlers, shaking each guy's hand. She is showing such grace during what has to be a wife's most difficult time. It gives me a chill. I've surprised myself by recognizing something like that. I'm not a wife, and who knows if and when I'll be one. And I've never had my husband pass away. But I'm in the midst of something inspiring today. Something I don't understand at all, because when someone dies, nothing should be inspiring. Right?

Mrs. Hillman crosses the mat and begins addressing each JV wrestler, as well. When she starts from the heaviest wrestlers toward the lightest, I realize she's going to be shaking *my* hand soon. I wipe away my tears. What in the world should I say?

My condolences for your loss...

Coach Hillman was a really nice man...

Sorry for my stupid newspaper quotes a few weeks back...

Again, I wipe my eyes as my brain scrambles to think of what would be best. Then, just as my thoughts start to spin out of control, Mrs. Hillman steps in front me and reaches out her hand. I reach out mine.

"Mrs. Hillman, I'm—"

"Melinda," she finishes. "I know, dear. My husband was a little old-fashioned, but he still spoke so highly of you. He would come home and tell me there's a girl on the wrestling team, Cole Radford's sister, who's as tough as some of the boys."

My eyes fill with tears, yet again.

"Believe me when I tell you," she says, "my husband was proud to be your coach."

I begin bawling.

Mrs. Hillman gives me a hug and walks back to the top of the wrestling mat. I'm sure she and her family shake hands with Mr. Newsome and other school officials, but I never see it. I'm still crying and my body is still shaking and I don't know what to think, and it isn't until Brook taps me on the shoulder and says into my hood, "Come on, Mel," that I realize the team has begun walking off the mat, through the gymnasium, and back from where we came.

Chapter 37

Cole's bedroom door is closed.

Even in the best of times it usually is, but this week I'm not sure I've seen it open even once from the moment we get home after practice until we leave for school the next morning. I've put my ear to the door a few times (even though he'd kill me if he caught me). Sometimes I hear music. Sometimes I hear him talking. I worry about him. My brother is strong-willed and thinks the world of himself, but I don't see how anyone gets through something like this alone.

I walk down the stairs and into the kitchen. My parents are having tea and talking about work, it sounds like. That's their usual way of relaxing at night. They stop and turn toward me.

"I heard the ceremony was very sad?" Mom says.

"Yeah," I say, grabbing a Vernors from the refrigerator.

"And practice?" Dad asks.

"We haven't had a decent one this week."

"That's to be expected," Dad says.

I open the can and take a sip of ginger ale. "There's

only so much crying, only so much emotion..." I'm not sure what more to say.

I think everyone on the team has reached a limit. We're burned out. It showed in the practice room. I tried to wrestle hard. I mean, if Coach Hillman really thought I was tough, then maybe I am. My brain was certainly telling my body what to do, it's just that my body wasn't listening, or it was listening but pleading, "Do we really have to do this *now?*" As bad as it got, Coach Geiger never raised his voice. Even when Connor strained his ankle taking a poor shot. I think Coach Geiger knew there was no point in yelling. He even ended practice early.

"Is Cole's door still closed?"

I nod.

Dad has an uneasy look on his face. "I certainly hope the varsity can get it together for the last two matches. Especially with the districts next week. Cole's sacrificed so much..." He shakes his head. "Well, maybe he can bring the team and your school something to get excited about."

I nod. "Maybe."

Chapter 38

"You should call him," Annie says, emphatically.

I'm sitting between her and Jade in the auditorium balcony. I don't know why Annie's brought up Stewart, except that there's still this suffocating pall of sadness in the school hallways and classrooms and the three of us just had to get away from it all for a while. I don't say anything, but it's not because I haven't thought about him. It would be nice to have him to talk me through Coach Hillman's death, or be a comforting shoulder to rest my head on—if we could find a way to get together.

"Twice Stewart's left a message for you," Annie reminds me.

"Maybe I should," I say.

"No," Jade says. "He doesn't deserve it."

"Give him another chance," Annie says. "At least let him explain why he ignored your calls on Saturday night."

"Why?" Jade asks. "Because you'd give Georgie another chance if you could?"

"Well—"

"See, she would," Jade says to me, with a dismissive frown toward Annie. "She forgets how miserable she was when Georgie broke up with her. Mel, honey, that's what I'm saying for you: Don't forget how you felt Saturday night when he blew you off. He didn't call or anything. So what if he's leaving messages for you now. It's too late."

Annie opens her mouth like she's going to say something, but she doesn't. I don't say anything either. I don't know if Jade is right or wrong. And I'm not sure how I feel about Stewart anymore.

After a few minutes in the silent auditorium, Jade takes a deep breath. "I hate seeing a friend get hurt," she says.

I'm pretty sure my parents have gone to sleep. I haven't. I'm so exhausted from being sad that my head's pounding, and as hard as I try to keep my eyes closed, I'm not getting anywhere near falling asleep. So I lie in bed, vaguely looking out my bedroom window at the sky.

I talked to Odessa on the phone earlier. She wanted to see how I was. I wished her luck for the end of the season. It was a short conversation, but it made me feel good that she cared enough to call.

With the time on my dresser clock creeping along, my mind has managed to cover a lot of things. One of those being Stewart. He hasn't left a third message. I don't know why I thought he would. Maybe, like Jade said, it's for the better. At least I've tried to convince myself of that. I could use a fresh start. Jade, Annie, and I can start scoping out new guys. And wrestling season is practically over, too. The JVs have practice until the districts, then it's optional while the varsity guys are competing in the post-season.

All in all, it was an okay season for me, I suppose. I sure felt a lot better about things following the clinic.

But, right now, that seems like forever ago.

Chapter 39

"You want me to *what?*"

And, that's exactly how I said it.

One minute, I'm dragging my exhausted self from the practice room toward the girl's locker room; the next, I'm hearing someone call out my name from down the hallway. I turn and see that it's Coach Geiger.

"Mel, wait a second," he says.

Oh, geez, what could it be *now?* It's Friday night, I really don't want to hear any more bad news about anything.

"Yeah, Coach?" I say.

He walks up to me. "How do you feel?"

Weary, drained, worn-out—pick one of them. "Uh... fine."

"How's your weight?"

"My weight?" I say. That's an odd question. "Okay, I guess. A few pounds under. Around 111, I guess."

"You looked good on the mats today," he says.

Looked good on the mats? Who's he kidding? I was just as distracted and sloppy as everyone else.

"That clinic must've been helpful," he says. "Good coaches, right?"

"Yeah, they were," I say.

"Great," he says.

Where's he going with this?

Coach Geiger takes a deep breath. "Look, Mel, I'm not going to beat around the bush. It's been an awful week for us. Losing Coach Hillman has been devastating. It's hit everyone on the team hard. I'm just not sure when, and how, we're going to recover. I'm not worried about the last two matches of the regular season, both teams aren't nearly as talented as we are. But the post-season I am worried about. If we're not wrestling on all cylinders for the districts, we won't be advancing guys—like your brother, Trey, and, hopefully, a half-dozen others—to the regions. We can't afford that. We need something that's going to breathe some life into this team, into this school."

Why's he telling me this?

Coach Geiger puts a hand on my shoulder. "I'm going to hold Connor out of the Livonia match on Tuesday night so he can get an extra day of rest. That leaves a spot in the varsity lineup open."

My heart starts thumping. "What're you saying?"

"I know you're certified to wrestle 106," Coach Geiger says. "You'd have to cut some weight. It won't be easy. And you'll have to get yourself ready mentally. That'll be harder. But I want *you* to fill that spot."

My throat tightens. "You want me to *what?*" I practically cough out.

"I want you to wrestle varsity."

"Varsity?" I say, feeling a bit woozy. "What will the guys think?"

"I don't care what they think," he says. "*I'm* the coach."

"I don't know..."

Coach Geiger straightens up. It's obvious he's completely unhappy with what I said. His eyebrows bend sharply. "Mel, have you been with the program for two years?"

"Yeah."

"And have you been to every practice this season?"

"Yeah."

"And do you work your tail off like every guy in the practice room?"

"I guess."

"There's no better way to honor Coach Hillman than for you to take the mat and represent Ashton at 106 pounds. Mel, I'm sure at some point during the next two seasons, assuming you keep working hard and improving, you'll wrestle varsity matches for us. Maybe even become a starter by your senior year. And when the time comes for you to take the mat in an Ashton varsity singlet for the first time, it'll be nice for you, and for the program. But on Tuesday night, there's an opportunity to do something truly special, at the seniors' last home match, at a time when your teammates and the school needs it the most."

I think I'm dizzy... *Don't fall over,* I tell myself. *Do not fall over.*

"Okay, Coach," I say, weakly.

"Is that a yes?"

My mouth opens, but nothing comes out.

"Well?" he asks.

I nod, slightly. "Yes."

Coach Geiger seems pleased. "Good decision," he says. "Go home and tell your parents. I'll announce it to the team on Monday. This is going to be a big moment for you. For all of us."

Chapter 40

But I don't tell my parents. Or Cole. I let it spin around in my head for a while. Like all night, and the next morning.

I'm going to wrestle varsity *in four days.*

Just thinking about it—which I've done, maybe, a thousand times since Coach Geiger told me yesterday—makes my stomach knot. Maybe I'll get lucky and throw up. Gotta drop five and a half pounds anyway.

Mom walks into the kitchen and searches the cupboards for a tin of coffee. When she sees me sitting in my sweats on the laundry room floor tying my sneakers, she gives me a curious look.

"You're up early," she says.

"Going running."

She glances at the kitchen clock. "Eight o'clock on a Saturday morning?"

I shrug. "Got some things on my mind."

Mom nods. I'm sure she thinks it's about Coach Hillman. Or that I'm still brooding over not being able to see Stewart. Like I'd waste any energy on him.

"You're going to Cole's match, right?"

"Yeah," I say. "And, Mom, it's *my* team, too."

But she's oblivious. "Your dad and I are leaving for West Bloomfield around noon," she says.

"I'll be ready."

She grabs a carton of eggs and a wedge of Brie from the refrigerator. "I'm making a cheese omelet. Do you want some for when you get back?"

"I'm not hungry," I say.

Even though I am. I'm starving, actually.

"Come on," Jade says to me. "What's the big news?"

I shouldn't have said anything. I should've waited. Sitting on the top row of the half-empty West Bloomfield gymnasium bleachers definitely isn't the place to tell your best friend that you have this major secret—and that she'll have to wait to hear what it is. But I couldn't stop myself.

"Can't tell you," I say, with a grin.

Jade tugs at my arm. "Give me a hint."

"Can't."

"Can't," she says. "Or won't?"

I'd rather get excited about the Ashton varsity, but it's kind of boring watching our guys beat the snot out of the home team. I thought there'd be more emotion, considering this is our first match since Coach Hillman died. In his honor, we are wearing black bands on our singlets, and West Bloomfield was gracious in calling for a moment of silence before the match started.

Only a few dozen of their fans showed up. Not that I blame them. They have a lousy team, so even though we're not wrestling particularly well, we still have yet to lose an individual match. Nate, our 152-pounder, is winning right now, and with Cole and Trey to follow, there's a good chance we'll shut out West Bloomfield.

"Tell me," Jade insists.

"Wait until tomorrow," I say. "Now watch." I nod toward the mat.

Jade pulls me close and puts her mouth to my ear. "Give...me...a...hint."

I nudge her away. "Look, I already told you. Come over for Sunday dinner tomorrow. My grandma'll be there. We should be eating around four o'clock. When you and my family are sitting down, I'll announce it." I can only imagine what Cole's going to think.

Jade suddenly has a huge smile on her face. "Oh, *noooo* way," she says. "It's about Stewart, isn't it? He came crawling back, didn't he? Promising never to hurt you again, pledging his undying love." Then she really hams it up, saying in a hushed but deep voice, "Oh, Melinda, how I've missed you so—"

"All right already," I say.

"My dear, the two of us were meant to be one—"

"Jade," I say. "Shhhh..."

She drops the act, only because she can't seem to stop giggling. And I can't either. It kind of feels good to laugh a little.

As Nate has his hand raised in victory, I watch Cole get a final word from Coach Geiger before he steps out onto the mat. For the past four years, no one but Coach Hillman has given him pre-match instructions. I was worried he'd have trouble getting back his competitiveness, but I shouldn't have. He looks as serious and determined as at any point this season.

"Let's go, Cole!" Jade yells.

I turn to her.

She shrugs and says, "What, I can't get excited for one of his matches?"

I shake my head.

"Hey, you don't want to tell me your big secret," Jade says. "Fine—then I'll just have to find something else to be interested in. Like your brother's match."

"Whatever," I say.

Thankfully, Cole wastes no time shooting in for the double-leg, lifting the West Bloomfield wrestler high, then slipping in the half when he brings him down to the mat. It's an impressive example of wrestling efficiency. In less than thirty seconds, Cole has decked his opponent.

Jade jumps to her feet—and almost out of her Crocs— along with the rest of the Ashton fans, clapping and shouting Cole's name.

I can tell from my brother's face that he's relieved. I don't know if he's taken Coach Hillman's death harder than the other guys on the team. How would you measure that kind of thing? It doesn't matter anyway. He's been dealing with it. Before, alone in his room. Now, out on the mat.

Chapter 41

Three and a half pounds to go.

Bet I lost at least a pound and a quarter on this run. I really pushed myself, going farther than I'd ever gone with Cole. And I didn't let the cold slow me. Or the fact that I'm totally starving. I just concentrated on the road in front of me. Those USGWA coaches probably do stuff like this every day. Maybe *twice* a day. They know how to sacrifice. They know how to set a goal and go after it. They know how to achieve. I'm just learning.

Stopping at our driveway, I hunch over to catch my breath. Grandma's car is here. I make my way to the back door. Inside, I give my grandmother a kiss hello, then untie my running shoes and peel off my layers of clothing. She comments on how thin I look.

"Grandma, a girl can never be too rich or too skinny," I say. "You taught me that."

"*That's* the lesson you learned from me?" she says with a mild frown.

In the kitchen, Mom and Dad are putting the final touches on the table for our Sunday dinner.

"Jade's here," Mom says. "She's up in your room."

"Thanks," I say.

"We're eating soon."

I won't be.

Stripped down to a long-sleeved T-shirt and thermal pants, damp with sweat, I walk through the kitchen and up the stairs. I expect Jade to immediately start bugging me about the secret; she can wait just a few minutes longer. But when I get to my bedroom, she's not there.

"Jade?" I say.

"In here," she answers from Cole's room.

I look in. "Let's go," I say.

"Relax, Mel," my brother says, snidely. "Why were you running anyway? Your season's done."

I smile, angrily. *Oh, wait my dear brother. Be a jerk all you want, but this Tuesday night I'll be sharing the varsity mat with you.*

I tug on Jade's arm. "Come on."

When we get into my room, I take off my shirt, thermals, and underwear and rummage through my drawers for a pair of sweats. "Sorry you had to spend even a minute with him."

"I don't mind," Jade says, sitting on my bed.

"You don't have to say that just because he's my brother," I say, finding something to throw on.

"I like your brother," Jade says.

"Whatever."

There's a pause before she says, "And, uh...I think he likes me."

"Likes you?" I scoff. "Likes you how? Like any girl he can get something off of?"

"No, like a girlfriend," Jade says.

I look over my shoulder. "What?"

"Mel, you know how you're going to tell me your big secret over dinner? Well, I kind of have a big secret, too."

I turn around to face her. "What *kind* of big secret?" I say, as my throat tightens.

"Me and Cole."

I take a deep breath. "You and my brother?"

She nods.

"And?" I say, gritting my teeth.

"We're going out."

"Going out?"

"Me and him."

"You and *my* brother?" I hear my voice getting louder, but I can't help myself. "Going out? Going out, as in dating? My brother? And you?" The words keep spitting out of my mouth. "I can't believe this. Have you guys fooled around?"

"Mel, I'm not—" Jade says.

"Well?"

Jade purses her lips. "Pretty much."

"What about our two-month rule?"

"It has been."

I feel dizzy. It takes me a few moments to compose myself.

"You've been fooling around with Cole for two months?" I say. "How could you lie to me?"

"I didn't lie," Jade says.

"You just did it behind my back, never said a word,

and pretended nothing was going on. You, my best friend, and Cole, my brother."

"I was going to tell you a while ago, but—"

"But what?"

"But you had that newspaper mess. Then the thing with Stewart happened. And then Coach Hillman. And you were so crazy with stuff."

"Me, crazy?" I say. "All this time you're giving me advice on how to deal with Stewart. And all that crap about 'truths'. So you screw up my relationship while yours apparently goes so well. Me, crazy? No, *now* I'm crazy."

Before I realize it, I'm pounding on Cole's bedroom door. "Get out here, your slutty girlfriend wants you!"

"Mel!" Jade shouts at me.

"You keep quiet, ex-best friend," I say.

Cole opens his door. "What's your problem?"

"What's going on up there?" Mom shouts from the bottom of the stairs.

I point my finger in Cole's chest. "Take your slut girlfriend," I say, grabbing Jade's arm, then pushing her at my brother.

"She's not a slut," he says.

"Take her," I say.

"Relax."

"Take her."

"Mel," Cole says, with an obnoxious grin, "are you having your period?"

This stops me for a moment, but only a moment. I

can hardly control myself. "You're a fucking asshole!" I scream.

"Melinda!" Mom yells. "Settle down!" She and Dad are now at the top of the stairs.

"No, I'm not going to. All the girls at school and he's got to pick *her*." I throw a nasty look at Jade. "Did you two know they're having sex?" I say to my mom and dad.

"Enough of this," Cole says. "We're leaving."

"Go! But before you do, mister big-shit big brother," I say. "You think you're so cool and all that. Well, I've got news for you. I'm wrestling varsity at 106 on Tuesday night."

"What?" Mom says. Or maybe it was Dad.

"It's true," I say.

"Varsity?" Cole says. "You?"

"You heard me," I snap, moving toward my bedroom. "Coach Geiger is putting me in the lineup. *Me!* I'm going to be the first girl at Ashton to ever wrestle in a varsity match. And no one, ever, is going to be able to take that away." Then, before I slam the door shut, I say, "And I'm doing it without any of you!"

It's been a couple of hours since my major meltdown. I'm sitting at my vanity, tired but still shaking, staring out my bedroom window as it slowly turns dark outside. Jade's been gone since right after I slammed my bedroom door shut. Cole drove her home. He hasn't come back yet. They even held hands before getting in his car. It makes me sick.

How could they do this to me? There are so many girls at Ashton more than happy to screw around with Cole. Instead, he's gotta go after *Jade*. And she's even worse, chasing after my brother behind my back. I know how she can be—flirty and sexy. What kind of friend does that, and then keeps it secret until it's turned into some kind of *thing*? I should've seen it happening; I should've realized what the two of them were doing.

There's a sharp knock on my door.

"Yeah?" I say.

Mom walks in. "Melinda, you've had plenty of time to cool off," she says. "We need to talk. Now."

"There's nothing to talk about."

Mom puts her hands on her hips and leans in toward me. "There's plenty to talk about!" *Whoa, she's pissed.* "You act completely out of control, swearing at your best friend and your brother, and then announce out of nowhere you're going to wrestle at a weight that, I'm pretty damn sure, is below what you're at right now—probably well below."

"You're an expert on wrestling?"

Oh, crap, I did *not* mean to say that.

"Listen to me, young lady," she says, a few decibels short of yelling. "You better take a moment to think about what you're saying and how you're saying it. You don't think I noticed that you've hardly eaten since Friday? You think I'm naive? You're starving yourself. I'll bet that's why you're acting so out of your mind."

"I'm not starving myself," I say.

"Oh, really? Then why don't you come downstairs and eat some dinner?"

"I don't want to eat."

"I know you do."

"I don't."

"You've got to be hungry."

"Why do you care?" I say. "You never bother Cole when he's cutting weight, no matter how miserable he gets. For four months, he can get sick and disgustingly pale and you don't say a thing. But I'm losing weight for one match—*one match*—and you're making this huge deal out of it. Is it because I'm a girl?"

"You haven't eaten in days," Mom says, brushing off my question. "That's why you're like this."

"I'm not like anything."

"So what's your excuse for the outburst?" Mom says, but she doesn't wait for an answer. "I have no idea what happened to you earlier, Mel. That's not *my* daughter. My daughter doesn't have a temper like that. My daughter doesn't use language like that. What were you thinking?"

"It's ridiculous that Cole and Jade are dating."

"Why?"

"Ma!"

"Get over it, Mel."

That shocks me. "You mean you're not the least bit worried about them having sex?"

"I'll talk to them about that," Mom says. "But I trust Cole and I trust Jade, who I've known since you two were little girls. I don't, however, trust you with an older boy, from another town, who I don't know at all. And, yes, I do worry about you more. The quotes in the newspaper. Being forbidden to date that boy. Everything that's gone on with Coach Hillman's passing. Then your awful outburst this afternoon. I think things are too much for you to handle right now."

"I can handle them," I say.

"Can you?"

I glance at my poster of Tricia Saunders. She looks so fierce. I wish I felt that way. I don't. But I can't let Mom know that.

"I have this opportunity," I say. "Coach Geiger wants me to be the first Ashton girl to wrestle varsity, and Tuesday night would be the perfect time. It's really a big deal. He's giving *me* the chance."

"Why?"

"Why? What's that mean?"

Mom frowns. "I don't want your coach using you as some kind of gender guinea pig."

"Gender guinea pig?"

"So he can make a name for himself."

"It's not for him," I say. "It's so I can make a name for *myself*."

Mom seems to think about this a bit. She sits down at the edge of my bed. "Come here," she says. I move next to her. She gives me a hug. "I respect you. Of course, I do. As a young woman, and as a wrestler."

"Thanks."

I lean my head on her shoulder and close my eyes. I feel comforted resting against my mom. We stay that way for a while, not saying a word.

"I wanted this to be a big moment for me. It was my turn to have our family hear about *my* good news. I wanted to be the star. I wanted everyone to be proud... Guess I pretty much ruined that."

Mom says nothing.

"And Grandma heard everything?" I ask, sheepishly.

"She did."

Great, just great...

"Are you sure you're ready for this?" Mom asks.

"I think I am."

"I don't want you losing more weight."

"Promise."

"You're lying to me."

"Only a little," I say, smiling a bit. "Just a few pounds more."

Mom shakes her head. "I don't like what happened earlier."

"I know," I say. "What am I going to do?"

"You have some apologizing to do."

"Yeah..."

"I don't think you have to worry about Cole," she says. "I doubt he even remembers what you said. But Jade, well, that might be a little tougher to fix. You said some mean things. Don't expect her to forgive you right away."

"And Grandma?"

"Yes, your grandmother, too."

I walk my grandmother to her car. She hasn't really said anything to me since I came down from my room. She's angry, or disappointed, or something...

"Glad you came over, Grandma," I say, opening the car door for her. I give her a kiss on the cheek. "Sorry you had to hear that stuff."

"Yes, so am I," she says. "More than you can imagine."

"It wasn't my fault," I say. "It was—"

"Please don't say any more," my grandmother interrupts me. "Melinda, you have to learn to take responsibility for your actions."

"I do."

"No, you're still a young girl," she says. "You're immature."

"But—" I stop myself.

"It's why I wanted you to work at DDI," she says, getting into her car. "Not to be mean, or to ruin your summer. But to have you acquire skills. To learn to act mature. Remember the day when we had you input companies? You should've been able to get through at least 230. And you know how I know this? Because that happens to be the same number of companies you had checked off on the list."

Oh, God, she knows about that? I hang my head.

"Is this what wrestling does to you? Lets you think you can just demean the job you were asked to do? Or tonight, do you really think problems are solved by yelling gutter language and carrying on without any dignity whatsoever?"

"No."

"Your mother told me you're probably not eating and very hungry. And very thirsty, too."

I say nothing.

"And every afternoon you're touching boys and being touched by them," she says.

"It's not like that, Grandma."

"Tell me how I'm wrong?"

"If you came to one of my matches, you'd see," I say.

"I want no part of that," she says. "I want to see you learn something useful, skills that will take you far in school and life."

There's no point in arguing. She still doesn't get it. And I certainly did myself no favors with my meltdown.

"Be careful driving, Grandma," I say.

I step back and watch as she pulls out of our driveway, then drives off down the road.

Chapter 42

I haven't seen Jade yet this morning. We usually meet at my locker before homeroom to gossip or compare homework. Safe to say, she's still pissed.

It's already an awkward start to the week, but no more awkward than the ride to school. I wasn't sure Cole would even drive me. But he did. Without a fuss. "Hope you're done being a maniac," was the only thing he said before backing out of our driveway. I didn't have to answer him, and he didn't demand an apology. Guys are like that, I suppose. It takes a lot to hurt their feelings.

Not Jade, though.

As Mrs. Portman takes homeroom attendance, I lay my head on the desk and close my eyes, and suffer through another awful hunger pang. I'm still a half pound over, so the pain's not going away. Neither is this insane thirst.

"Are you okay, Mel?" Mrs. Portman asks. "Do you need to go to the nurse's office?"

"I'm fine," I say, knowing a trip there might put my chance to wrestle in jeopardy, then add, in a hushed voice, "Just a little tired."

Mrs. Portman nods.

A few minutes later, the intercom comes on. "Good Monday morning, Ashton students," Ms. LaFleur gives her usual greeting. "A few reminders for this week... Thursday is the deadline for the upcoming AP test... Checks are due at the main office... Students interested in trying out for the spring theater program can contact Mr. Neddy... The season's final wrestling match will be at home tomorrow night... Come cheer on Melinda Radford, as she becomes the first girl at Ashton to compete in a varsity match..."

I raise my head and look around the classroom. Everyone is staring at me. I'm not sure what to make of their expressions. Most seem surprised; some perplexed; a few smile.

How in the world did Ms. LaFleur know?

I feel a tap on my shoulder.

When I turn around, Julie Palmer asks, "Was that a joke?"

"Why would it be?" I say.

She shrugs. "Okay, cool."

Jade avoids me the entire day. I check, and re-check, our secret spot in the auditorium balcony. And the school's back stairwell. I watch for her between classes, and even walk up and down the second-floor hallway three or four times in hopes of seeing her. We don't cross paths in the bathroom, or in the cafeteria. Of course, she could be out sick but, more likely, Mom was right when she said fixing things with Jade was going to be really hard.

Guess I'll try to call her tonight, though I wonder if she'll pick up. I've got practice to worry about now—my last before tomorrow night's match. And I have to face my teammates. God, I hope they're cool about this. I put on my wrestling shoes and grab my headgear, then walk out of the girls' locker room. When I turn the corner, I see Jade.

I stop.

She's down the hall, outside the practice room, standing with Cole. I step back behind the corner and watch the two of them. They're smiling. And close. Touching hands. Jade looks *so* happy. God, I hate to admit it, but I'm totally jealous. Stewart and I were like that once.

Jade reaches up on her tiptoes and gives my brother a kiss on the cheek before walking away. Then Cole kneels down to tie his wrestling shoes. He's smiling, too. I notice his eyes follow her.

Someone bumps my shoulder. "Hey, Mel," Brook says. "You ready?"

"Hope so," I say.

We walk down the hallway and into the practice room, noticing "The Robert J. Hillman Wrestling Room" now painted above the door.

Not long after, Coach Geiger has the team sitting in a semicircle on the champions mat.

"Good match on Saturday night," he says. "West Bloomfield wasn't very talented, but considering our own circumstances, I'm pleased with how we wrestled. This is an important week for our team, and our program. The districts begin on Friday. And we have Livonia tomorrow night. Last match for you seniors. We're a little banged up physically, so I'm sitting Connor. He can use an extra day of rest. As you heard this morning, Mel will be in the starting lineup."

A few of the guys nod their heads. Then Brook shakes my hand, while Georgie gives me an encouraging (but still annoying) punch on my arm. They're all kind of playing it cool. At least no one objected. Not even Lionel. That's fine. I'll show all of them I deserve the chance.

"Mel," Coach Geiger says, staring at me. "Take a look."

I raise my eyes. He points to a space on the practice room wall.

"I've got two plaques sitting in my office," he says. "One has an engraving of your name and you being the first female at Ashton to compete in a varsity match. The other has your name and you being the first Ashton female to compete and *win* a varsity match. Which one I hang will be up to you."

Then he blows the whistle. "Let's get to work, Ashton. Start warming up."

And, for the first time in my two years on the team, I don't have to find a spot on the other mat. I stay right where I am. Next to Trey. Next to Connor. Next to Nate. Next to my brother, and the rest of the varsity wrestlers.

Chapter 43

I can't fall asleep. It feels like I have a fever, but I'm way too dehydrated to sweat. Every few minutes, I have to curl up in ball to fight the hunger that keeps coming back without the decency of a warning. So I try to distract myself by visualizing moves.

Imagining my stance...

Ready for the ref's whistle...

Moving on my feet...

Balance...

A good setup...

Drop-step...

And finish...

Cover for the takedown...

Control my opponent on the mat...

Attack for back points...

On bottom, escape to my feet...

I go through it all again—for, like, the umpteenth time. I'm still boiling hot, dizzy, and I keep tossing and turning, so much so that poor Owings gave up sleeping beside me hours ago.

Finally, I push aside my comforter and turn on the light. I find a pair of sweatpants and a T-shirt, grab my wrestling shoes, then quietly leave my bedroom.

I'm not surprised to find Cole in the basement practicing his drop-steps. But I am surprised when he tells me to throw on my shoes and work with him. So I do.

We alternate shots, working on our singles and doubles. Cole uses motion and misdirection to set up his takedowns; I tie up an arm and shoot in. And though he's much bigger and stronger than me, my brother knows how to give me just enough resistance to make it realistic, but not too much to stop me from completing the move.

We go for fifteen minutes, then work down on the mat, drilling stand-ups and switches from the bottom, and pinning combinations from the top.

Afterwards, Cole tells me to take a break. He stretches, while I sit on the basement stairs.

"How's your weight?" he asks.

"Quarter pound over."

"You haven't eaten much."

"Nothing," I say.

"And you're thirsty as hell."

"Like I'm dying."

Cole seems to approve of that. I might've even seen him smile. He tosses me a half-eaten energy bar from his equipment bag.

"Take a few bites," he says.

While we have this moment together, I want to tell him that I saw him and Jade together before practice and

I really think they look like a good pair. But he's in that zone, I can tell, focused on only wrestling and tomorrow night's match. So when he asks if I'm ready for more, I simply nod and get back on the mat.

Chapter 44

I open my eyes.

My first thought: *Oh, God, I'm wrestling* varsity *tonight.*

My second thought: *I feel like I'm going to barf.*

And, oh yeah, I'm totally exhausted. I'm not sure how much sleep I finally got last night, but it wasn't enough by a long shot.

I crawl out of bed, cough a few times, then give Owings a scratch on his head. I open my bedroom door and hear my parents in the kitchen. They're not saying much. It's the day of a match. I grab a towel from the hall closet and walk in the bathroom. Before I turn on the shower, I notice something taped to the mirror.

It's a newspaper clipping.

I look closer.

A short article from the *Detroit News* high school wrestling section. Today's. A few lines are circled in pen.

I pull it off.

"History is expected to be made tonight at Ashton High, one of the state's finest wrestling programs," it reads. "Sophomore Melinda Radford, younger sister of co-captain Cole Radford, is scheduled to compete at 106-pounds against Livonia High, marking the first time a female competes in a varsity match for the school. It will also be just the second time in state history that a brother and sister are in the same varsity wrestling lineup."

"Dad, why'd you put this—" I start to say, but before I can finish, my mouth starts to water.

Oh, no...

I slam the bathroom door shut and lean my head over the sink. An instant later, my stomach convulses. But nothing comes out. Which is almost a good thing because a full-blown yak is loud and the last thing I need is for Mom and Dad to hear. My mouth waters again and, for a second time, I dry heave.

I raise my head and look in the mirror. My eyes are bloodshot, and my face is pale. I'm a mess—a total mess. I turn on the shower and step in, feeling relief as the water cools my body. I even let the water spray into, and flow out of, my parched mouth. Until I know what my weight is, it's as close as I'll come to drinking anything.

A few minutes later, Cole bangs on the door. "Hustle up, Mel," he says. "And don't forget the dress code."

I almost forgot.

It's Ashton tradition that varsity starters wear a tie and jacket to school the day of a match. I suppose I could put on something blandly nice, but since I'm practically dying of starvation and dehydration on the inside, the least I can do is look totally fabulous on the outside. So, after I'm done in the bathroom, I put on an outfit from St. John Collection that I had set aside long ago for just such an occasion—a white blouse, with steel-gray fitted pants under a wool knit jacket, and finish it off with a black silk tie, loose at the collar.

One final thing.

I reach inside the cover of Owings' bed and pull out the essay I had written for Mr. Williamson. I unfold the paper. I had written at the top: What I Want to Accomplish in Wrestling. Later tonight will fulfill the first and second of those goals.

"Mel, let's go," Cole calls out.

I leave the essay on my vanity, grab my equipment bag, then check myself in my bedroom mirror. Sleek. Fashionable. Hot.

Before I leave I take a long look at Tricia Saunders. Fierce. Relentless. Ruthless.

I can be all of it. I hope.

Jade has her arms around me; mine are wrapped around her. It's one of *those* hugs, a hug between two best friends who never ever want to hurt each other—even if one stupidly did—the kind that means everything in the world, but doesn't need any words to explain it.

Cole gave up waiting. That's okay, Jade and I aren't done yet.

Eventually, she says, "We better get to homeroom." Then she asks, "How you feeling?"

"So awful you can't imagine," I say.

She looks me up and down. "You look a little pale, but your outfit is amazing. Definitely have to let me borrow this sometime."

"If I make it through the day, you can have it."

We both smile.

"Nervous?" she asks.

"Like I'm going to pee in my pants—if I actually had something to pee," I say. "But let's talk about something else. Tell me, how'd you manage to hide all yesterday?"

"Pretty good, right?" Jades says.

"I looked everywhere."

"Not everywhere, my dear Mel," she says. "I found a new secret spot."

As we approach the front entrance, I notice people looking at me. But not in that there-goes-the-social-pariah kind of way, like after the mess with the newspaper quotes. People are smiling and nodding, wishing me luck, saying they'll be at the match tonight.

"You're like a freakin' rock star," Jade says.

When we walk in the main hallway, it's even crazier. Some girl yells out, "Chick power!" and every teacher that walks by gives me a "Good luck, Mel." If I wasn't so damn nervous, it'd be totally cool.

I tell Jade I've got to go weigh myself, but before we split off from each other, I say, "Going to tell me where the new spot is? And don't say you can't because it's only for you and Cole."

Jade smiles. "It's only for you and me."

"And you'll be at the match tonight?"

"I'll think about it," she says, with a wink.

When I get to the wrestling locker room, I open the door and ask if anyone's around. Just Cole. I walk in and quickly get stripped down to my bra and underwear, with my brother standing guard at the door. Thank God for the two-pound allowance at this point in the season, I think to myself. I know I'm going to need it. I step on the electronic scale and hold my breath.

After a few unnerving moments, the scale displays: 105.75 lbs.

I've got a quarter pound to play with. I can eat something. Maybe a candy bar or two. Maybe a piece of cheese and a few crackers.

Cole waits at the door for me to get dressed before letting Trey and the other starters into the locker room. I get a pat on the shoulder from each as I leave for homeroom.

It's been a long, long day. I've had a bunch of them lately, but this is the longest. I have a few minutes to myself, in the back corner of the girls' locker room. I can hear basketball players and winter track athletes walking about, but other than a nod or a knowing smile when they pass me on their way to the showers, I'm left alone to prepare for my match. I made weight with a half pound to spare, and now I'm feeling the rush of energy from a turkey wrap that I finally got to eat. It's the best I've felt in days. Of course, that just means hunger and thirst are no longer a distraction, and now I can focus completely on the fact I'm more nervous than I've ever been in my life.

I make a final check of my headgear and the laces on my wrestling shoes. I shut my locker, sit back, and take a few deep breaths. Be ready for that first half minute, Odessa always says. Start tough, then things will settle.

I look at the clock.

Ten after five.

I put the hood of the varsity warm-ups I borrowed over my head, exit the girls' locker room, and make my way to the wrestling locker room. I open the door, give an obligatory, "Girl coming in," then walk over to the bench. Nate and Max scoot over. I can feel the tension. I notice my brother in the corner, shadow wrestling, while a few others are stretching. Most, however, are sitting silently, pensively.

The door opens and Coach Geiger walks in.

My stomach flutters.

"Good, we're all here," Coach Geiger says, after seeing me. "Not a whole lot to go over. On paper, Livonia isn't very strong; this should be an easy victory. But we need to be thinking about tonight as a prep for the districts. The Livonia coach and I agreed to start the dual meet at 113. Mel, that means your match will be the last one of the night."

Now my heart's thumping like crazy.

"I was assured your opponent—this kid, Gomez—is not going to forfeit. In fact, he's eager to wrestle," Coach Geiger says. "He's a sophomore, too. His record is under .500, but the Livonia coach tells me he's gotten better as the season's gone on. Should be a tight match, Mel, but you should beat him."

Nate taps me on the leg with his fist.

"Get yourselves ready," Coach Geiger says. "Then let's get out there."

After Coach Geiger leaves, Cole and Trey tell the team to get in weight-class order.

"Headgear on and hoods up," Cole says. He looks at me. "Ready?"

"Yeah."

Single file, we move down the hallway and around the corner to the practice room. Mr. Williamson is standing outside the door. He gives me a nod. Then, as is Ashton tradition, we circle the practice room—I glance up as I pass the space on the wall where Coach Geiger said he'd hang my plaque—then head toward the gymnasium. Fans are waiting outside the side doors. When they see us, they begin clapping.

"Go get 'em, Ashton," someone calls out.

Another shouts, "Big match tonight!"

"Let's go, Mel!"

That's Jade's voice. I raise my eyes. She's taking pictures. (Probably of Cole, but I don't care.) Annie and Odessa are there, too. Then I see Mom and Dad. And *Grandma?* Oh, God... I look away, just as my eyes start to well up.

When we get to the gymnasium side entrance, Cole cracks open the door. I recognize the song our school band is playing, it's that old one Mom likes so much: "Girls Just Wanna Have Fun." Then the music quiets and the lights shut down. One after the other. Leaving a single ceiling lamp above the mat. Cole raises his hand. Two drummers step forward, and a drum roll begins.

A roar from the crowd fills the gymnasium.

In the semidarkness, I follow Cole and Trey as the team walks in lockstep toward the mat. Cameras are flashing. Ashton fans are stomping in the stands. And yelling. The sound is startling. My heart's racing. So's my breathing. We circle the mat once, then pair up. Alex and I alternate shots with each other.

The band begins, "Man! I Feel Like a Woman!"

Oh geez, they're really milking this.

After our short warm-up, both teams line up for introductions. It's the first time I get to see what my opponent looks like. Not that it makes a difference. You can't judge what's inside a wrestler by how he looks on the outside.

"Ladies and gentlemen..." the PA announcer begins. "Welcome to Ashton High for this evening's dual meet, as our hometown Eagles face the Livonia Patriots... Nine days ago, Ashton was hit with the tragic loss of Bob Hillman, our beloved teacher and wrestling coach. Since this is the first home match since his passing, we ask that you observe a moment of silence in his honor..."

For a half minute, the gym is quiet.

Then the announcer continues. "Tonight's match will begin at the 113-pound weight class. Wrestling for Livonia will be Jacob Feldman... And for Ashton, Alex Yarrow..." The crowd cheers its approval as the two wrestlers cross the mat to shake hands.

"...At the 120-pound weight class, from Livonia, Dimitri Popov... And for Ashton, Michael McCoy..."

I try to stay in one place, but I can't keep my feet still. I hop from one foot to the other, shrug my shoulders, stretch my arms. I always imagined my first varsity match would be something special to remember, but my brain is way too much on hyper-drive to remember a thing. I sure hope someone gets this on video. Then, as I roll my neck for, like, the hundredth time, I catch a glimpse of someone in the shadows.

Stewart?

I roll my neck again, trying not to seem like I'm looking. But I am. Then I squint. I don't see him, though.

"At the 160-pound weight class, from Livonia, Joe Burke... And for Ashton, Cole Radford..."

After shaking his opponent's hand, Cole looks at me on the way back across the mat. I nod to him, then glance into the shadows again. No Stewart.

The introductions go on. As they get closer to the 285-pounders—with my weight class, right after—Ashton fans begin a new cheer.

"Let's go, Mel!" Then a bass drum pounds. *Boom, boom, ba-boom...* "Let's go, Mel!" *Boom, boom, ba-boom...*

Until, finally, it's my turn.

"At the 106-pound weight class, from Livonia, Marco Gomez... And for Ashton, Melinda Radford..."

The crowd roars. I can hardly feel my legs underneath me, and I definitely can't hear myself think or breathe or anything. I move across the mat, getting a close-up look at my opponent, shake his hand, then turn and head back to my teammates.

I'm behind our bench; across the mat, Gomez is behind his bench. Once or twice, we catch each other's eye.

As expected, Ashton clinched a team victory midway through the dual meet when Trey pinned his opponent, putting the score at 35–3. From that point, it was just a matter of time before my match came up. The 220-pounders went quickly. The 285-pound match is going even quicker.

Cole comes up behind me. He hardly broke a sweat in his win—another first-period pin. I like having my brother next to me. It doesn't make me more nervous, just the opposite.

"You gotta own the moment," he says.

I nod, then set my headgear, adjust my sports bra, and tug at my singlet until everything feels right. And, as the third period ends, with an Ashton victory at 285, I walk over to Coach Geiger.

"Mel, I'm proud of you making it to this point," he says. "But it's not enough. You're a better wrestler than this guy. Go out there and show everyone." He gives me a slap on the back.

The crowd starts the chant again. "LET'S GO, MEL!" *Boom, boom, ba-boom...* "LET'S GO, MEL!" *Boom, boom, ba-boom...*

I jog out onto the mat and stop at the small circle. Gomez is waiting for me.

The referee steps in. "Don't stop wrestling until I say so," he says. "Ready?" Then he blows the whistle.

And everything goes silent.

No crowd. No drums. No teammates. No coach.

I circle to my left, waiting for Gomez to come at me hard. But, oddly, he doesn't. Where's the half minute of hell? Instead, he circles, too, mirroring what I'm doing. Backing up, when I come forward; coming forward when I step back. For a moment, I'm confused. Is he scared? Playing possum? He does a halfhearted drop-step that I hold off. Then another. And when I think he's left an opening, I shoot in for the single. But he blocks that.

Eventually, we tie up, then push and pull each other, until I step outside of the large circle. The referee blows his whistle.

"Out of bounds. Let's start again."

I look over at Coach Geiger. He points to the clock and says, "Twenty seconds left. Take a good shot."

Off the whistle, I do.

I'm in on a double. Gomez puts in a wizzer, but then hesitates, giving me a moment's opportunity to get him off his feet. There can't be much time left. I keep driving, and he keeps scooting his hips. Just as we near the edge of the circle, I throw in a half. He turns to his stomach.

"Takedown, Ashton," the referee shouts at the buzzer.

2–0.

I stand up.

Whoa, I'm winning!

I can feel the crowd's reaction in the vibrations through my wrestling shoes. I glance at Coach Geiger. He's clapping. And my teammates are on their feet.

I choose bottom to start the second period. The referee waits until I'm set, then motions to Gomez. When he's set, too, the whistle blows.

I try for a stand, but Gomez drags me down. Then I try a switch, but he blocks that. We do the same thing again.

Then a third time. His strength, which I didn't feel when we were on our feet, suddenly overwhelms me. I'm not sure I can make it the rest of period, fighting him muscle for muscle. He pulls in my left arm, then breaks me down to the mat, keeping his weight on me the whole time. I try to move my hips so I can get back to a base, but I can't.

I push off the mat with my arms. Major mistake. Gomez sinks in a half. Not deep, but deep enough. Then he comes out to the side. If I could hear them, I'm sure my teammates would be yelling for me to look away. I've already done that. But Gomez isn't giving an inch. He's cranking my head down, wrenching my shoulder. I feel my body getting to perpendicular.

I can *not* give up back points.

I force my head in the opposite direction and brace with my free arm. But Gomez keeps grinding me down. I'm getting tired. I know it. He knows it. My neck hurts, and I'm not sure I can take the pain in my shoulder anymore. Then with one more drive of his legs, I can feel my body wilt. I go over. My shoulder blades edge toward the mat.

But I hear the whistle.

"Out of bounds," the referee shouts. "No back points."

I sit up and see that my shoulders were just outside the circle. *Geez, I totally got lucky.*

"Mel," Coach Geiger yells, getting my attention. "Eleven seconds left. Just hang tough."

So I do. We restart at the center circle. And, shortly after, the second period ends with the score unchanged.

Gomez chooses bottom to start the final two minutes.

I look at Coach Geiger. "Let him up," he says. "Then take him down."

Off the whistle, I let him escape.

The score's 2–1.

I want to wrestle on my feet, where I can use my quickness to my advantage. But, suddenly, the half minute of hell that I expected at the start of the match arrives. Gomez comes at me hard, shooting in deep for a double. I cross-face and sprawl, dropping every bit of my weight on top of him. He tries to suck my legs in tighter, but as he does, I turn my hips, throw in a wizzer, and knock him off balance.

We separate for a few moments, but he shoots in again, this time on the single. We scramble across the mat, then—thank, God—out of bounds. I'm practically out of breath and can hardly pick myself up off the mat.

Then the referee makes a call that I didn't want to hear. "Stalling, Ashton," he says, raising his fist to signal the warning. "Gotta keep working."

I look at the clock—thirty-one seconds left—then at Coach Geiger, who shouts, "You shoot, Mel. You shoot!"

At the center circle, the referee starts us, again. Gomez charges at me. Out of desperation more than anything, I lower my level and drop-step into his midsection. I hang on to both his legs. My arms are jelly. Gomez sprawls hard, breaking my grip. I switch to a single-leg and desperately hold on to that.

Out of the silence, I hear my brother's voice as clear as if he were right next to me. "Ten seconds, Mel..."

I keep holding the leg.

"Five seconds..."

As if everything in the world depends on it.

"Two seconds..."

Everything.

"Time!" the referee shouts. "No takedown."

Finally, I let go of Gomez's leg and crumble to the mat.

I did it!

I won, 2–1.

It wasn't the prettiest, but victory is mine.

And now I can hear the crowd going crazy, and I can see my brother Cole and my teammates jumping up and down. And I can feel my eyes swell. Gomez offers his hand and pulls me up off the mat. He's hugely disappointed, I can tell, but gracious in defeat. We stand at the center circle on either side of the referee.

And my arm is raised in victory.

With the dual meet over, my teammates mob me at the center of the mat. Hands tousle my hair and pat my back, and I don't mind so much being touched by so many guys. And I hear their shouts of approval.

"Great job, Mel!"

"The first of many!"

"You kicked ass!"

Eventually, they lead me off the mat, with my brother's arm over my shoulder. Coach Geiger, smiling widely, shakes my hand.

"You made me look good, Mel," he says.

"Thanks, Coach."

Chapter 45

My grandmother is taking my friends and me out to dinner. I told her we'd probably be talking about wrestling a lot. She smiled and said she'd do her best to follow along.

I'm thrilled I don't have to think about cutting weight again until next fall. Cole, on the other hand, has already driven home. He still has to watch what he eats. And I'm sure he's going running later. The thought of that makes me admire his discipline and dedication even more. I sacrificed for one match and thought it was a nightmare; year after year, he does it for the entire five-month-long season.

Coach Geiger gave us a quick talk when the team got back to the locker room. He didn't have much to say. It was an easy victory, of course, and the rest of the varsity was already thinking about the districts this coming weekend.

"Up and down the lineup, we wrestled well tonight," he said, then looked directly at me. "Nicely done, in a very tough spot."

A few of the guys nodded in agreement.

"You know I only had one plaque in my office, right?" he said. "The one with you being the first female to *win* a varsity wrestling match for Ashton."

I'm not sure I believe him, but it's a nice thought anyway. Then it's time for me to leave so the guys can weigh themselves, take showers, and get dressed.

I return to the girls locker room. I don't feel like taking a shower or changing. A part of me doesn't ever want to take off my singlet and warm-ups, though I know how weird that sounds and Jade would certainly draw the line there. So I throw on Juicy Couture fleece sweats, grab my equipment bag from my locker, and meet Odessa, Jade, and Annie waiting in the hallway.

Odessa puts her arm around me. "Girl, I am *so* glad we're not in the same weight class," she says. "I wouldn't want to face you in a match."

"You don't have to worry," I say. "I'm thinking of retiring."

"Retiring?"

"I'm undefeated," I say, with a smile. "I think I might want to stay that way forever."

"You mean we don't have go through all this next year?" Jade says. "Thank God."

We laugh.

Then Jade grabs my arm. "Uh-oh, Mel," she whispers. "It's *him*."

"Him who?"

She turns me left. "Him."

It *is* him. Stewart. Standing against a wall. He gives me a quick wave and a kind of sheepish expression.

Annie leans into me and whispers, "Mel, he's cute."

I look back at the three of them.

"Go," Jade says, giving me a little push.

"Yeah?"

"We'll be in the car," she says. "Don't be too long, though. You know how your grandmother can be. If we're not careful, she'll have *us* working at DDI this summer."

I stand there. Stewart moves toward me. Yeah, he *is* cute. Handsome, really. I almost forgot how much so.

"Finally got to see you compete," he says to me. "You're definitely good. A real badass."

"Thanks," I say, and maybe it's the high I feel from winning, but then I cut right to the chase. "So, why are you here?" And he better not say he's here for someone else.

"I came to watch you."

"How'd you know?"

"Read it in the *News,*" he says. "Couldn't miss history being made."

"Yeah...history."

"Anyway, I'm glad I was here."

"So, how is everything?"

He shrugs. "Okay," he says. "Sorry about your coach. I read that, too."

"Did you read about how you turned out to be a jerk?" I say. It comes out way nastier than I meant.

"But I'm not," Stewart says.

"What happened?"

"I left messages for you."

"Yeah," I say. "After you blew me off."

"You never returned my calls."

"Stewart," I say, with my newfound toughness, "what happened?"

"I got fired," he says. Sheepishly, it seems.

"Fired?"

"Yeah."

"From Crystal Fog?"

"That night when we were supposed to go out," he says. "I thought I'd work a few hours in the afternoon to make some extra money. This bigwig leaves his car—a charcoal Maserati, a beautiful car. When I went to park it, I hit an icy patch in the parking lot. It only skidded a little. But it was enough to bang up the front end. The club manager fired me on the spot. When my dad found out, he was so mad I thought he was going to kill me. He took away my car and grounded me. I couldn't make it over."

"So, you don't call?" I say. "I waited all night."

"I knew I wouldn't be able to take you out," he says.

"Like that matters to me?"

"It matters to me," he says. "I'm the guy."

I shake my head. "What you did was pretty lousy."

"Mel, I lost my job *and* my car. I felt like a loser."

"And you made me feel like a loser, too."

"Sorry," he says.

"You said that."

"I mean it."

"How'd you get here?"

"My friend from school," Stewart says. "He knows a guy on the Livonia team, so I got a ride from him."

I'm done grilling Stewart. He's got all the right answers. They always say an elaborate excuse is the most believable, but I don't think Stewart would lie to me. Of course, I didn't think he'd ever blow me off, either.

I pull him to the side of the busy hallway. "What do we do now?"

"I don't know," he says. "I wasn't sure I'd get to speak with you. To apologize."

"And you have."

"And you've accepted?"

I purse my lips, then smile. "For now."

"For now?"

"Gotta lotta makin' up to do, Guv'nor," I say.

His eyes light up.

"It's been a good night for me," I say. "And I guess I was wrong for not returning your calls. So, yeah, you deserve a second chance. But only *one* second chance. I've got to get to dinner. Call me later. I'll probably answer."

"Only probably?" he says, with a smile.

I step toward him, reach up on my toes, and give him a kiss on the cheek. He smells good, just like I remember. I turn to go, but then stop. He smells *really* good.

Without another thought as to whether it's right or wrong, I throw my arms around him and press my open mouth against his. For a few moments, right there in the school hallway, we make out big time. When I finally pull back, his eyes are still closed.

I say goodbye and skip out the school exit to the parking lot, practically floating, where my grandmother and friends are waiting. I'm going to have to convince Mom to let me see Stewart, but I'll worry about that later. Besides, I'm sure Jade will have a plan.